THE WORLD AS HE SEES IT

(PERSPECTIVES #2)

A.M. ARTHUR

BRIGGS-KING BOOKS

BLURB

The World As He Sees It (Perspectives #2)
Love knows no limits...but fear could keep them from seeing it.

Gabe lives a double life. As Gabriel Henson, he works multiple jobs to support his remorseless, alcoholic mother. As Tony Ryder, he does internet porn for extra cash and regular safe sex without complications.

Yet when he encounters a scared young man freaking out in a night club, he's compelled to reach out. Ever since then, the memory of that young man has haunted him.

Tristan Lavalle lives his life thirty minutes at a time. After a traumatic brain injury three years ago, he gets through his day recording his life in spiral notebooks and sticky note reminders.

A month after Tristan's embarrassingly public meltdown, another chance meeting with Gabe sparks a warm, emotionally fulfilling email relationship. Both men crave more, but fear of the next step stands between them.

Until Tristan gets the opportunity to take part in a clinical trial that could improve his memory—if the side effects don't kill him. But for Tristan, the possibility of a real life with Gabe is worth any risk...

COPYRIGHT PAGE

DEAR READER,

This book is for everyone who fell in love with Tristan as deeply as I did. The idea of writing a book from the perspective of a young man with short term memory problems was daunting, to say the least. I wasn't entirely sure I could do it, so I started with Gabe first. Eventually, Tristan spoke up and his voice was finally there, ready to tell his story and find his happily-ever-after. He wouldn't settle for anything less than that.

I hope you enjoy this unusual love story.

Much love,

A.M. Arthur

1

Gabe Henson picked at the label on his bottle of Samuel Adams lager, more interested in getting the square of paper off in one piece than in drinking the mostly full beer. The club's pulsing music seemed far away, not penetrating like it usually was. He ignored the throng of good-looking dancers behind him and shut down the occasional attempt by an unfamiliar face at buying him a drink. The regulars knew him, and they knew when to leave him the hell alone.

Like right now.

He hadn't come out to Big Dick's to find a hookup. His boss preferred his models not to have sex for a few days leading up to a scene, and Gabe had one tomorrow. He only was at Big Dick's, surrounded by other gay men, so he wasn't sitting at home with his mother, worrying about the upcoming scene.

And yet that particular anxiety had taken a backseat to another incident less than an hour old. He couldn't scrub his memory of the image of the frightened, golden-haired boy who'd cowered in a corner of the break room, completely unaware of anything except the name of a friend who'd know how to help him. Although "boy" wasn't very kind. He was at least twenty-one if he'd gotten inside. Bear hadn't let a fake ID slip past him since the day the bar opened.

Tristan.

The name didn't suit. It conjured up images of a long-haired Brad Pitt riding horses and seducing Julia Ormond. The Tristan from tonight reminded him more of Alex Pettyfer, minus at least fifteen pounds and with shaggier, slightly blonder hair. Not to mention a healthy dose of fear in his eyes. Eyes haunted by something that was none of Gabe's business, but had caused Tristan short-term memory loss, according to the friend.

Gabe couldn't imagine living with such a debilitating condition. What sort of desperation had sent Tristan into the bar alone, knowing sooner or later he'd forget where he was and why?

And why the hell can't I stop thinking about him?

He'd extended an offer of free drinks to both Tristan and the friend—Joel? No, Noel—but he doubted they'd take him up on it.

"What's up, bub?" Pax asked while he scooped ice into a shaker. "Who pissed in your shoe?"

"Fuck off," Gabe retorted without anger. Pax had been bartending at Big Dick's for over four years, and they'd always gotten along, despite Pax's mystifying habit of changing his hair color once a month. Last month he'd gone full-on skunk black and white. This month it was cobalt blue.

Pax snickered over a bottle of tequila. "Someone's going through a dry spell."

"I don't need details of your personal life, thanks."

"Oh, bub, I didn't mean me."

Gabe rolled his eyes. He wasn't going through a dry spell—exactly. He'd been having pretty regular sex for the last eighteen months. It just wasn't the kind of sex he wanted to be having—the real, nonporn kind. Even his very occasional hookup didn't count, because he felt as disconnected from his partner afterward as he did when he left a scene.

Not that he disliked or regretted his job. He liked sex. He liked having sex, and getting paid for it was a bonus. Even porn sex could have its own levels of intimacy. He was best friends with one of the guys he regularly did scenes with. But at the end of the day, that intimacy wasn't real. It didn't keep him warm at night. It didn't go out for coffee with him after a movie. It didn't turn into an actual, trusting relationship.

And maybe that was the point.

"There's a hot blond number at the other end of the bar," Pax said while he shook his drink. "Don't think he's a regular, if you're looking for fresh meat."

"I'm not looking tonight, thanks." Gabe pried another few inches of the damp label off the glass bottle. Nearly done.

"If you say so."

Pax moved off to pour his drinks, replaced almost right away by Gabe's dad. The white sequined vest cast a sparkly reflection all over the bar, and Gabe tried not to squint too much. He loved that his adopted dad, Richard Brightman, was comfortable enough in his sexuality and with his looks to wear something as hideous as Richard Simmons-inspired sequins, but that didn't stop Gabe from having fantasies of burning them all in a bonfire.

"What's got you tied up in knots, kiddo?" Dad asked.

Lying to him was harder than lying to Pax. "Thinking about that Tristan guy."

"Yeah, that boy has got himself a case of real bad luck. At least he's got a friend to look out for him."

"Right." Another bit of the label came away. Then another. Aware of eyes on him, Gabe looked up. Dad hadn't moved or redirected his attention. "What?"

"Don't."

Irritation prickled his scalp. "Don't what? It's not against the law to peel beer labels."

"That isn't what I mean, and you know it. Leave this Tristan kid be, he's not your problem."

"I am not making him my problem."

Dad leaned in so he could lower his voice. Keep family shit private and all that. "You hanging out here with that look on your face means you're thinking about him. You want to fix him, don't you?"

"I don't even know him."

"Yeah, well, I know you, Gabriel."

"Meaning?"

"Meaning you can't fix your mother, so you keep looking for other people you can fix."

Gabe's hand jerked, tearing the label off and leaving the last corner. Angry now, he wadded up the ruined label and tossed it onto the bar top. "I do not want a lecture about Debbie, okay? Leave it."

Dad raised both hands in mock surrender. "I don't want to lecture you. You've listened to all of my lectures, kiddo. I just wish you heard me sometimes, is all. We both do."

"We" included Richard's partner and Gabe's bio dad Bernard "Bear" Henson. He'd been Bear all of Gabe's life, and he always would be, even though technically he should be "Dad". Dad had as much history with Gabe's mother Debbie as Bear did, and they both understood the burden Gabe continued to bear. Gabe couldn't give up on her. She didn't have anyone else.

"I do hear you, Dad. I hear you both when you talk, and then I make my own decisions. Isn't that how you guys raised me? To think for myself?"

Dad let out a frustrated grunt. "You're a pain in the ass, you know that?"

"You raised me that way too."

He grinned. "Damn right, I did. Now are you going to drink that beer or let it go flat?"

"It's probably already flat, but I get the point."

"Good. It's Friday. Actually, it's Saturday but let's not get technical. Go have fun."

"Thanks."

Gabe spun his stool around so he could watch the dancing bodies while he sipped his warm, slightly flat beer. He really shouldn't be indulging the night before a shoot. Beer didn't make him bloat up the way it used to, especially if he stuck to one, but he had to look his very best on camera, no exceptions.

The beer was more of a prop than anything else. The last time he indulged a little bit, he'd let the person he was there with drink himself into a blackout. Shane had seemed like a decent guy on a run of bad luck, desperate to let loose a little, and he had. The demons Gabe had seen in Shane's drunk eyes were the only reason Gabe had decided to forgive him for being an asshole about waking up in Gabe's bed. So hungover he'd practically accused Gabe of sleeping with him and lying about it.

That had pissed Gabe the fuck off. Maybe they'd fucked twice on camera for a payday, but Shane—or Colby, his stage name— didn't fucking know him. He had no right to judge Gabe. Gabe didn't need to get a guy drunk off his face in order to get laid, and he hadn't been wasted with a hookup in more than two years. He'd learned his lesson.

And Shane/Colby could stay the fuck out of his life.

So why the hell had Gabe agreed to bottom for him tomorrow?

The usual reason he took risks: money. They'd get a lot of downloads for a badass top like "Tony" finally taking one up the ass.

He'd been stretching all week with his fingers and a plug, but damn if he wasn't still nervous as hell. The only time in his life that he'd ever bottomed had been a painful disaster—probably not unusual for two drunk and inexperienced fifteen-year-olds.

A mop of shaggy golden-brown hair caught his attention, far out on the dance floor. Gabe sat up straighter, straining to catch the man's face, pulse jumping. Surely it couldn't be—no. The face was all wrong. Chiseled and tanned.

You're an idiot. Tristan isn't coming back, and he's definitely not doing it tonight.

Gabe checked his watch. After two in the morning. Last call was at two forty-five anyway, and he had to be up early for a ten o'clock call time. As much as he preferred the chaotic peace of Big Dick's, it was past time to go home.

The unlocked front door didn't surprise him anymore, but it had instilled a new instinct to enter his home slowly and carefully. Check around for open cabinets or upturned couch cushions. New damage that wasn't caused by a drunken rage and might indicate an intruder. Debbie didn't remember the little things like locking the front door and flushing the toilet.

He prayed for the day when she forgot how to walk to the nearest state store.

The front room didn't appear much different than when he'd left eight hours ago. A pile of unfolded laundry on the couch. Pizza boxes on the coffee table already overflowing with Debbie's magazine subscriptions. The familiar odors of cigarette smoke and sour wine mixed with something greasy and old. He locked the front door, then followed the smell into the kitchen. Half a dozen white takeout boxes littered the kitchen table, some of their contents sprawled on the old metal table. A few black flies buzzed around the mess.

"Fucking fantastic," Gabe said to the ceiling. Her room was overhead, but she'd probably drunk enough to sleep until noon the next day. She always ordered lo mein when she made a conscious choice to try for a blackout. Something had upset her tonight, and he'd hear all about it when he got home from his scene tomorrow.

The trash can was overflowing. He pulled that bag out and tied it off. Shoved the Chinese cartons into another bag, along with the box of red wine on the counter. It was half-full, and he'd catch hell tomorrow, but he didn't care. Tonight he seriously didn't fucking care. He hauled the trash bags out the back door and stuffed them into the cans by the steps. Then he spent ten minutes tracking and smashing the black flies with a plastic swatter.

He fucking hated flies.

After a quick blast of air freshener, he turned off the lights and went upstairs. Debbie's room was the first door, and it was wide open. He peeked inside because the bedside lamp was on. The bed was messy, the sheets all over the floor, but no Debbie.

Irritation overrode concern. It was late, he was exhausted, and he had to deal with her wherever she'd passed out for the night.

His room was out of the question. He kept the door locked when he wasn't home—not only so she didn't unearth his porn stash and sear her eyeballs, but also because he simply didn't trust her. He didn't trust her not to steal the Burberry watch he indulged in after his first scene and hock it for booze money. He didn't trust her around any of his things, so he kept them locked up when he wasn't home.

At the end of the hall, the bathroom door was ajar. He flipped on the light. Debbie was asleep on the bathroom floor, wrapped up in her yellow robe. He dropped the toilet lid with his foot, then flushed the evidence of her dinner and drinking. She hadn't vomited on the floor or herself—good luck for which he was insanely grateful.

As much as he wanted to leave her there, he needed to shower in the morning, and that wasn't happening with his mother passed out on the linoleum. In these moments, Gabe thanked the universe that he'd gotten his build from his father. All six foot two and 210 of him could pick up five foot three, buck-nothing Debbie with little fuss or stress.

The woman couldn't eat six cartons of noodles in a week. Such a waste of money.

She didn't stir during the short walk to her room, or when he put her down. The sheets took a minute to get in order. He checked that there was a trash can on both sides of the bed, turned off the lamp and shut the door.

Business as usual in Debbie Harper's house.

Somewhere in the back of his mind, Bear gave him a sad smile and said, *It's not your job, Gabriel. It's not your job.*

Gabe didn't disagree. He also didn't know how to quit.

What else did he have to do with his life if not take care of his alcoholic mother?

He had to give Colby credit for being as gentle as possible. Agreeing to bottom for the first time since he was fifteen had been an agonizing decision for Gabe, but the payday for first bottom during a three-way was his deciding factor. Chet even had mercy on him by allowing him to pick who topped him. Even though Gabe was good friends with his other scene partner Jon "Boomer" Buchanan, Boomer was sometimes a clumsy top.

Colby—he still had a hard time referring to him by his real name while working—was a decent guy who did porn like someone was holding a gun to his head. His story intrigued Gabe, but he'd never asked. Today had been Colby's last shoot, anyway, so it didn't matter. If Colby/Shane came to work at Big Dick's as a dancer, then Gabe would make an effort.

Gabe had prepped for a long time in the shower that morning. Colby did quite a lot of manual prepping on-screen, and Boomer had rimmed him for a while, which had felt fantastic. The actual penetration had hurt, but not unbearably so, and Gabe managed to come. Chet was happy with the footage, so Gabe chalked it up as a win and escaped to the upstairs shower to clean up.

Jon would call him later to make sure he was okay with how

everything went, because he was a good guy like that. They regularly worked out together, and even though they'd filmed more than half a dozen scenes, there was zero romantic anything between them. And that worked for Gabe. He liked having a friend who listened to his crazy family problems, didn't judge and didn't expect sex in return for his time and attention.

After a quick shower to wash away the day's sweat and bodily fluids, he slipped into a pair of running shorts and a T-shirt from his gym bag. His phone flashed at him. Six missed calls, all from Debbie. No messages. Gabe glared at his cell phone, wanting his sudden flash of irritation to erase every single call record. When it didn't, he used his finger.

Deleted.

Chet was waiting for him by the set house's front door with a check in hand. "Excellent work today, my boy, very good film. Here's the advance you asked for."

Gabe hesitated in taking the check. Chet was an anomaly in the porn industry because he paid his models one of two ways. First was cash upfront, no royalties, which was industry standard and the get-money-fast option that people like Colby usually took. Gabe was a royalties guy, which usually meant no money upfront, but he earned a decent percent back on all downloads. Debbie's latest stunt with the unsecured loan had made Gabe stoop to asking Chet for an advance against today's video.

"I appreciate it, Chet." Gabe tucked the slip of paper into his gym bag.

"If things are getting tight, I can fit you in more than twice a month."

"I'll think about it." He still received regular monthly payments from his library of past scenes, but padding his collection might move that decimal point over one more place. "Call me when you need me again."

"Take it easy, Tony."

Gabe took in a deep breath as he left the house, and exhaled long and slow on the walk to his car. It was a ritual he used to shed himself of Tony, the guy who walked into that set and did his job, fucking like a champ and always with a smile. Sure, Gabe enjoyed himself. Regular sex without any of the baggage, and always, always safe. All of the models were tested for STDs regularly, and nobody fucked without a rubber at Mean Green Boys.

Two years ago, Gabe had contracted a pretty gross case of oral gonorrhea from a hookup he'd blown and then fucked. Despite Richard's status, the incident had finally wised Gabe up to the dangers of casual sex, and he'd gone without for a while. He met Jon at the gym one afternoon, and after their paths crossed several times in one month, they started regularly working out together. Gabe had enjoyed the friendship, and he'd learned Jon was fastidious about avoiding infection.

One day after showering together, Jon had joked about Gabe "being in porn with a cock like that". Gabe had laughed it off, even after Jon went on about the benefits of good, regular sex with very little risk. A few days later, Gabe got a call about doing a modeling interview with Chet Green. It went well, Chet threw dollar signs at him, and that was that. Signing on with Mean Green Boys had been a bit of a no-brainer—plus he needed the money that he couldn't get as a career waiter.

His drive from the residential home in Camp Hill, across the Susquehanna on the Capital Beltway, and then north to his place on Harris Street took about twenty minutes. He tried to ignore traffic and the other drivers, tried to ignore whatever his mother wanted so badly that she'd called him six times without leaving messages. He rolled down the windows and concentrated on the hot July air and the humid, oily odor of the city.

He'd worked up a good sweat by the time he parked in front of the aging blue house. The yard needed to be tended. He put that on this afternoon's mental to-do list. Physical exertion would help him forget the faint discomfort in his ass.

Something inside the house shattered before he could slide

his key into the lock. The knob turned, which told him she'd been out at least once since he'd left for the shoot, because he always locked the door behind him. They had a basement full of old QVC packages from before he'd wrangled all of Debbie's credit cards away, and they didn't live on the best side of town.

He stepped into chaos. The complete opposite of the relative order from the night before. Cushions were off the sofa, magazines littered the floor. A dining chair was on its side. Movies and books were scattered across the carpet near the television. From the door, he couldn't see the source of the shattering sound.

"Mom?"

Debbie stormed out of the downstairs bathroom, her robe fluttering like a cape, curly red hair wrapped around her head like a frizzy shower cap. She stabbed a finger in the air as she sailed toward him like a snorting bull. "Where is it? Where did you put it?"

Gabe held up his palms and took a step to the side. "Where did I put what?"

"My wedding ring! You took it off while I was sleeping, and you hid it somewhere. Where is it?" Wine-soured breath puffed in his face. He had nearly a foot of height on his mother, but she still somehow managed to seem bigger than him. More domineering, just like when he was a kid and she knocked him around.

"I didn't take your ring," Gabe said. "You hocked it when I was thirteen, and you accused me of stealing it then just like you're doing now."

"I had the ring last night."

He despised these mornings. Hangover-inspired rants about events from long ago, usually something that she'd decided was Gabe's fault. The wedding ring had gone missing more than ten years ago after a particularly nasty fight between Debbie and Bear, and she'd blamed them both for taking it. Bear had eventually tracked the ring down to a local pawn shop, whose owner swore Debbie sold it to him herself.

One of the fun side effects of excessive alcohol abuse was memory loss.

"You haven't had the ring for ten years," Gabe said. "All that happened last night was me picking you up off the bathroom floor and putting your drunk ass to bed."

Her hand snapped out, quick as always, and cracked hot across his cheek. His head didn't move because she didn't have that kind of strength anymore, but the slap hurt. She tried again, and he caught her wrist, his temper flaring. He squeezed until she whined, and then he let go.

Her big green eyes filled with tears. Her chin trembled. On a long wail, she fled the living room. Her footsteps thundered upstairs, ending with the slam of her bedroom door.

Gabe rubbed his face where his cheek still stung. Then he started cleaning up her mess.

Again.

2

Big Dick's. Big Dick's. Big Dick's. Big dicks. Big dicks. Big—why I am I thinking about big dicks?

Tristan Lavalle blinked out of the windshield at the scenery going by, somehow both familiar and new. He wasn't driving, which was a good thing. He hadn't driven a car in a long time. Since the accident. The accident was why he couldn't remember why he'd been thinking about...something. Dicks?

Except it hadn't been an accident. It was simply easier and less rage-inducing to think of it as an accident instead of what it had been. Or what he'd been told it had been, since he didn't remember that, either.

Noel was driving. Noel was his best friend in the world, and they hung out on a regular basis even though they didn't live together anymore. College was over. He and Noel weren't roommates with Billy and Chris, but they visited sometimes too. At least he was pretty sure they did.

He studied Noel's profile, hoping something hit him. A familiarity with the situation, or even with what he was wearing. His short-term memory was pretty much nonexistent but he knew he had moments of familiarity. Mostly with people, now with a few places. They happened a lot with Noel, and a lot in...that place he lived that wasn't with Noel and Billy and Chris.

Benfield. Yes. He knew that. Mostly old people. Not many like him.

Noel's clothes struck him as odd. Noel was a police officer, and he wasn't wearing his uniform. When he came to visit, Tristan couldn't remember but he was pretty sure he didn't wear skin-tight black jeans and a dark green sleeveless tee. Party clothes.

Tristan glanced down at this own attire. Dark blue jeans. Not really tight, but then again none of his clothes really fit right. His black tee said "Kiss Me, I'm Cute". Billy had given him that shirt for his nineteenth birthday.

Nighttime. Party clothes. They were going out.

His notebook was open in his lap. Tristan didn't want to refer to it yet. He wanted to try and get this on his own without the copious notes he'd probably taken. His entire life since the accident was chronicled in a never-ending series of spiral notebooks. Notebooks and sticky notes all over his bedroom walls. Calendars and reminders on his laptop to do everything from take his meds to eat breakfast.

I'm completely broken, but everyone keeps trying to fix me.

Especially Noel. Noel had been there that night. Noel had been hurt too. Tristan's family had written him off for being gay, but Noel had always been there.

"Can you turn the air up a little, babe? It's hot back here."

Tristan flinched at a voice both unfamiliar and totally déjà vu. He and Noel weren't alone. A lot of the times recently they weren't alone because Noel was seeing someone.

Think. Think. Think. I know this.

Noel fiddled with the air conditioning buttons on the car's dash. "Better?"

"Yeah, thanks."

Noel turned off the highway and into the brightly lit city.

Harrisburg. They'd gone to college here. He knew the city, and he loved coming to visit. He didn't need memories of trips to know in his heart he loved this city. The museums and the river and City Island and everything about it.

He glanced at the person sitting behind Noel. Dark hair and eyes. Super cute. Boyfriend. Tristan had been studying certain portions of his notebooks, trying to absorb details of this guy. Name. Occupation. Family. So many little things his damaged brain couldn't record. Specific details lost forever, unless inked onto paper.

He did know the man, though. He felt that familiarity in his heart, not with his mind. Tristan also knew something terrible had happened to him recently.

Don't ask. Read the notebook.

Aug.8—Going to Big Dick's with Noel and Shane. Late birthday cele-bration. Missed birthday last week because Shane's brother died. Be sensitive tonight. Shane. Big Dick's. Birthday.

Oh. Duh.

He'd never met Shane's brother—even without checking his older notebooks, Tristan felt the truth of that in his heart. But Tristan's own brother had died in high school, and he knew some of that pain. His wasn't the same as Shane's. No one's loss was ever the same. Everyone grieved differently. He was glad that Shane had Noel.

"I said I'm sorry, right?" Tristan asked before common sense could censor the words.

Shane stared at him, eyebrows knitted together. "For what?"

"Your brother. I can't remember his name, and I can't remember if I've seen you since the funeral, and if I didn't say it,

16   A.M. ARTHUR

then I'm really sorry for your loss." The word vomit made him feel idiotic, and like maybe he had said that all before.

If he had, Shane didn't mention it. He smiled, but his eyes stayed sad. "Thanks, Tristan."

"I wish I'd met him."

"Everyone liked him, so I'm sure you would have too."

Something in Shane's tone made Tristan drop the conversation. They were going out to Big Dick's for Tristan's birthday. Happy thoughts only. And Shane probably didn't need the reminder. He lived with the pain every day. For a few hours tonight, he needed to forget.

Forget. Ha ha.

Tristan focused on the nighttime city streets, catching the occasional glimpse of something he knew from before. An exit sign. A restaurant. A busy intersection. His focus slipped, and he glanced at the notebook entry for a reminder.

He'd been twenty when the accident happened, so he'd never been to Big Dick's before. Rumor was the bouncer was an expert at catching fake IDs, so he and Noel had never bothered trying. And he didn't feel like flipping back through hundreds of pages of handwritten text to find his answer. "Have I been to Big Dick's before?" he asked Noel.

"Once," Noel replied. He squirmed, uncomfortable with the question.

That made Tristan nervous. "What happened?"

"About two months ago, you decided you wanted to go to Big Dick's on your own, to prove to yourself that you could."

Tristan dropped his forehead into his palm. He was impulsive on the best of days. His memory problems only exacerbated the stress those impulses put his friends through. "I freaked out, didn't I?"

"A little bit. You lost your notebook, and you didn't know anyone. The owner called me, and I drove out to pick you up. Nothing happened to you, Tris."

I bet I wanted to get laid.

Tristan didn't need to check his notes to know he hadn't had sex since before the accident. Three years was a long damned dry spell. Not that he could remember the dry spell, exactly. He sensed the passage of time, of course. He could look at Noel and the ways he'd changed and know it was way past college, only it would take a while to remember exactly how long past.

Somehow he innately knew three years. Déjà vu sense at work?

So yeah, dry spell. Then again, who'd want to have sex with a guy who'd probably forget what they were doing halfway through and freak the hell out on him? No one.

Loser.

At least I can dance for a while without forgetting. And Noel will be there. I'll be safe.

Noel was his touchstone. No notebook needed to know that. Or to know his parents weren't around. Noel had been his one constant through everything. Tristan wouldn't be able to function without him.

"I must have felt terrible for dragging you all the way to Harrisburg in the middle of the night," Tristan said. "You don't live there anymore."

Noel nodded, his cheeks pinking up like they did when he was remembering something he didn't like. "You did feel terrible. But I didn't mind."

"Yeah, right. You shouldn't have to babysit me. And I shouldn't have gone out alone." Tristan considered flipping back through his notebook to see if that night was in this one. To figure out his mindset. Except he knew what it was, because he felt like that most of the time.

Lonely. Horny. Scared.

Sick and tired of his broken brain. Desperate to be whole again.

All of the above. All the time.

"If I make a scene tonight, I am so sorry ahead of time."

Noel squeezed his knee. "I called the owners last night. They remembered you and they know we're coming. Their employees know."

Humiliation flamed his face. "Shit, Noel, really?"

"I didn't do it to embarrass you. I did it to keep you safe. It's actually a good thing, other people knowing about your disability."

Dark eyes flashed in his mind. They didn't belong to anyone in particular. He saw them occasionally and for no good reason. Kind, dark eyes. A warm smile.

"Have I made any new friends lately?" Tristan asked.

"Friends? No." Noel took an exit into another part of the city. "I mean, you've been meeting new people when we go out places. You've met some people in Stratton."

"Okay."

Noel parked in a pay-by-the-hour garage instead of on the street. Tristan took another look at his notebook for additional clarification, then used a marker to write *Noel, Shane, dancing* on the backs of both hands. He'd look kind of silly but it would help.

The late hour didn't diminish the sweltering August heat, and Tristan worked up a good sweat walking. Shane and Noel both looked crazy sexy in their club clothes, and even sexier walking side by side. He was happy for Noel. Happy his best friend was in love and enjoying himself.

He was also stupidly, insanely jealous.

He stuck close with his stupid, insane jealousy because the streets were teeming with people of all ages, heading into and out of the different restaurants and clubs. They turned down a quieter side street that was more like an alley. Halfway down the block a few guys hung out against a stone wall, most of them smoking cigarettes. An industrial door with no sign or markings was being guarded by a big, burly bear of a man in a black leather vest.

"Hey, Officer Carlson," the bouncer said. He had a deep voice to match his broad body. "Nice to see you again."

"Hi, Mr. Henson," Noel said.

"Bear, son. Everyone calls me Bear."

"Right. This is my friend Tristan Lavalle."

"A right pleasure."

Tristan shook Bear's hand, surprised by the gentle grip. "Hi." He glanced at Shane, who didn't seem at all annoyed at being left out. "Um, that's Shane. Noel's boyfriend."

Bear grinned. "Yeah, I know that one all right."

"You do?" He reached for a notebook he didn't have, then looked at Noel for answers.

"Shane dances here once a week," Noel said. "He got the job through Bear's son Gabe."

"Oh." He didn't bother asking if he'd already been told that. Probably. Every single piece of information that was mildly important to his life had been repeated to him at least, oh, eighteen times. Minimum.

"Enjoy yourselves, boys," Bear said. "First drinks are on the house."

"Thank you," Tristan replied.

Noel pulled the door, and what had been a distant bass became an impressive thumpa-thumpa in Tristan's chest. The interior of the club was wide and deep, with a high ceiling decorated in strands of red and blue lights. Strobes and other lighting flashed around the dance floor, which seemed to make up most of the floor space. A small U-shaped bar stood to the right. In the rear were what looked like raised platforms. Two hot guys in red short-shorts were gyrating together on one of them.

This is the kind of dancing Shane does? Shit.

He was probably twenty kinds of hot up there.

Someone jostled past them, reminding Tristan to keep moving forward. Noel was hustling them straight for the bar. Tristan couldn't drink alcohol because of his antidepressants and anxiety medications, and Noel was driving so the only person able to drink much was Shane.

Lucky bastard.

Not that Tristan was going to mourn his dry night. Men. Everywhere around him, a sea of hot men. All kinds of eye candy. Every age, height, weight, shape and body hair amount. He observed and mentally drooled over the flesh on display. The air smelled of liquor and sweat and sex, and good Lord he was starting to get lightheaded from it all.

Noel nudged them closer to the bar. A middle-aged man with gray hair and a pink sequined vest gave them all a big, toothy smile. "Noel and friends," he said. "Richard Brightman, pleased to officially meet you, Tristan."

"Hello," Tristan said. *Officially meet you* implied they'd interacted before, but the man's name meant nothing to him.

"I'm Bear's husband. We own the place."

"Oh. It's a great place. I'm pretty sure this is my first time. I like it." Noel flinched.

Okay that was wrong. When was I here before?

"So what are we drinking tonight?" Richard asked. "First round on the house. Samuel Adams for you, Shane?"

"Yeah, thanks," Shane replied.

Richard knows because Shane works here.

"I'll have a vodka tonic," Noel said. "Tris?"

"Virgin margarita," Tristan said. He loved margaritas, and while a virgin wasn't as good as one with Patrón, he couldn't mix with his meds.

"Coming up," Richard said.

The music changed to a faster, sharper beat. Tristan's hips rolled in tiny motions, instinct bringing out his love of club dancing. Of getting into it with another dude, all writhing bodies and gyrating hips. Arms and legs. Sweat and heavy breathing.

Wonderful arousal stirred in his gut, heating his blood

already. He might not be getting laid tonight, but damn it, he was going to have some fun.

"Hey, you guys made it," said a sexy, sultry voice.

Tristan glanced over his shoulder to see who the voice had spoken to, only to find himself staring into a pair of kind, dark eyes. Kind, dark eyes belonging to a stunningly handsome face. Black hair. Tan skin. Tall and well-built. A walking wet dream who was smiling like they were old friends.

Holy fucking hell, he's gorgeous.

"Hey, Gabe," Shane said.

Gabe.

Those kind, dark eyes never broke from his, and Tristan couldn't look away. Gabe was a stranger, and yet somehow familiar.

His eyes. The eyes I see. We've met.

"We've met," Tristan said before he could think twice.

Gabe's eyebrows twitched. "Yes, we have. Do you remember that?"

"I remember your eyes."

"You remember my eyes?" He didn't sound surprised or weirded out by that. More like pleased that a detail had actually stuck.

It pleased Tristan all over the place. "That's weird, right? I remember your eyes, but I couldn't tell you what I had for dinner tonight."

"I guess I made an impression."

"It's easy to see how you might." Hell yes, Tristan was flirting. Hot guy. Dry spell. He was out to have a good time. "I'm guessing we met here?"

"Yeah, we did." Gabe glanced at Noel, who apparently knew this story, because he nodded at Gabe. "About two months ago, you came to the club alone."

Dread crept over him. "How badly did I embarrass myself?"

"Not badly. Once my dad called Noel and he explained everything, it was okay. I'm glad I was here to help."

He was leaving out a lot of details that Tristan wouldn't remember in half an hour, and he wasn't entirely sure he needed to hear them. Possibly for the second, third or tenth time. Instead of pressing the issue, he took a long sip of his margarita, savoring the pop of lime and salt on his tongue. Then he looked Gabe in the eye and asked, "You wanna dance?"

Gabe's grin was immediate and blinding. "Definitely."

Tristan chugged the rest of his drink, then plunked the glass down on the bar. He grabbed Gabe's hand and led the way into the sea of moving bodies. Arms and hips bumped and brushed. Music poured through him, setting the beat as he turned to face Gabe, who was already moving. A white tee clung to what was probably a perfect six-pack. Black jeans hugged his ass and outlined a nice package.

So fucking hot.

And his for now, so Tristan let go of Gabe's hand, closed his eyes and danced.

Noel Carlson leaned one elbow on the bar top while his free arm snaked around his boyfriend's waist. He and Shane stood there watching Tristan come to life on the dance floor.

Fun, flirty and impulsive, Tristan had been impossible not to love from their first encounter in college six years ago. Occasionally lovers, always the best of friends, they'd spent the first three years in each other's pockets. Helping each other study, picking on each other's choice of dating material, being a shoulder to lean on in the hard times. Noel treasured every memory of that Tristan.

The summer before their senior year, he and Tristan had been walking home from a late movie and were jumped by four drunk assholes. Noel ended up with his chest carved to pieces from a broken whiskey bottle. Tristan had been left with a traumatic brain injury that compromised his short-term memory. Thirty minutes was usually the maximum amount of time before information or a moment between them was lost to him forever.

In the three years since, Tristan had improved in some ways. Shane coined the term déjà vu sense. He innately knew certain things, such as the time period since the bashing, the fact that Noel was a police officer and lived in a different town than him, and that he was in a relationship.

Hearing him say he remembered Gabe's eyes had been a shock for Noel. The night Noel received a call from Richard, telling him that Tristan had gone to Big Dick's alone and was freaking out, was burned into his memory forever. The fear over what had happened and the state Tristan would be in. The anger at himself for not thinking to take Tristan out. Horror at hearing Tristan say he wished that he'd been killed by that whiskey bottle.

Noel had heard that tearful remark more than once, and it hurt every single time. He knew Tristan was unhappy living at an assisted living center surrounded by the elderly. He didn't know how to help him, except for small steps like tonight's outing.

"He looks so happy," Shane said.

"I know."

Tristan was writhing to the beat of the song, occasionally snaking an arm around Gabe's shoulders or waist. Gabe had a few inches in height and a solid thirty pounds of both weight and muscle. Tristan was five ten, but he was skinny as hell because he accidentally skipped meals frequently enough to piss Noel off. He'd spoken to the staff at Benfield about it more than once, and most recently he'd threatened legal action if they didn't make sure Tristan was properly taken care of.

Noel had that kind of power, only he'd never told Tristan. Because of Tristan's mental state, his parents had maintained power of attorney and paid for all of his medical expenses. Last week, a lawyer for Justin Lavalle had couriered over documents giving Noel the power of attorney for Tristan. His parents would continue to pay for his room and expenses at Benfield, but they no longer wanted to be informed about or responsible for his care.

After Noel had spent ten minutes ranting his rage to Shane, he'd signed the papers. At least someone who genuinely loved Tristan was in control of his health and future.

He just hadn't figured out how to tell Tristan about it. Yet another reason for Tristan to consider himself a huge disappointment to his parents.

Tristan's dancing faltered. He looked around, a little wide-eyed, then down at his hands. Gabe said something. Tristan smiled, and then everything went on like normal.

Memory slip.

"It's kind of weird," Noel said, practically shouting into Shane's ear to be heard over the din.

"What's weird?"

"Tristan out there dancing with a porn star."

Shane choked on his beer hard enough that Noel had to snag a napkin off the bar so he could blow his nose. "Asshole."

Noel laughed. "I wasn't trying to kill you, I swear."

"Yeah, right." He leaned in, his breath tickling Noel's ear. "In a few minutes, you're going to be out there dancing with a porn star too, you know."

"Former porn star."

"Pedant."

Shane had gone into Internet porn a few months ago as a means to pay off a huge debt he owed for medical expenses, and to take the burden off his ailing brother Jason. The porn had torn at Shane's soul and nearly kept him and Noel apart. But in the end, the debt was paid and Shane was free of it. He'd even landed the dancing job at Big Dick's thanks to his association with Gabe on set. The only thing it hadn't done was save Jason's life. He'd passed away from a massive heart attack while Noel and Shane were making a birthday cake for Tristan.

Some days were harder than others, but Shane was putting the pieces back together, and Noel would do anything to make it easier on him.

"The word former is very important to the label," Noel said. "It says that no matter what happened before, now you're all mine."

Shane's soft smile was worth more than a hundred verbal "I love you's". "Yeah, I am. Let's dance, officer."

Noel finished off his vodka tonic before joining Shane in the throng. He'd seen Shane dance. He wasn't getting out of this club without a hard-on.

3

During the next three hours of ridiculously frenetic dancing, Gabe reminded Tristan of his surroundings four more times. Not bad really, since Noel said the memory usually went after thirty minutes or so. Maybe it was the energy, the dancing, or even Gabe himself. It didn't matter, because the blond man in his arms was having the time of his life, and Gabe was thrilled to be a part of it.

The first time he saw Tristan huddled on the floor of the break room, red-faced and freaking out, Gabe had wanted to comfort him. To hug him and try to figure out why he was so scared. But Tristan had flinched away from him, like he'd flinched away from his dad, so he'd let him be. It wasn't until Noel arrived and fully explained the situation that Gabe started getting angry.

Angry that Tristan was living such a difficult life, and that an attempt to go out and find some companionship had ended in fear and tears. His anger had only been compounded by Tristan's confession, overheard as Gabe was leaving the break room. "Why didn't they just kill me with that fucking bottle?"

So many things in one sentence. He'd wanted to make it

better somehow, even though Tristan wasn't his to fix.

He never imagined he'd end up dancing with Tristan at Big Dick's, both of them sweaty and sporting wood. And judging by the hard length currently thrusting against his thigh, Tristan had been blessed in that area. Tristan's hands were everywhere. Clutching his shoulders, raking down his back, occasionally dipping low enough to squeeze Gabe's ass. Gabe returned the favor, enjoying his own manual exploration of Tristan's writhing form. On the thin side of lean, very little muscle definition, but so much control.

Most of the time Tristan danced with his eyes closed, seeming to rely on instinct to keep him from bumping others or stepping on Gabe's feet. But the moments when he did open his eyes, flashes of bright blue sparkled and showed his utter joy at what they were doing. He was nothing like the scared boy from their first meeting. This Tristan was confident and alive.

And ten kinds of hot.

Don't go there.

He couldn't help it. Tristan was exactly his type: blond hair, fair skin, a few inches shorter. Smaller enough in stature that Gabe could really get his arms around him to snuggle after a nice, long fuck. The kind of postcoital time that usually came with relationships, and it had been a long time since he'd tried his hand at that. Not that he was contemplating a relationship with Tristan. He'd known the guy a grand total of four hours, all of which Tristan would forget by morning.

Christ, that must suck so bad for him.

"Hey, stranger!" Marty Gibbons bounced his way past Noel and Shane, grinning to beat the devil. And he'd spoken to Tristan.

Tristan faltered on the beat. "Hi?"

Marty picked up dancing right next to them, as though he'd been invited into their bubble. "I'm so surprised to see you. I figured after last time you'd never set foot in here again."

"We've met?"

"Sure have, but don't worry. Gabe told me about your memory problem, so I don't mind that you've forgotten me. I'm Marty." Marty spoke in a flirty way that made Gabe's skin prickle with irritation. Sure, maybe the pair had been about to get something on before, but tonight Tristan was dancing with Gabe. And even though he liked Marty well enough, Marty was far too self-centered to be good for someone like Tristan.

Tristan needed attention and focus, not a guy whose favorite topic was himself.

"Gabe told you?" Tristan asked.

"Well, you did kind of freak out on me, and he didn't want me to think you were high or anything. Memory problems suck, yeah?"

"Yeah."

"Wanna dance?"

"I'm already dancing. With Gabe."

Something like pride made Gabe's chest swell. He liked that Tristan was enjoying their time together.

"You sure?" Marty asked with a jerk of his hips. "We had a pretty good time before."

"I'll have to take your word on that," Tristan replied, with just an ounce of sass.

Gabe stole a glance at Noel, who was watching them intently while his body still moved with the poetry that was Shane dancing. Shane was a natural and he'd been a fantastic addition to their Monday theme nights. He'd gotten a lot of attention all night from regulars who recognized him, but he was staying firmly in his boyfriend's arms.

That kind of devotion made something deep inside of Gabe ache for a connection to someone.

"Well, if you change your mind," Marty said, "you come find me."

"Uh huh."

Gabe silently cheered when Marty drifted into the crowd. Tristan's arms snaked around his waist, forcing their chests and groins together. Pleasure tickled its way down his spine at the pressure against his erection. A sliding, grinding pressure that was taking things from nice to *wow*. The tempo of the music changed from frenetic "must dance" to a sexier "oh yeah" that signaled the start of the last hour of business.

Tristan danced like a man with a very definite plan for how things were going to proceed, and Gabe didn't know how to throw on the brakes. He didn't want to, not really. But he also didn't want to take advantage or put Tristan in a position to freak out again. He'd hated seeing Tristan so upset. Gabe wouldn't allow himself to be the cause of another episode.

Because, as expected, Tristan's motions faltered and his expression went distant, confused. He stared at Gabe, then glanced around him until he spotted Noel and Shane. He looked down where their erections were grinding together, and his face flushed.

"Gabe," Gabe said before Tristan could ask or wonder. "We've been dancing for about three hours."

"No wonder I'm so sweaty." Tristan relaxed and fell back into the beat. His arms were looser around Gabe's waist, and that was okay.

"Want something to drink?"

"Yeah, actually. I'm kind of feeling the burn."

Gabe missed the press of Tristan's lean body the moment they pulled apart. He kept hold of one of his hands, though, threading them through the throng, over to the bar. Dad already had two bottles of water waiting.

"Thanks," Tristan said as he accepted one of the bottles. "Do you have an open tab?"

"Yep. Plus that's my dad, so I get a hefty discount."

"You don't get served on the house? That seems like the best perk with a parent that owns a bar."

Gabe laughed. "No, I insist on paying something. It was a battle, believe me. My other dad hates it but he understands. I like standing on my own two feet."

Something in Tristan's eyes shuttered. "Must be nice."

"Which part?"

"Both. Parents who care about you and being able to stand on your own feet."

Hell. Way to go, idiot.

"I never came out to my parents before the accident," Tristan said. "It would have just been another way I disappointed them. After the accident, they obviously found out. Noel says they haven't visited me once, and I know in my heart that it's the truth."

Accident. Getting bashed wasn't an accident.

A flash of anger at Tristan's nameless, faceless parents settled in his gut. "I'm sorry." Trite but Gabe didn't know what else to say.

Tristan shrugged, then sipped his water. "It bothered me for a long time. I don't really think it does anymore. Everything from before is so clear in my head, but it also feels distant. It's weird."

"I bet it is." Gabe couldn't imagine the immense frustration of restarting your life every half hour. Not knowing who you were with, or why you'd walked into a room. It would drive him crazy. "Noel seems like a good friend."

"He's the best." Tristan sought out his friend in the crowd, his smile brightening. "We met our freshmen year in college and we've been best friends ever since." That smile dimmed. "Noel was hurt too that night. He doesn't like to talk about it so I don't know what happened to him but he was hurt."

Gabe glanced out in time to see Shane spin Noel around in a complicated move that had a few folks watching. Curiosity demanded he ask Noel more about the "accident". His complete enjoyment of this conversation with Tristan kept him still. "I'm sorry that both of you were hurt."

"Thanks." Tristan tilted his head in an assessing way. "I don't think I do this a lot."

"Do what?"

"Talk about myself with complete strangers."

"Well, we're not complete strangers." He glanced at the clock above the bar. "We've known each other at least five hours now."

Tristan chuckled, a soft, raspy sound that sent tingles down Gabe's spine. "So I can upgrade you to incomplete stranger?"

This time Gabe laughed. "I don't mind, if it means we get to keep talking."

"Definitely. I don't think I've made very many new friends these last few years."

"Then consider one made."

"Excellent. As long as you're not offended when I forget your name in a little while."

"I haven't been offended yet." Gabe leaned in so he didn't have to speak so loudly. "Anyone who gets offended once it's been explained to them isn't worth your time or your friendship."

Tristan's broad smile was a thing of beauty. "Thank you. Sometimes I forget the world is bigger than my room at Benfield."

"The world can be anything you want it to be. You have a limitation, sure, but that doesn't mean you have to let it hold you back from experiencing things."

"I know. It's one of the reasons I'm seeing Noel more. I know I've been to see him where he lives. I don't remember the trips, exactly, just a sense of having been there."

"That's definitely a start. So is coming here tonight."

"Yeah." Tristan fiddled with the plastic ring around the bottle's neck. "I wanted to get out and to dance and be normal for a while. I honestly don't think I expected to make a friend."

"Well, I'll tell you a secret. I'm a pretty introverted guy, so making new friends isn't something I do easily."

"Really? You seem like the guy who knows everyone and talks to anybody."

Gabe shrugged. "I can be that guy. I guess growing up with two dads who own a bar helps you get to know people. And people know me by association. Doesn't mean I'm actually friends with them. Like Marty."

"Who?"

Shit. "Not important."

"Please don't do that."

"Do what?"

Tristan's smile was gone, replaced by an intense stare that was almost accusatory. "If I ask a question, please answer it. Don't treat my memory problem like it doesn't matter."

"That's not—" Except it was what he'd done. "I'm sorry. Marty's a regular here. He came over while we were dancing a while ago. He's someone I know, but not someone I'd hang out with or call a friend."

"Thank you." His expression smoothed out. "So what do you do when you're not hanging out here? Are you in college?"

"No, I graduated a few years ago. Communications degree that I've yet to use."

"So what do you do for a job?"

"I'm a waiter. And I have a bartending license so I help out here once in a while when they're shorthanded. Nothing fancy but it helps pay the bills." No way on earth was he going to admit to his other job. Gabe wasn't ashamed of doing porn, but the job wasn't something for casual conversation.

"Is there something you'd rather do?"

"Sorry to say, no. I got a Communications degree because I could do almost anything with it, maybe go to grad school. I just never found a passion for anything." Plus his home life was exploding all over the place, and keeping his mother under control had become another full-time job. "What about you?"

"I never graduated." Tristan tapped his fingers on the bar top. "I was premed because that's what my parents told me to take. One of their sons would be a doctor no matter what."

"You have a brother?"

His whole face went blank. "I did. He died when I was thirteen. Alex was my parents' pride and joy. He was smart, athletic, had scholarships. When he was gone, all of their expectations for him got dumped on me."

"Man, that fucking sucks. I'm sorry." Gabe needed to refocus the conversation. "If you'd had a choice for a major, what would you have picked?"

"Animation." The excitement was back in his voice and his blue eyes. "I loved drawing and Pixar films, and I wanted to get into animation and storytelling. But my dad wouldn't have ponied up tuition for that, so I did what he wanted. Didn't get either one of us anywhere."

"Have you tried taking classes?"

"What's the point? I'd never remember what the instructor said. I can't concentrate on anything long enough to complete a project. I'd forget what the hell I was doing or why I had to finish it."

"Sorry, I didn't really look at it that way." Gabe felt like an ass for constantly highlighting Tristan's limitations. He wanted Tristan to be happy, to find something he enjoyed doing, instead of wasting away his life in an assisted living center.

"I see things differently than most people," Tristan said. "Don't worry about it." He gulped down the rest of his water. "You know what really sucks?"

"Tell me."

"I'm really enjoying our conversation, and I hate that I won't remember it."

"I can write it down and email it to you. What's your cell number?"

"I don't have one anymore."

Gabe blinked. He didn't know anyone his age without a cell phone. "You don't?"

"I didn't need it. I never left Benfield, so Noel always called me directly."

"Oh." Duh. "But you have an email address?"

"Sure. I don't really use it much."

Gabe tugged his cell out of his pocket and opened up his email. "Give it to me."

Tristan spelled it out for him.

"Brannon Rules?" Gabe had to know. "Who's Brannon?"

"Ash Brannon. He's a Pixar animator. He worked on *Toy Story* and *Toy Story 2*. *A Bug's Life*. *Over the Hedge*. It's silly but I'm a fan, and it's the only email address I've ever had."

"It's not silly. Not if it's something you love."

"The nice thing is that I know those films by heart, so I can still watch them now and not get lost. It's only new movies I can't watch."

"I'm glad you still have something you can enjoy."

"Yeah. Except watching them is kind of depressing too, because I get all excited about a career I'll never have."

Gabe had probably reached his limit of "I'm sorry's" for the night, so he held another one back. "You feel like dancing some more?"

"Sure. I need to take a piss first."

"Bathrooms are in the back. Make sure you use the one on the right."

Tristan grinned. "The one without the favors, you mean?"

Gabe nearly choked on his water.

"Hey, I'd heard of this place long before the accident. I'm guessing by your reaction that it's true."

"Yeah, it's true." Gabe couldn't find much amusement in the fact, since the bathroom with the bowl of condoms and lube sachets was where Tristan had had his meltdown.

"You ever use that one?"

"Hell no. My dads are pretty open-minded guys, but I don't like the idea of having nearly public sex with them both thirty feet away."

Tristan laughed, then slipped into the crowd. Gabe watched him thread his way through dozens of dancing bodies, occasionally knocking away a grabby hand that made Gabe want to follow him so he could body-check a few guys. He almost did anyway, just in case the memory switch flipped again. But he'd seen the writing on Tristan's hands. Hopefully that would be enough.

Gabe, waiter, sometimes bartender, no idea for the future, Gabe, two dads, Gabe, hot as hell, my new friend, don't forget, waiter, Gabe.

Tristan kept the litany going, desperate for every crumb he had tumbling around in his head. Every small scrap of information from his conversation with Gabe, because it wouldn't stay. He was having so much fun. He hated that it would end, only to restart and end again, until he eventually went home and it was gone forever.

Except he's emailing me. I'll have it to read and reread.

He just had to remember to check his email in the morning. He should have asked Gabe to remind him before they parted ways, or to tell Noel to remind him. He'd do that as soon as he got back from the bathroom.

The door on the left was temping, if only to see the infamous favors for himself. Something kept him away, though. A pang of nerves he couldn't explain.

The bathroom on the right reeked of familiar things—sweat and musk and urine. Men still made out in the corners and against walls, but the single pairs of feet behind the three stall doors told him that heavier stuff was restricted to one area. He slipped up to a urinal, purposely ignoring the interested looks being tossed his way.

Years ago, the interest would have had him flirting up a storm with anyone who was cute enough for the effort. Tristan loved going out and meeting new people. He never turned down a party invitation, and he'd had a pretty active sex life. Memories he leaned on whenever he wanted to rub one out. One of his favorite fantasies was of the first time Noel fucked him. It had been a little awkward because they were already friends, and transitioning from friends to relationship was weird. But they'd laughed their way through it, they'd both come, and good Lord, Noel had a great dick.

Tristan redirected his thoughts before they made it difficult to piss away whatever he'd drunk tonight. He did his business and washed his hands. On his way out, someone crowded him against the wall and put a hand by his head. The guy was his age but obviously intoxicated, and Tristan had no idea if he knew him or not.

"Hey, hot stuff. Did you ditch the bodyguard?"

"What?"

The guy got close enough that Tristan could feel his body heat and smell the alcohol on his breath. "Gabe. Finally get tired of him? Need new blood?"

"I'm taking a piss, and then I'm going back to Gabe. Do you mind?"

"Sure do. I saw you first."

Okaaaaay. "Yeah, well, I have a mind of my own and I can make my own choices."

"Choices you don't remember making later. How do you know you really want Gabe?" The dude grabbed Tristan's dick and squeezed.

Tristan jumped, then gave the guy a hard shove. He stumbled into someone else, who kept him from falling over. "Fuck off, guy." He slammed through the bathroom door, irritated by the drunk fucknut's grabby hand. He could take care of himself, but goddamn he hated people who got wasted and groped strangers without permission.

Except I guess I'm not a stranger to him.

Still didn't give him the right.

He glanced around the crowded dance floor, a little uncertain now that his thoughts were flying on a whirlwind of annoyance.

Gabe.

Right. He'd left him at the bar.

"Hey, you okay?" Gabe appeared beside him, that gorgeous face wrinkled up with a frown.

"Yeah."

"You sure? You look mad."

"Something weird happened in the bathroom."

"Marty again?"

Marty. A regular. Someone Gabe knew but wasn't friends with. "Possibly."

"I saw him go into the bathroom, and you hadn't come out yet."

"Then yeah, probably Marty." Made sense.

"What did he do?"

Tristan shrugged it off because he didn't need Gabe to defend him. "He got handsy. I took care of it. My brain might be scrambled but I'm not exactly helpless."

"I never assumed you were."

"No? You followed me to the bathroom to wait."

It was hard to tell on his tanned skin, but Tristan was pretty sure Gabe blushed. A silent admission that he'd been checking up on Tristan.

"I don't need someone to save me, Gabe." His frustration level rose another degree. "Living like this is fucking hard enough without people treating me like I'm a child."

"That wasn't..." Gabe flailed for the words. "I'm sorry."

"Good."

"And I don't think you're helpless, and you are far from a child. I just...I got a little protective. I like you."

Some of Tristan's frustration floated away on a little bubble of genuine surprise. Gabe was protective of him. Gabe liked him.

This is some kind of fantastic dream, and I'll wake up any second.

"In that case, you're forgiven," Tristan said.

"Thank you. Like I said before, I don't make friends easily. I want to keep the ones I've got."

"Hey, guys," Noel said. He and—Tristan glanced at the words on his hand—Shane appeared beside them, both sweaty and disheveled. "I hate to say it, but time to call it a night."

Disappointment curled around Tristan's heart and squeezed an unhappy pang. "Shit, really?"

"I'm wiped, and this one"—he pointed at Shane—"has to work in the morning."

"Noel, can you take a picture of us, please? I want to remember this. And Gabe."

Noel quirked an eyebrow, but he did produce his phone as asked. Tristan looped his arm around Gabe's waist, enjoying the warm press of his muscular body so close. Gabe did the same, giving Tristan's hip a gentle squeeze. Tristan didn't have to force his smile for the photo.

"Hopefully I'll see you again," Tristan said.

"Yeah. Look for that email in the morning, okay?"

"Noel, make sure I leave myself a note to check my email in the morning, okay?"

"Okay," Noel said. To Gabe, he said, "Thanks for making him smile like that."

Gabe nodded. "It was my pleasure. Take care of him."

"Always do."

Tristan reluctantly followed Noel and Shane around the dancing mass, toward the front door. He glanced back once to find Gabe still watching from the rear of the club. He waved. Gabe waved back.

Maintaining his connection to Gabe was important to Tristan for so many reasons. Tonight was the first real step toward normal that he'd made in a long time, and even though his memory issue would never go away, he had new hope that the future would be a little less lonely.

Gabe.

4

09/06
10:34 a.m. _

Tristan—

You're probably surprised and confused to receive this email, and that's okay. My name is Gabe Henson, and we met for the second time last night at Big Dick's, a nightclub in Harrisburg. Your friends Noel and Shane took you out for your birthday, and from what I could see, you had a wonderful time.

I say we met for the second time because the first was about two months ago. You came to Big Dick's by yourself, and you had a moment where you forgot what was going on and where you were. Noel came and picked you up, but you and I met briefly. I brought you water because you were upset. Please don't worry too much about that night. You didn't get hurt. You didn't do anything to embarrass yourself.

Since Noel told us why you reacted the way you did, I knew up front when we saw each other last night. I had a great time with you. We danced for hours. We chatted by the bar for a while, and I promised you that I would email you our conversation (well, it will have to be the condensed version, because I don't have a photographic memory) so you could have that information. So these are the things we talked about.

We talked about what I do for a living. I'm a waiter and infrequent bartender. I did graduate college with a degree in Communications that I never used. I'm not sure what I want to do with my life, but career waiter isn't it. My dads own Big Dick's. My bio dad, Bear, is the bouncer at the door, and my adopted dad, Richard, usually works the bar. They love and accept me and my choices. You didn't ask me my age, but I'll tell you anyway. I'm twenty-four, turning twenty-five in December. Yes, winter baby.

You talked about yourself a little. You told me about your love of drawing and animation, and that watching Toy Story *makes you sad sometimes. I hate that something you used to love makes you sad, but I understand why it does. It reminds you of before. I'm sorry that talking about it with me made you a little sad, but I'm grateful you shared that part of yourself. You told me you don't get to meet a lot of new people. I really hope we can stay friends. You were a lot of fun to talk to, and you're one hell of a good dancer.*

Noel took a photo of us together on his phone. If he didn't send it to you yet, make sure you harass him for it. And maybe get him to send it to me too. My cell # is at the bottom of this email.

I know you don't remember me, but I'd love it if you wrote me back. I think maybe both of us could stand being a little less lonely. —Gabe

–

09/06

11:59 a.m. _

Hi Gabe—

It feels weird to be emailing a total stranger, even though I have the photo of us open on my laptop. I really hate I don't remember dancing with you because judging by your brand of hot, we must have had a fantastic time. (Is it okay that I called you hot? I probably did in person, at least once, because I'm a huge flirt when I don't feel self-conscious.) Anyway, thank you for your email and for letting me know what you already told me about you. And the stuff I told you about me.

I bet the way my memories work is confusing. It confuses me a lot too. Details fly away. It sucks. But I have this thing that Shane calls my déjà vu sense. It's like I instinctively know things without actually remembering the event or when I learned it. Like I know Noel lives in another town. And I'm starting to know Shane—at least, when I see him now I know that I know him but I don't always remember his name. It's the same with most of the staff here at Benfield. Familiar faces but no names. I'm going to study your picture so maybe if we get together again I'll have that déjà vu with you. That would be cool.

So you told me what you do for a living. Unfortunately, I don't really do anything. I listen to a lot of music. I read mostly magazines and short articles in newspapers. I don't watch much TV, except for short things like news segments or sitcoms. Sometimes game shows. I used to watch The Price is Right *a lot when I was a kid, so I'll go out to the TV room and watch it when the other residents put it on. I don't like the new host very much, but it's entertaining. The new* Family Feud *guy, though? OMG, he is the funniest thing ever.*

They do activities here for the residents, but they're mostly geared toward old people. Which makes sense because I live with a lot of old people. I was looking through some notebooks to find interesting things to tell you and I found a day when an elderly man named Scott insisted I was his grandson James. Getting old must suck. My calendar says there is a painting class at two o'clock. I think I'll go to that. Me telling you about animation has inspired me. Thank you.

This is fun. I hope you write back. —Tristan

09/07
1:15 p.m. _

Tristan—

It's Gabe again. I'd have written back sooner but I had to fill in for someone last minute at my waiting job, so I ended up working a double. I hate that. It's exhausting and physically demanding, but more money, so there's a bright side. Right?

So how did the painting class go yesterday? I'll pause a moment while you find your notebook entry and remind yourself. *grin* Please tell me about it, even if you didn't enjoy yourself. I'm curious.

I've got the rest of the day off for a change. I'm usually scheduled on Sundays because it's a busy day, and my boss says I have the kind of face that draws in customers. I take it as a compliment, but I'm pretty sure she's flirting with me. Too bad I bat for the other team, right? My buddy Jon (you've never met him) tells me I get hit on so much by girls because I'm very straight acting. What the hell does that really mean, anyway? Is there a straight or gay way to act? Really? I act like me.

Hope I hear from you soon. —Gabe

09/10
8:45 p.m. _

Gabe—

Hey! I'm sorry it took me a few days to reply to your message. My sticky note reminding me to check my email every day fell off the wall, so I didn't see it. I only remembered because I found printouts of our emails on my desk. I print them out so I can read them whenever I want, even if I'm not on the computer.

So the painting class. Apparently I enjoyed myself. In my notes, I wrote that I wasn't the youngest in the room. Another resident named Charlie was there. He's nineteen, and he is severely mentally deficient (the nurse said "retarded" was rude), and that's why he lives here. He painted spiders. I don't know why. I don't have a painting in my room (according to the notebook, I'm going to finish it in class this Saturday) but apparently I painted a guy's face and described the details. When I looked at the photo of us, I realized it was you. Maybe déjà vu is working already? I look at your photo a lot, I think. Why wouldn't I?

Sorry, flirting again. It doesn't seem as real, I don't think, since you aren't in front of me. But I like having your words to look at too. They help me feel not so alone.

Tomorrow is Thursday. Thursday is the day I hang out with Noel. We go out and do things, and it's always fun. I feel normal around Noel. He gets it. He was there.

I never told you that, did I? The night of the accident, Noel and I were out together. I remember up to that part. I don't remember us getting bashed. But he told me enough that I know he was hurt too, so I went back and found where I'd written it down. After these three guys beat my head in with a bottle, they used the broken end to cut up Noel's chest. He got a lot of stitches and he still has scars. The cops never found the guys who hurt us. I get angry about that sometimes. We never got justice and it fucking sucks. I just hope those assholes didn't hurt anyone else like they hurt us.

Sorry to end on such a depressing note.

Why didn't the toilet paper cross the road?

drum roll
It got stuck in a crack.
LOL. —Tristan

—

09/10
9:35 p.m. _

Ha! Thanks for the chuckle. I needed it. Longer email tomorrow. —G

—

09/11
10:13 a.m. _

Hey T—

I'm glad you enjoyed the painting class and that you're going back on
Saturday. It's kind of amazing that you painted my face. I forgot to tell
you (no pun or anything) that when we hung out last Friday night,
you told me you remembered my eyes from the first time we met. It
was really cool, and it makes me very glad our lives have intersected.
Bear (my bio dad) always tells me that the people we meet are in our
lives for a reason. Sometimes for a long time, sometimes for an hour, but
everyone affects us in some way.

I won't take up much of your time. You probably won't read this
until tonight anyway. I hope you enjoy your day out with Noel. You
two have a special bond, and thank you for telling me more about the

assault. I *hate* that you guys were hurt and that you never saw justice. Is that why Noel is a police officer?

I've got to work in a few hours, so I'm going to hit the gym. Later! —G

09/11
11:45 p.m. _

G—

I'm wired tonight for some reason, which is why I'm emailing you back so late.

Noel and I had a fantastic day. Even if I don't remember it, I know by how I feel later, and I feel great. Looking over my notes, we drove out to Lancaster today. Spent some time at the outlet mall (that thing is huge). Lunch was good. I had a big bowl of chicken and dumplings, and Noel had chicken-fried steak with mashed potatoes. Good Amish-style food.

It's kind of weird reporting these things from my notebooks. But it's also kind of cool knowing someone else actually cares what I do with my time. I know Noel cares. He keeps track of my activities, my mood, that I'm eating when I'm supposed to. But you're someone brand new and you care. It makes me feel less isolated.

Noel even asked about you, and I told him we'd been emailing. He loves that I made a friend, but sometimes I think he's hiding something. It's hard to tell. Did you guys have a fight I wasn't told about? Or was told and forgot to write down?

I hope you had fun working out. Oh, and yes, Noel became a police officer because of the accident. He was already majoring in criminal justice, so he signed up for the police academy after graduation. He *loves his job, even though his hours are weird. But he doesn't have to work Thursdays, so that's our day. And every Sunday afternoon. Maybe you could come visit with him one day. If you have time. —T*

09/12
3:23 a.m. _

T—

We must be on the same wavelength. I can't sleep. I'm glad you had a good day with Noel yesterday. You deserve it. Thanks for telling me about it. Believe it or not, I've never had chicken and dumplings. My dads were both pretty simple cooks. We ate a lot of baked chicken and mashed potatoes. Bear makes a killer lasagna for special occasions. My mother knew the number to everyplace nearby that delivered. I do a lot more of my own cooking now, especially after seeing what goes on in restaurant kitchens sometimes. Yuck. Plus I like to stay fit, so cooking lets me control what's in my food.

Bored yet? I'm rambling about food because I can't freaking sleep. And I have this sudden, weird craving for popcorn. The kind you get at the movies that's coated in that fake butter stuff. Damn. Now I'll never fall asleep.

Here's a joke for you: What did the duck say to the bartender?
drum roll
"Put it on my bill."
You're rolling your eyes, I can tell. Anyway, 'night, Tristan. —G

09/12
8:45 a.m. _

Morning Gabe!

I guess I finally passed out at some point. I woke up feeling kind of disturbed and I don't know why, so seeing your email and remembering you gave me a nice little rush. I'm sorry you couldn't sleep last night, but thank you for writing me.

I'm only awake because my doctor called and scheduled an appointment this afternoon. He wants Noel there. He says he wants to discuss a new treatment option, but he wouldn't give me any more details, so I'm kind of bouncing off the walls. Usually our treatments consist of memory exercises and crap like that, but this seems different. Maybe I'm just being extra-hopeful. I don't know.

I'll let you know what finally happens. —T

PS—What do you call an alligator in a vest?
drum roll
An in-vest-igator.

_

09/12
10:34 a.m. _

GOOD LUCK! —G

_____

5

Noel's appearance in Tristan's doorway nearly made him drop the stack of notebooks he was moving from his bed to the desk. Noel was dressed casually and didn't seem upset or in a hurry, so not a bad news delivery.

"What day is it?" Tristan asked. He could have sworn it wasn't one of their visiting days, but what the hell did he know?

"Friday." Noel folded him into a warm, tight hug. "You nervous?"

"About what?" *Great, what did I forget this time?*

"We're meeting with Dr. Coolidge today. He said he has a new treatment option."

"Oh." *Oh!* "Really? What is it?"

"He didn't specify."

"Cool. Okay. When?"

Noel glanced up at the clock on the wall. "In about five minutes, so we'd better start walking."

"He came here?"

"Yep. Trip out just for you."

Something about that made Tristan more hopeful than usual. He couldn't swear to it but he had a sense that he went to Dr.

Coolidge's office for their appointments, because his neurologist didn't operate out of Benfield. "Well, let's not keep him waiting. Maybe someone has developed a miracle cure for my scrambled brain."

Noel chuckled. "Maybe."

Tristan passed familiar faces as they walked. Familiar hallways too, even if he didn't remember any specific occasion walking down them. Or chatting with anyone. An old man called him James twice before giving up.

Weird.

He followed Noel into a small room near the nurses' station. It had a table and chairs, kind of like a conference area only smaller. Fake potted tree in the corner. A painting of mountains and trees on one wall. Boring.

They sat on the same side of the table, and Tristan put his hands under his thighs so he didn't start tapping them. It annoyed Noel.

Dr. Coolidge. Dr. Coolidge. Good news, please, good news.

Almost right away, two men entered the small room. The first had that déjà vu familiarity thing going on, so Tristan pegged him as Dr. Coolidge. Young, with short brown hair and a blue polo instead of a suit.

Interesting.

"Good afternoon, gentlemen," Dr. Coolidge said. "Tristan, Noel, this is a colleague of mine, Dr. Noah Fischer."

Tristan and Noel stood up long enough to shake their hands. Dr. Fischer had a firm, friendly grip. He seemed older than Dr. Coolidge. They all sat down, the two docs on the other side of the table.

"Dr. Fischer is a fellow neurologist who's been reviewing your case," Dr. Coolidge said, speaking directly to Tristan, which was nice. When he was a kid, the doctors always spoke to his parents, never to him. "He's recently brought something to my attention that I'd like him to present to you both."

"Okay," Tristan said. "I can't promise to remember it all if takes longer than thirty minutes to explain, but I'll listen."

"That's why I asked Noel to come to this appointment. You'll need to make this decision together."

The words carried a kind of heaviness that worried Tristan, and he was glad to have Noel there instead of his parents. He was pretty sure they never visited him, and they probably would have taken the meeting via conference call. Noel being with him was better.

"A decision about what?" Noel asked.

"Neuroscience is a constantly changing field, and we are on the cutting edge of medicine," Dr. Fischer said. "We have to be because there are still so many things about the human brain that we don't yet understand. Traumatic brain injuries like yours, Tristan, are especially big mysteries to us. Some people are hit hard in the head, and they have no ill effects beyond a headache. Others lose memories, motor functions, the ability to speak."

"Tell me something I don't know," Tristan said. He knew his limitations, thank you very much.

"I work for a company called MindCorp. We develop new protocols for brain-related injury or illness, and we've had several go on to be approved by the FDA. Many companies focus on quality of life protocols for these types of injuries, such as temporary improvement for Alzheimer's patients. At MindCorp, we focus on treatment protocols, and for the last few years, I've been working with a team specifically on permanently improving memory function in relation to traumatic brain injuries. We've passed out of the animal testing phase, and we've completed phase one of a clinical trial that has shown promising results."

Tristan's heart skipped and his palms began to sweat. "What does promising results mean?"

"It means that forty percent of participants showed an improvement in memory retention."

"Can you dumb it down a little more, please?"

Dr. Fischer smiled. "In one case, a patient with a similar history to yours had complete restoration of his short-term memory."

"What?" Tristan stood up so quickly that his chair flipped over backward. "Are you shitting me?" Noel grabbed his hand and squeezed tight. Tristan couldn't look at him. He couldn't stop staring at Dr. Fischer and the hope he'd just tossed into Tristan's lap.

"Please don't jump the gun, Tristan," Dr. Fischer said. "That was one instance out of a large pool of participants. But other improvements were shown in terms of memory retention, and we're very hopeful. We're ready to proceed with phase two. Dr. Coolidge submitted you as a candidate, and I agree you're an excellent choice."

Tristan gaped, Noel's hand his only lifeline to reality. This wasn't happening. This wasn't real.

"What happened to the other sixty percent?" Noel asked.

"No change to their cognitive abilities," Dr. Fischer replied. "They simply did not improve. The good news is that they didn't get worse, either."

"What about side effects?"

"Somewhat typical things like dry mouth, constipation, headaches, occasional dizziness."

"And atypical things?"

I'm so glad Noel's here because I can't think well enough to ask this important stuff. Headaches I can deal with.

Dr. Fischer's smile dimmed a bit. "Out of the forty percent who showed improvement, ten percent of those participants experienced seizures, anywhere from mild to severe."

"Seizures," Tristan said. "That sounds awful."

"They can be scary, yes, as well as life-threatening. One patient did choose to quit the trial because of the frequency of his seizures."

"Please tell me it wasn't the person who got their short-term memory back."

"It wasn't."

He glanced down at Noel, who was watching the doctors with his cop face on full-force.

"What other risks are we talking about?" Noel asked.

"Unfortunately, we can't determine that at this time," Dr. Fischer said. "Phase one showed us some side effects, but that's why we do more than one trial and with a wide array of patients with a variety of histories. Everything that makes Tristan unique, from his genetic makeup to his age and his diet, can change the side effects in an instant."

"So I could be the lucky guinea pig who gets warts all over or something gross like that?" Tristan asked. Partly joking. Kind of serious, because warts freaked him out.

"Let's hope not." Dr. Fischer slid a manila folder across the table. "I've put together an informed consent form for you that details everything we've discussed. I want you to study it, talk to Noel about it, and then let me know your decision before September twenty-ninth."

"Is that when you start?"

"Yes."

"Will I have to go a hospital somewhere?"

"No, the medication can be administered by the staff here. The main difference in your routine will be additional medical testing on a weekly basis. I've already reached out to the staff at Mercy Hospital, which is the nearest facility with the needed equipment. We'll meet there once a week and review your overall health and any changes in your memory capacity."

"Mercy is only a few miles from where I live," Noel said.

"Really?" Tristan asked. "Cool."

"If he does experience side effects that require treatment, who pays his medical expenses?"

"All of that information is in the consent form," Dr. Fischer said. "But his medical expenses would be covered by MindCorp up to ten thousand dollars."

"So worst case scenario is seizures or no real change," Tristan said. "Best case is I'm normal. I could have a normal life."

"It is possible, Tristan. It's also possible you'll go through this and nothing will change. So I urge you to think carefully when making this decision."

His mind was already half made up, but Noel would tell him to wait and discuss it more. Noel was careful like that, while Tristan was the impulsive one. It was why they worked so well together. "What do you think, Dr. Coolidge?"

"We've worked together since your hospital stay, Tristan," he replied. "I've seen you improve over the last few years, in terms of cognitive function and general mental state. However, these last few months your psychiatrist and I have also seen a downturn in your overall outlook. You've been more depressed in your sessions with Dr. Patrone, and the staff has reported more frequent outbursts of anger."

Oh great. I'm losing it and I don't even know it.

Noel squeezed his knee.

"So you think I should do this?" Tristan asked.

"I wouldn't have passed your information over to Dr. Fischer if I thought otherwise."

"Will the staff here know about the trial?" Noel asked.

"The administration, the on-call doctors and the head nurse will know, so they can be aware of any potential side effects," Dr. Fischer said. "I don't want to inform the general nursing staff. We need their unbiased feedback on any memory improvements they may or may not see."

"Do I take pills every day or something?" Tristan asked, his excitement over the possibility of getting better growing with every new question asked. Every new answer given.

"You'll receive an injection in your hip twice a week, Monday and Thursday, in the morning. The injection site may be sore for a few hours. We'll also need you to undergo a complete physical evaluation at Mercy before we begin the trial."

"And how long will I participate in the trial?"

"Phase one ran for six months. For phase two, we are asking for a nine-month commitment."

"Okay."

"It sounds as though you're leaning toward a yes."

"I want to do this." Tristan knew in his gut he wanted to do it, and he would. He had to. "But I still need to talk to Noel about it."

"I understand. Let Dr. Coolidge know your decision, and he'll contact me."

"Thank you."

Tristan stared at the closed door after the two doctors left, not quite believing that the conversation had just happened. Noel's chair scraped, and then he was standing across the table from him, arms folded. His face was a weird mix of scared and hopeful.

"I need to do this, Noel."

"I know you do. That's why it worries me so much."

"What does?"

"The possibility that it doesn't work. I know you, Tris. You will be heartbroken if you go through with this and nothing improves."

"Forty percent is decent odds, though, considering, right? I mean, if it was ten percent, then maybe not, but forty is good. That's like one out of three."

"What about the seizures?"

"It wasn't everyone who got better." Tristan circled the table and put his hands on Noel's shoulders, as much for himself as for his friend. "Please. I hate living like this. In bits and pieces. Forgetting everything, writing down everything. Not knowing who's a stranger and who's a friend. I don't want to get hurt more and I don't want to die, but this isn't really living. It's a chance I have to take."

Noel's blue eyes glimmered and he blinked hard. "I know.

You're my best friend. I want you to be happy, but I don't know what I'd do if I lost you."

"You won't."

"Okay then. Let's go back to your room and get this written down before it's gone."

Tristan's heart thumped hard. He was going to do this. In a few weeks, he'd start a clinical trial that could give him his life back.

Please, please God, let this work.

Gabe lugged the two reusable shopping bags' worth of groceries out of the backseat of his car, oddly energetic for having just spent the day fucking a new guy on the Mean Green set. Usually he was exhausted after a shoot. Instead, he rode the endorphins to the store and stocked up on a few things. Even the annoyance that was grocery shopping at a supercenter didn't bring him back down.

He still hadn't heard from Tristan about his meeting with the doctor, but it had only been a few hours. He probably hadn't seen the sticky note reminder yet.

The front door was unlocked, the television blaring what sounded like *Judge Judy* before he even opened it. Debbie was sprawled on the sofa in her bathrobe, hugging a pillow, staring vacantly at the TV screen. She didn't move or seem to notice his arrival, which was fine by him. When she was zoned out at least she wasn't yelling.

He dumped the grocery bags on the counter next to a stack of envelopes. Unopened bills. The sight of them had stopped making him angry once he accepted the inevitability of it. No matter what he did, she found a way to spend money she didn't have. They were lucky they hadn't lost the house yet.

Once the groceries were put away, he tossed some cold

chicken into a wrap with a smear of hummus. Easy dinner that
went down with a glass of water. In the living room, a sitcom
rerun came on, adding canned laughter to the background.
Debbie hadn't moved once.

He moved to stand in front of her. Not even a blink. "Debbie?
Have you eaten today?"

Nothing.

While he preferred her quiet to ranting, the whole point of
living there was to make sure she took care of herself. And he was
pretty sure she was wearing the same clothes she'd worn
yesterday.

He heated up a can of tomato soup. Got her sitting up with a
tray on her lap. She ate by rote, not seeming to taste it or really
care that she was doing it. Better than nothing. He cleaned up the
kitchen, then led her upstairs. By the time they were in the bathroom, she'd come around more. Enough that he trusted her to
actually shower, so he left her alone.

His phone dinged with an email alert.

Tristan.

He unlocked his bedroom door and went inside to read it,
buoyed by the sight of his new friend's name on his screen.

*I probably could have sent this sooner but every time I reread today's
entries I get scared and excited all over again. And now that Noel called
Dr. Coolidge and said I'm in, it's official and I want to tell you.*

*On September 29, like two weeks from now, I will begin partici-
pating in a phase two clinical trial for a drug that might improve my
memory. One person in the first study ended up totally normal. There's
a forty percent chance I'll improve, which is good, I think. Only a little
less than half of everyone improved, and I'll do almost anything to not
live like this anymore. Noel and I talked it out forever because there are
side effects, but nothing really deadly. He's nervous and I'm nervous,
but oh my GOD! What if it works?*

Anyway, that's what the appointment was all about. Hope you had a good day! —T

Gabe reread the email twice, his excitement rising with each passing moment. Tristan had a real chance at leading a normal life. They could sit down and have long conversations that Tristan would be able to remember in an hour. He could stop living his life thirty minutes at a time.

"Please, God, let this work." He hadn't been to mass in years, but he made the sign of the cross anyway. "Tristan deserves it."

6

Tristan snapped the binder clips together, sealing in the latest printed email from Gabe. He kept each one, even the emails he sent to Gabe, printed in order, in a binder, so he could read them whenever he wanted. Apparently they'd been emailing daily for the last couple of weeks. The binder helped remind him he had a friend out there. A smoking hot friend, judging by the only photo he had of them.

Today's latest email was dated September thirtieth, sent at twelve thirty p.m. He scanned the page again, reminding himself of the contents. His eyes caught on the third paragraph's first line. *Do you feel anything yet? I know it's early, but I'm really pulling for you.*

He wasn't sure what that meant, so he flipped back to an email from the day before.

Right. Drug trial. Memory improvement.

"I guess I'm not feeling anything," he told the page. One day after the first injection was way too soon. He probably had it written down somewhere about the time frame for improvement, but he didn't feel like searching.

"Good morning," Noel said from behind him.

Tristan jumped and nearly dropped the binder. Noel and his boyfriend stood just inside of his room, both of them grinning like they had a secret. Tristan stared at the black-haired man next to Noel, willing his name to come.

Nothing.

"Shane," he said before Tristan could even ask.

"Right, yes." Shane sounded familiar enough. "What are you guys doing here? It's Tuesday."

"We have a surprise for you," Noel said. "Wanna go on a road trip?"

"Definitely." Anything that got him out of Benfield for a while. "Do I get to know where? I'll probably forget by the time we get there."

"Nope. Complete and utter surprise."

"Okay, cool." Tristan grabbed his current notebook and a pen. "Lead the way."

He signed himself out at the front desk, then followed the pair to Noel's car. No one really said anything, and judging by the way Noel and Shane kept tossing looks back and forth, it was a pretty big surprise. Tristan tapped his fingers against his knee and watched the scenery go by.

"So did you have any soreness from the injection yesterday?" Noel asked. He met Tristan's eyes in the rearview.

"Um, hold on." Tristan flipped back through yesterday's entries. "A little bit. Kind of like a dull ache, but only for about an hour or so."

"That's good."

"Might last longer the more frequently I get the shots."

"We're all pulling for you," Shane said. "Sincerely. I hope this helps."

"Thank you. Me too." He liked Shane because he was considerate, and because he made Noel so happy. He was also a little jealous, because they had something Tristan might never have if the treatment didn't work. Not everyone was as patient as Noel.

And Noel was easier because Tristan remembered him from before the accident.

Tristan would never have to ask him what his name was.

They were on the road for a while before he spotted a sign for Stratton. "I know that name, don't I?" he asked.

"You sure do," Noel said. "This is the town where I live. You've been here half a dozen times or so."

"Cool. What are we doing today?"

"That's part of the surprise."

Do I know about a surprise? A surprise for me?

He stayed quiet instead of looking like a fool. Noel drove into a small town nestled in the hills. Shopping center, fast food, nice homes. Typical small-town Pennsylvania without being too poor. They ended up in a neighborhood of boxy, midcentury homes with cut lawns, trash cans by the sidewalk and older-model cars in the driveways.

"Do I know someone who lives here?" Tristan asked.

"Actually, yes you do," Noel said.

"Okay."

Noel pulled into a two-car driveway in front of a small, single-story home. White paint, blue trim. Neat hedges. A simple brick stoop. The front lawn was cut, if a little small, and there was no garage. Nothing about it seemed familiar at all. Both men got out, so Tristan followed them up a brick path to the front door.

Instead of knocking, Noel stuck a key in the knob and pushed open the blue front door. He went inside first, practically vibrating with energy. Tristan followed, with Shane right on his heels, as bubbly as Noel. Tristan stared at the pair, who looked ready to explode with whatever their secret was.

"Am I supposed to guess who lives here?" Tristan asked. The walls were bare, revealing evidence of nail holes and recently removed artwork. No furniture to speak of in the boxy living room, or to the left in the small dining room. "Are they nomads?"

"We live here," Shane said. "I've already sold the trailer. We closed on the house yesterday. Noel wanted to bring you here to tell you."

"You bought a house?" he asked Noel, disbelief making everything a little fuzzy. "Really?"

"Yes." Noel's eyes shone with emotion. "We're moving in this week."

"We'd sleep here tonight but the bed won't be delivered until tomorrow," Shane said. "It even has a guest bedroom. It's the perfect size for us. And maybe a dog."

"You're getting a dog?" Tristan asked.

"We've discussed it."

"And made no decisions," Noel said.

"And I get to decorate the whole place, because Noel says he doesn't really care as long as I stay away from animal prints."

"He hates animal prints, especially in clothes," Tristan said.

"For good reason." Noel steered him down a short hallway and into a kitchen. With no appliances.

"Damn, you guys got a fixer upper, huh?"

"It was a good price," Shane said. "And I've got the money to fix it up the way we want." His expression darkened briefly. Tristan didn't ask why, or where he'd gotten a wad of cash for home renovations. For all Tristan recalled, Shane could be a closeted millionaire.

Except that probably wasn't it, because Noel grabbed Shane's hand and didn't let go.

Conversation switch, stat.

"Do I get to help fix it up?" Tristan asked. "I can paint and stuff."

"Oh, you are definitely going to help," Noel said. "Once the interior designer here decides on paint colors, we'll make a weekend of it or something."

"Sounds like fun." And terrifying. "Um, have I spent the night anywhere but my room since the accident happened? I don't feel like I have."

Noel shook his head. "No, you haven't."

"So it will be an experiment for all involved. I mean, if I freak out in the middle of the night you can always take me home."

"Nah, that would be like giving up. I'm never giving up on you, Tris."

"Even if I'm like this the rest of my life?"

"Even if." Noel used his free hand to thump him under the chin. "But I thought we were being positive? If this treatment works, you won't be like this forever."

"Treatment?" *I'm doing something new?*

"Yup." Patient as ever, Noel explained the clinical trial.

"Forty percent is good odds," Tristan said. "I could have a real life."

"Yes, you could. That's what we're all praying for. So you want to see the rest of the house?"

"Definitely."

After a quick tour of the upstairs, Noel led him through the kitchen and out the back door. The instant he saw it, Tristan understood why they'd picked this particular house. The front lawn was small, but the fenced-in backyard was huge. Three large oak trees stood near the rear of the property, providing a nice area of shade. A wide brick patio gave them the perfect place to host summer barbecues.

And the pool. An in-ground pool, covered at the moment, but Tristan knew what it was. A shed stood near it, probably for equipment and stuff.

"Dude," Tristan said.

"Yep." Noel bounced on his toes, clearly pleased with himself.

"You've always wanted a pool."

"And now I have one."

"The big jerk didn't tell me that," Shane said. "When I demanded to know what was on his wish list for a house, he said he didn't care."

"And that was true," Noel replied. "Having or not having a

pool wasn't a deal breaker. But it definitely made me lean toward this house."

"Since it's practically October we aren't going to bother with it this year, but come next spring? Pool party. Major pool party."

"I am so here," Tristan said.

Noel laughed. "You'd better be."

"This is all so cool. I'm really happy for you guys." He side-eyed his best friend. "Look at you, settling down. Who'd have thought?"

"Hey, I always wanted to settle one day. You were the one who always said variety was the spice of life."

Tristan shrugged. "Okay, so I'm a slut. You weren't exactly a monk, you know."

"Oh yeah?" Shane said. "I want stories."

"How about food instead?" Noel said. "Dixie's Cup for lunch?"

"Well, it'll be hard to fix lunch here without a stove. And don't think I'm letting him off the hook. I still want stories about your college conquests."

"College days are clear in my mind," Tristan said. "Ask anytime."

"I will get you back for this," Noel said to him.

"Bring it, Carlson."

On the ride to Dixie's Cup, Tristan wrote down every detail he remembered about Noel's new house. Even though his relationship with Shane sometimes made his jealousy sit up and take notice, Tristan was thrilled for Noel. He loved seeing his best friend so happy and settled. He loved the small house and the big backyard. Even more, he loved the idea of visiting them both there.

Of taking more steps toward actually living his life, rather than simply existing in it.

Gabe stuffed his gym shorts into his workout bag on top of his sweaty T-shirt and sneakers. He hated wearing his smelly clothes home from the gym, even though the locker room made him feel self-conscious. Which he'd never admit to his gym buddy Jon, because Jon would tease him endlessly about the big bad porn top afraid of someone ogling his bare ass.

Jon didn't give a shit. He spent more time in the locker room totally naked than in any other state of dress or half dress. And he had plenty to be proud of—sculpted six-pack, perfectly defined V, everything smooth and hairless. Plus he was blond and had a boy-next-door adorableness about him that made him perfect for porn.

He also had a great ass. Gabe had been there several times, always in a professional capacity. As much as they got along outside the Mean Green set, and as well as they played off each other on set, they had no personal chemistry. Not that it mattered if they did. He couldn't seriously date a guy who was fucking other guys, and he didn't care if that made him a hypocrite. If he ever found someone to be serious with, Gabe would tell him about porn. They could dump him or deal.

I wonder what Tristan would think.

He doubted that Shane had ever told Tristan about his stint in porn, so there was no predicting Tristan's reaction. He seemed like an open-minded guy.

Not that it mattered, because unless this drug trial actually worked, they had no real chance of anything beyond an email relationship.

"Earth to Gabe," Jon said. "You gonna close the locker, or are you willing it with your mind?"

Gabe blinked at his friend, who was actually dressed and standing with his own gym bag slung over one shoulder. Gabe shut the locker door a little too hard, and the noise echoed in the mostly empty room. Midafternoon on a Tuesday wasn't the gym's busiest time of day.

"Who's got you so distracted?" Jon asked as they headed for the exit. He was as tall as Gabe, not quite as broad in the shoulders, and he winked at anyone who let eye contact linger. Jon actually enjoyed the infrequent moments when he was publicly recognized for his porn.

Gabe occasionally signed an autograph or two himself. Tony Ryder had a fan base.

"No one," Gabe replied. So far, Tristan was a secret known only to his dads, and he wanted to keep it like that.

"Liar. I've seen you zoned out from fatigue and from worrying about your old lady. This was a new kind of zoned out. An *I'm thinking about someone hot* zoned out."

"I'm not thinking about anyone. Shut up so we can go get our smoothies."

Jon made a clucking noise that said he was leaving it for now, but not forever.

Protein smoothies from the gym's café had become a ritual for the last year or so of working out together. Jon had confessed to a previous history of an eating disorder brought on by a bad relationship, so Gabe had committed to helping him stay on track. While being physically fit was necessary for modeling, Jon wanted to take care that he didn't slip back into old habits of overworking and skipping meals.

Their gym had a small café that served a variety of smoothies, cut fruit and salads. Gabe's favorite was the chocolate protein smoothie. Jon liked to change things up and try different combinations. Today he ordered the Citrus Sunburst.

"How's Henry doing?" Gabe asked as they settled at an empty table.

"He's in good spirits." Jon sipped at his smoothie, elbows on the table. "The last round of chemo is this week, and his doctor is encouraged."

"That's excellent."

"Yeah."

Jon's best friend and mentor, Henry Pearson, had been diagnosed with prostate cancer several weeks ago, and his doctors were aggressively treating it. Gabe didn't know the whole story between the mismatched pair, only that Henry was roughly thirty years older than Jon, and Henry had been his first gay friend after being kicked out by his parents at age eighteen. Gabe also knew that Henry meant the world to Jon and that watching him go through cancer treatments was incredibly painful.

Another reason why he was glad he knew about Jon's eating disorder. Anorexia was about control, and cancer was far from a controllable thing.

"I'm going to go see him tonight," Jon said. "He's been bitching about wanting to watch the newest Marvel movie, so I promised I'd bring it over."

"Sounds like fun."

"I hope so. He's got that metallic taste in his mouth again, but he insists that popcorn is one of the things that overpowers it. Apparently he eats so much of it that his air popper is giving him fits."

Gabe chuckled. "He'll have to put a new one on his Christmas list."

"Yeah." Jon's smile flickered. "Fucker better be here for Christmas."

"He will be." Gabe couldn't really promise that, but it got Jon smiling again.

"Henry would be the first one to tell you he's okay with dying, but damn it, I'm not ready to let him go."

"Nothing wrong with that." Gabe was lucky that he'd never experienced real loss in his twenty-four years. He loved his dads and couldn't imagine life without them. They'd had one scare with Richard when Gabe was twelve, but other than that he was doing well on his meds. And even though his mother was a pain in the ass on her best days, he loved her too.

Gabe's phone pinged with an email alert. Tristan.

"Okay, there's the look again," Jon said. "Who is he?"

"Huh?"

"You just got that same look you had in the locker room. I know you're holding out on me, pal. Spill it."

"Not a chance."

"You know I'm going to keep pestering you until you tell me."

"I also know that I am far more patient than you, so your curiosity will be more annoying to yourself than your pestering will be to me."

Jon crossed his arms and sulked. "Jerk."

"Hey, a guy's entitled to some privacy."

"Says the porn star."

Gabe glanced around, because Jon had said that a little loudly. No one seemed to be paying attention. "Emotional privacy, dumbass. And maybe shout it next time."

Jon shrugged. "I'm not ashamed of it."

"Neither am I, but I also don't go around advertising it."

"You should. You'd get more dates that way."

"Yeah? When was the last time you went out?"

Jon proved his maturity by blowing a raspberry. "I don't need the emotional complication of dating right now."

"Ditto." Gabe occasionally craved the connection and wonder of waking up next to someone he loved, but not enough to take that plunge again anytime soon. The emotional scars that Andrew left behind were still fading.

"Oh, hey, did I tell you? Benny's coming back to shoot week after next."

"Yeah? He's feeling better?"

"Loads, apparently."

One of the goofiest, most flirtatious models at Mean Green, Benny Taylor had decided two months ago to start PrEP. He'd had to go on a filming hiatus when the side effects became too much for him. His system must have started acclimating if the nausea and dizzy spells were going away.

Gabe had only ever given brief consideration to the HIV prevention drugs available, but the long list of short- and long-term side effects had turned him off the idea. He didn't have sex outside of his regular scenes, and except for one time, he always topped. And he'd never had a condom break.

"You ever think about taking something like that?" Jon asked.

"Thought about it. Not for me."

"Yeah, me either. The last thing I need is something else to make me hate food." He checked the time on his phone. "Dude, I gotta bounce. See you Friday."

"See you then."

Gabe opened the email, always eager to know what Tristan was up to.

G—

Noel and Shane bought a house. A real house with a huge backyard and a pool, and just rereading my notes gets me excited again. It has two bedrooms, and once the guest room is fixed up I can stay overnight. It will be my first time sleeping anywhere except Benfield since the accident, so that's awesome. I hope I don't wake up and freak out on them. And they asked me to help paint and decorate and stuff. Did I mention they had a pool? (haha, I know I did, but I love it, I love swimming.)

We went to lunch, and I spent the rest of the afternoon with them, and now I'm back at Benfield. Nothing else really exciting. I really wanted to tell you about the house. I hope you're having a good day. I look at your photo often enough that your face is becoming familiar at first glance. Not as familiar as Shane but I've known him longer and see him in person more frequently. Maybe we can hang out for real again.

October is tomorrow. It's kind of depressing to look at a calendar and realize another month down that I don't remember. But the house makes me happy again, so there is that. Later. —T

Gabe read the email twice, as was his habit when a new one showed up. Tristan's excitement over the new house leapt off the screen, and it excited Gabe. He was also happy for Shane, who finally seemed to be moving forward with his life.

Maybe we can hang out in person again.

"Maybe we can," Gabe said.

I hope we can.

7

11/01
3:14 a.m. _

T—

I'm impressed that I'm still awake enough to write you but I guess I'm wired from the party. We had a huge turnout at Big Dick's (the bar in Harrisburg that my dads own and I occasionally bartend) for the Halloween Bash, so I was helping out until close. Some of the costumes were amazing, and I attached a few photos of my favorites. Take careful notice of the second photo. I think you'll find sexy Woody and Buzz Lightyear to your liking.

I didn't dress up. I've never really done the whole costume thing. I did wear a black T-shirt with a skull on it, so that kind of counts, right? It's Halloweeny.

We also hosted a costume contest, hence the huge turnout. Partici-pants paid five bucks to enter, and we're donating all proceeds to Chan-

nels Food Rescue, which delivers donations to food banks. We awarded prizes (a punch card for ten free drinks at the bar) in three categories: Scariest, Sexiest and Most Unique. Everyone paraded out at ten, and then we put ballot boxes at the bar, so people could write their choices on the card they were given at the door (no ballot box stuffing or cheating).

Scariest costume was a guy named Ben who went full-on zombie. Makeup, latex, rotting flesh, bloody clothes. It was movie-worthy stuff. I wish I'd been able to snap a picture for you. Sexiest was a guy I know from the gym. Everyone calls him Steel and it's probably because of his abs. A perfect eight-pack and they were on display (along with everything else) because his costume consisted mostly of body paint, glitter and fake leaves glued in various places. He called his getup a Tree Sprite, and he took our one rule (no bare penis) literally. No clothing other than the leaves-covered g-string was touching his skin. Sexy as hell.

Most Unique was pretty punny. Guy named Malcolm glued mini cereal boxes all over a suit and pants. Every cereal box had a tiny knife or ax embedded, and a blood splatter. What was he?

Personally, I would have voted for the guy who wore about a hundred paint sample strips in dozens of shades of gray. Yes, he was Fifty Shades of Gray. Ha ha.

My dad made up a few Halloween-themed drinks for the night that sold well. No one got too drunk or got into a fight, so that's always a plus on holidays. Maybe by next year you'll be able to come out on your own, and we'll have a good time. —G

—

11/01
9:36 a.m. _

G—

Cereal killer! Epic costume!

I'm sorry I missed the Halloween Bash at Big Dick's last night. It sounds like you had a great time. Noel wasn't able to take off because it's Halloween, and he's a cop, and he has to be out there in case people do stupid shit. And let's face it, people will always do stupid shit on Halloween. When I was a kid, the day before Halloween was called Mischief Night, and it was when teenagers went out and toilet papered their neighbor's house, or threw rotten eggs at their car. I never did, because if I'd been caught my parents would have grounded me for the rest of my life, but a lot of my friends did. Did you do Mischief Night?

Now that it's November, I guess everyone is starting to think about the holidays. Do you do anything big and special for Thanksgiving? I checked back, and every year I've spent it with Noel. He doesn't fly back to Arkansas. He only does that for Christmas, and only on Christmas Day, early, so he can spend Christmas Eve with me. When I read stuff like that, it makes my heart hurt. Noel is an amazing friend to me, and all I ever feel like is a burden.

OOHH! I can't believe I forgot to mention this (ha ha): I think I may have had a minor bit of progress, thanks to that drug trial. Today I remembered breakfast is served at eight o'clock. I didn't have to look at my schedule! It was surreal to have it pop into my head, and when I checked the schedule I was right. I can't remember lunch, but dinner is...thinking...five thirty? *checking, brb*

YES I AM RIGHT!

HOLY SHIT!

Sorry but I have to go call Noel! Talk to you later! —T

The train-whistle ringtone that Noel had set for Tristan's phone at Benfield scared him into rolling right out of bed. He hit the floor with a solid thud that made Shane cry out somewhere above. Tristan called so rarely that his heart was pounding before he could accept the call.

"Hey, are you okay?" Noel asked.

"I'm super fucking fantastic!" Tristan's voice was pitched high with whatever had him so excited.

Noel took a second to focus on the alarm clock. Quarter to ten in the morning. He'd only been home and asleep for two hours. Shane stared down at him from the bed, dark hair sleep tousled, his eyebrows slanted. "Okay, what's going on?" Noel asked.

"I remembered what time breakfast and dinner are. I fucking remembered those two things!"

"You did?" He scrambled to his feet, ignoring the ache in his backside from the landing on his room's hard floor. "Shit, Tris, really?"

"Yes. I knew, but I couldn't think of lunchtime, but then I did think of dinnertime all without having looked at my schedule. I think it's working. Could it be working? It can't be a fluke. God, please don't let it be a fluke."

"Calm down, you're babbling. Deep breaths."

"Okay, what?" Shane asked.

Noel explained while Tristan breathed heavily into the phone. Shane's entire face lit up with the news.

"Did you write it down just in case? That you remembered this?" Noel asked.

"Of course I did."

"Okay, good. You need to call Dr. Fischer and let him know. This is your first real breakthrough."

"It is, isn't it? I figured as much. I don't have any notes nearby about remembering anything else, so yeah, this is it. Holy shit."

Pure joy seized Noel's heart. His throat closed and his eyes stung. Tristan wanted this to work so badly, and it appeared he was getting his wish. A tiny portion, but it was a start. Besides the weekly appointments, they'd gone to Mercy Hospital twice since he began the study in order to do full neurological assessments with Dr. Fischer.

Memory game tests, physical exams and blood work. Both times Tristan had left discouraged because he'd failed the memory tests.

Maybe it wouldn't happen with the snap of their fingers. Maybe it began with the small things, like remembering a time on a sheet he'd looked at every day for years.

"I don't know what to say," Noel said. "I'm so fucking happy for you. I really hope this is the first step."

"Me too. I know it's not a cure, and I know I can't expect to remember something new every day, but Noel...I don't...shit." Tristan's voice got rough, on the verge of his own tears.

"Be happy, Tristan. Let yourself be happy over this."

"I will. Gah!"

The cry of pure joy made Noel laugh.

"I have to call the doctor before I forget or something," Tristan said.

"I'll remind you, believe me."

"I know you will. Gah! Bye."

Noel laughed again as he hung up, then tackled Shane to the bed with a shouted, "Best news ever!"

Shane planted a hard kiss on him. "It's amazing news. The drug trial is working."

"Looks like."

"Maybe one day I'll walk into his room and he'll know my name."

"I hope so." Too wired to sleep anymore, Noel rolled back out of bed. The smallish master bedroom didn't have the width or depth that he needed to pace, so he settled for bouncing on the balls of his feet.

Shane turned on his side, head propped on his hand. "You look like a kid who's just been told Santa's making a personal stop for milk and cookies."

"It kind of feels that way. Three years. Three years, and he might start getting his life back."

"You will too."

Noel startled. "I have a life."

"Yes, you do, but your life has centered around Tristan ever since you guys were bashed. He'll always be your best friend and important to you. I know that. But one day, if Tristan really gets his short-term memory back and goes out into the world again, he won't be your responsibility anymore."

"I know that in my head."

"It's getting your heart to catch on?"

"Yeah." Noel wanted Tristan well more than anything else in the world.

Please, God, give this to him. He deserves it and so much more.

Gabe hauled the black garbage bag out to the trash cans behind the house, shivering the entire time. The weather had gone from Indian summer to cold and windy overnight, and he was still getting used to grabbing his jacket for simple chores. Like carrying out the remains of Debbie's Friday night binge— Chinese food cartons and a wine box.

At least the gnats would start dying. All they needed was one good frost to take care of the little fuckers.

Debbie had been passed out on the couch when he got home from Big Dick's earlier in the morning, so he'd left her there, written to Tristan about the party, and then crashed for a while. The sound of Debbie hitting the wall outside his room on her way to the bathroom had woken him again, so he stayed up and started cleaning.

Her bedroom door slammed a little after ten, right as he was carrying out the trash.

Let her sleep.

He went back inside and hosed the downstairs with room

freshener. Once it was properly fragranced with lilacs, he checked his phone for messages.

His very dead phone, because he hadn't plugged it into the charger when he got home.

"Fantastic."

Tired and frustrated by the life he'd chosen to stay in, he trudged back to his room to plug the damned thing in. That done, he booted up his game console, and then logged into his email. The message from Tristan made him smile and dulled the sting of his morning. The contents at the very end made his heart pound and his hands sweat.

He remembered something.

Gabe hadn't known Tristan long, but he understood the importance of this morning's breakthrough. He could only imagine Tristan's phone call to Noel, the two of them celebrating the news.

He hit Reply.

11/01
10:09 a.m.

T—

The fact that you remembered not only what time breakfast is served, but also dinner, is AMAZING news. I am so thrilled. Look at me smiling in that photo you have, and imagine it ten times wider. I'm rooting for you so hard.

I am not ashamed to admit that yes, I went out on Mischief Night. I was a bit of a hellion in high school, and I probably gave both my dads gray hair from some of the shit I pulled. My friends and I did some amazingly stupid things, like setting off firecrackers under people's windows and setting them off inside of carved pumpkins. I probably made a lot of little kids cry because their hard work turned into burnt pie filling. Sometimes I think back and am amazed I never ended up in juvenile detention.

Do you know what Skype is? Search for it when you have time. If your computer is new enough and has a camera, we can talk to each other over a video feed. It's different than the phone, because we'd be able to look at each other. Maybe it will help with you remembering me.

Gabe's heart gave a funny lurch at the idea of speaking to Tristan face-to-face again. Or a reasonable facsimile thereof. He didn't Skype too often, because pretty much everyone he called was on the same cell carrier, so why bother? But he'd talk to Tristan. He'd give him another lifeline into the real world, the thriving world outside the walls of Benfield. Outside the restrictive walls of his own mind.

He wanted to be that lifeline so badly, and he had no idea why.

After adding his Skype info, he rambled a bit about a few more of his Mischief Night prank days. Reminiscing was fun. He didn't see the guys he used to know much anymore. They'd fallen out of touch after high school ended, and while Gabe looked back fondly on the friendships, he didn't miss them. He rarely thought about them, except during moments like this.

Those thoughts inevitably circled back to the whirlwind of being fifteen and embracing the fact that he liked boys. So many things in a matter of months. First kiss with a guy, first blowjob, first getting naked, first guy he fucked.

First guy who fucked him.

Last guy for almost ten years too.

Gabe stared at the unfinished email, so many memories and thoughts bubbling to the surface. Allowing a boy who was way too drunk and way too eager to fuck him had seemed like a good idea at the time. As good as any idea a horny fifteen-year-old can have. Gabe hadn't started working out yet and was still two growth spurts away from his current height, so he'd been unable to make him stop.

It hadn't been nearly as awful three months ago when he did his bottom scene with Shane. He'd been attentive and careful, giving Gabe hope that maybe with the right partner he'd enjoy it. For now, he was content to top the shit out of his scene partners at Mean Green.

None of that went into his email to Tristan.

Nothing else seemed important to write, so Gabe signed off and sent the latest communication. Then he signed on to Skype, put his laptop aside and grabbed his game controller. Time to do something mindless until he worked the club tonight.

A plan that got shot down by his ringing phone. For a split second, he glanced at his laptop, irrationally hoping that Tristan had been on his computer and so eager to talk that he'd already set up Skype. His moment of joy was cut down by the name on his phone screen. Chet.

"Hey, man," Gabe said.

"Tony, baby, how are things?" Chet asked in his trademark seductive purr. The man defined silver fox in a way few could, and he knew how to turn on the charm.

Good thing Gabe didn't go for older men. "Same shit, different day. What's up?"

"I have some potentially exciting news for you. I got a call from a producer for Puppy Farm, out in New York. They're interested in you."

Gabe blinked at the wall. Puppy Farm was one of the fastest rising gay porn studios in the country, and they were quickly becoming the hottest ticket in the industry despite being only a few years old. In his two years doing scenes for Chet, to his knowledge—because someone would have bragged about it—no one from another studio had ever called for a Mean Green Boy before.

"They're interested in me?" he said, mostly to confirm he hadn't completely misheard Chet.

"Yes, they are, and before you ask, they want you to top."

"Why me?"

Chet laughed. "You don't give yourself enough credit, baby. You make the screen sizzle when you handle the guys you fuck. And you have the kind of big dick that audiences love to see pounding a tight little hole."

Gee, he paints such a lovely picture of my profession.

Except it wasn't his profession, exactly. Gabe enjoyed doing porn, but he didn't want it to be his identity. The same way he didn't want waiting tables to be his future career. He hadn't figured out his goals yet, and doing a scene with a studio as big as Puppy Farm could bite him in the ass sometime down the road.

Hell, any of his porn could.

"It's cash upfront, of course, but they're making a nice offer," Chet added.

"How much?"

When Chet told him, he nearly said yes on the spot.

The entire reason he needed the extra cash was sleeping it off down the hall. He'd have to be gone at least one, maybe two nights, and he couldn't leave Debbie alone. His dads wouldn't stay with her, or allow her to stay with them. He'd never ask Jon to bear the brunt of her madness, not with Henry so sick.

"How much time do I have to think about it?" Gabe asked.

"Think? What's to think about?"

"It's a big deal, a lot of exposure I'm not sure I want, and it's hard for me to get away, okay?"

"Look, try and let me know something by the end of next week, all right?"

"Okay, thanks."

Gabe hung up. Chet had never gone out of his way to grow

the studio, but saying yes was a big chance for Chet. Tony Ryder getting featured in a Puppy Farm scene meant more potential subscribers to Mean Green. He understood that, and he didn't want to make Chet look bad to another producer by saying no. But this was Gabe's choice. He wasn't going to make it lightly.

He glanced at his silent laptop, willing it to ring. Willing it to give him someone to talk to for a little while. Even if he couldn't get advice on this from Tristan, he still desperately wanted to talk.

8

Gabe jerked awake, disoriented from having fallen asleep in the middle of the day. The ringing sound repeated itself. He fumbled for his phone only to find a black screen.

"What the hell?"

Laptop. Skype.

Tristan was calling him.

He pulled the laptop closer and answered the call. Tristan's smiling face filled the screen, as boyishly handsome as Gabe remembered.

"Hey, bad time?" Tristan asked.

"No, I dozed off." Gabe shifted into a more comfortable position. "It's good to see you."

"You too. Your photo doesn't do you justice."

A pleasant warmth spread through Gabe's chest. "Thanks. Neither does yours."

Tristan laughed. "It feels so weird to flirt with someone again. I haven't done this in a long time."

"Glad to be of service. It's no hardship, believe me. And I should apologize."

"For what?"

"For not thinking of this sooner. We've been emailing for two months."

"Could have been worse." Tristan's smile twisted up in one corner, giving him a very sexy smirk. "You could have thought of this tomorrow."

"Good point. So you remembered breakfast and dinner times. That's fantastic."

Tristan bounced, which made the laptop shake. He must have been sitting on his bed. The wall behind him was covered in sheets of paper and sticky notes. "I know, right? And it's still there. Breakfast at eight and dinner at five thirty. This is the first new memory I've made in three years, Gabe. Like an actual memory, not my déjà vu sense."

"Are you sure? How did you know about the déjà vu sense?"

Tristan blinked. "Fuck me."

Yes, please.

"What's wrong?" Gabe asked, keeping the other thought to himself.

"You're right. I know I didn't read about déjà vu in the last thirty minutes or so. Oh shit!"

The laptop bounced again, giving Gabe a view of the ceiling. In the background, Tristan was producing excited, cheering sounds that made Gabe laugh out loud. If ever Gabe had to describe pure joy, it would be Tristan in that moment.

"This is crazy," Tristan said as he righted the laptop. He'd changed positions, his back against a bed, so he'd probably gone down to the floor. "I can't believe the trial is working."

"When do you see your doctor again?"

"Hold on a sec." Tristan put the laptop down. He returned in less than thirty seconds. "Sorry, had to check the calendar. I have an evaluation on Tuesday, but I did call him today. I don't remember if he was excited, but who cares? I have enough excitement for everyone. Probably for five or six people."

"Nothing wrong with that. It's a big deal."

"It's a huge fucking deal." His smile flickered. "I guess the only downside is that if the drug is working, I could have seizures."

"Nah, don't worry about that. Focus on the positive." Gabe didn't like the idea of Tristan on the ground, seizing uncontrollably. He'd seen his mother have a seizure after drinking so much that she'd given herself alcohol poisoning, and it had been nightmarish. "Did your doctor give you any idea of how quickly you'll progress?"

Tristan looked to his left, probably conferring with one of his notebooks. "He said once memory function has begun to improve, it can be two to six weeks before significant improvement is made."

"Did he define significant improvement?"

His attention returned to Gabe. "It means I can go out on my own without forgetting where I am and who I'm with."

"Excellent."

"So if that happens, do you want to go out with me in two to six weeks?" Tristan ducked his head, at once forward and shy in the action.

Gabe's heart skipped. The ballsy invitation only made Tristan more appealing. "Yes, I would."

"Good." He bit his lower lip in an adorable way, then glanced to the left again. "Oh, I wanted to ask because I couldn't find it in any of our emails, but do you have any siblings?"

"No. I'm an only child." Gabe had never gone into the intricacies of his parents' relationships, because it wasn't something he wanted written down. And he didn't want to go into gory details when Tristan would likely forget it all anyway. "My mother and biological father split when I was really young, and it wasn't on the best of terms."

"Because he came out?"

"Yeah. They never really became friends again, which I guess isn't unusual for divorced couples."

"It would probably be more strange for them to be best friends."

"Definitely." Not that it had ever been likely. Too many hurt feelings were involved from all parties, including Gabe. And because he didn't want Tristan to think he was uninterested or rude, he added, "You told me about your brother. A little bit, anyway, when we first met."

"Oh. Okay good." Tristan's expression went momentarily sad, then smoothed over. "You want to know something weird? Even though I accept that the accident happened more than three years ago, I still feel like I just saw my parents a few months ago. I went home for the weekend, because it was my father's birthday. Mom made chicken Alfredo for dinner, because that's his favorite, and she made lemon bars for dessert because they're mine."

Something in his face unfocused as he went away into the memory, speaking as much to the past as to Gabe. "She makes them homemade, not some mix from a box. And with real lemons, not concentrate. It makes them extra tangy. I can eat a whole pan. She said I did once, when I was five, and I had a sick stomach all the next day. No one else makes them as good as she does."

And he hadn't had one in years, because his parents all but disowned him. Such a sweet, funny soul who deserved so much better.

Gabe had no idea how to make lemon bars, but he made a mental note to research it. How hard could they be?

"We talked about school after dinner," Tristan continued. "I was about to finish my junior year, and Dad had already decided I was going to Penn State for med school. I didn't get a choice, he said, because he was paying for it. I didn't fight him. All I wanted was to get through school and then do whatever the hell I wanted to do with my life. And when I agreed with him, everything was always pleasant. No harsh silences like those first few months after Alex died. No disappointed glares. Sometimes I think he suspected I was gay, but thought if he ignored it, like he ignored that I wasn't as smart as Alex, it wouldn't be true. I'd be the smart, straight son who was going to be a doctor. If I've seen them since, I obviously don't remember it."

More than anything in that moment, Gabe wanted to reach into his laptop and give Tristan a hug. He didn't want to add to Tristan's state of melancholy, but he also never wanted to lie to him. "Noel told me that your parents haven't visited you since the hospital."

Tristan nodded, his blue eyes too shiny. "That sounds right. Noel would have told me if they had."

"It's their loss. They still have one son, and they can't see far enough past their bigotry to love you like you deserve."

"How do you know what I deserve?"

"Because I'm a good judge of people. I can see past bullshit pretty well, and you, my friend, are a genuine person. You've got a good heart."

His cheeks pinked up. "Okay, we are so definitely going on a date now."

"Yes, we are. In two to six weeks."

"Awesome. Give me a minute."

Gabe's view was suddenly blocked by a close up of lined notebook paper and scrawled words too out of focus to read. The page shook a lot. Tristan was writing all of this down. Gabe waited patiently, glad Tristan thought to do that, so he had their conversation notes for later.

After a few minutes, Tristan put the notebook away. "So I made up a cheat sheet of all the things I've collected about you, and you're a waiter. Tell me a story about that."

"A funny story or a terrible story?"

"Surprise me."

Gabe had worked in food service for years, so he'd seen and heard it all, and had pretty much everything said to him, from racial slurs—a grouchy old man once called him a spic, and Gabe wasn't even Hispanic, he just tanned well—to very clear come-ons. Unfortunately, most of the come-ons were from women. He'd nearly lost his temper more times than he could count, and he'd seen assholes get a decent comeuppance in return.

"So I've worked in a few places over the years," Gabe said. "One of them was this fifties style all-night diner, and I was one of the few guys who waited tables there so I got a lot of the overnight shifts. The owner liked having dudes around in case disruptive drunks came in looking for a greasy dinner."

"Makes sense," Tristan said. "Did you like overnight?"

"Not really. It's the reason I started drinking coffee, though. Anyway, this one Friday night, around eleven or so, this bus pulls into the parking lot. An entire team of high school soccer players gets out, all of them hooting and being rowdy because they'd won some kind of regional championship. And they are absolute assholes to me. Changing their minds on orders, talking back for no reason, making fun of the place. When the food comes, they're throwing shit around, tossing pickles at the windows to see if they'll stick. Basically being dicks and wrecking the place.

"After they've been in the place a good twenty-five minutes, finally their coach comes into the diner and sees what's going on, and he nearly shits himself. His face was epic. He lets out this bellowing 'What the actual fuck?' that, I swear to God, made the windows rattle."

Tristan leaned in closer, his eager face filling the computer screen.

"The coach starts lecturing them about manners, sportsman-ship and good behavior. And then. Then! This is the best part." Gabe grinned at the memory of the pride he'd felt that day. "The coach helps me bring out the mop bucket and a ton of cleaning supplies, and he makes his team clean the entire damned diner."

"You are shitting me." Tristan hooted. "That's fantastic! Oh my God, I wish I could have seen those kids' faces."

"I loved every minute of it. And I got a really good tip."

"I would hope so. I don't think I could ever be a waiter. I don't have a very good brain-to-mouth censor. I'd be fired after the first dumbass said something rude to me."

"Good thing animators don't deal with the general public then."

Tristan's eyebrows arched. "I told you about that?"

"Yes. The night we danced together at Big Dick's. I could tell how much you enjoyed it by the way you talked."

"I still think about it sometimes, and it always depresses me. Except not so much recently, I don't think."

"That's because you've been going to art classes every Saturday."

"I am?" He glanced around his room until his gaze settled somewhere. "That's right. I bet that's why I have that painting of your face on my wall."

Gabe grinned. "You put me on your wall?"

"Wouldn't you?"

"I'm not really my type."

Tristan laughed. "Tall, dark and handsome?"

"Nah. I prefer blonds."

"Lucky me." He tilted his head. "Have you ever thought of modeling?"

Gabe's heart gave a funny lurch. He had no intention of telling Tristan that he already was an adult model, but he also didn't want to lie. "I'm not very good at taking direction. And I don't think I'd want to see my face on a billboard or the side of a bus." Doing videos once or twice a month for a small company was one thing. Finding larger fame was quite another, and the exact reason why he hadn't given Chet an answer about the Puppy Farm inquiry yet.

"Earth to Gabe," Tristan said, waving both hands in front of the monitor. "Where'd you go?"

"Sorry, lost in thought. Did you ask me something?"

"I asked if you were an introvert or more of an exhibitionist."

"Combination of both, I guess. It depends on the situation. When I'm at Big Dick's I don't like to be the center of attention. My dads own the place, and I need to set a good example."

"So tell me about a time you were an exhibitionist."

Gabe was unashamed to admit that he had more than one example. Unfortunately most of them involved Andrew, and he wasn't going down that road of past heartbreak today. "I came out when I was nineteen, and I fucked around a lot for the next four years or so. This one night I was working at the same diner as before, and this guy comes in with a group of people. He spends the entire night cruising me. Like so obviously cruising me that his friends even started teasing him. So this one time I'm refilling water glasses, and he bluntly asks if I ever take smoke breaks."

"Oh my God." Tristan's eyes lit up with delight, probably guessing exactly where the story was heading.

"I very nearly say no, I don't smoke, until I get it. So I say, 'Yeah, I'm about to take one right now. Out back by the trash cans.' I go through the kitchen to the back. It's pretty well lit out there, but there's a three-sided cement block enclosure that provides privacy from the parking lot. And the cooks aren't paying any attention. So this guy walks around from the front of the diner, drops to his knees and gives me a fucking blowjob right there."

Tristan made a delighted sound. "That sounds so awesome. I've never done anything like that. Did you blow him back?"

"Nope. He finished me off, then wiped his mouth and left. His table was gone when I got inside, and they'd left a good tip."

"Holy shit, that's the best story." Tristan was practically vibrating with excitement. "Noel doesn't talk about his sex life, because he's always been private about that stuff, so it's refreshing to hear someone else in the world is getting laid."

"There are people getting laid a lot more frequently than I am."

"Not a casual hookup kind of guy anymore?"

"Not for a while. That thing kind of lost its appeal."

"Have you ever had a long-term boyfriend? I'm asking because if it was in your letters, I didn't note it on my cheat sheet."

Gabe had never mentioned Andrew to Tristan. Andrew wasn't a happy memory. "I had one. It lasted for about a year, but it wasn't meant to be." Way too polite a description for the situation, but whatever.

"I've never had one, either. In college, I didn't want one and it would have been awkward anyway, because I wasn't out at home. And then this happened." He gestured outward, at his room. "No one wants to date a guy who won't remember them half an hour later."

"But you're starting to remember things. Don't blow off the boyfriend thing just yet."

"Oh I'm not." Tristan licked his lower lip in a very unsubtle way. "Not anymore."

I bet when he's in full-force flirt mode no one can resist him.

Gabe's dick was certainly starting to take notice, much like it had that night dancing at Big Dick's. He'd masturbated to that memory quite a few times. He'd even used it while he fluffed himself before his last shoot. Every single thing about Tristan was fucking sexy as hell. He desperately wanted to see him in person again.

"Listen, maybe one of these Thursdays when you hang with Noel, you guys can come to the city and I'll hang out with you too," Gabe said, a little rushed and in one breath.

Tristan's smile went from seductive to excited. "Definitely." He reached over to scrawl something. "Actually, give me a few. I need to write down that blowjob story and a note to ask Noel about Thursday."

"Sure." The time Tristan spent writing, Gabe spent watching him. The way his eyebrows dipped into a V. The way he stuck the tip of his tongue out while thinking hard. A small mole on his left jaw. A second one a few inches lower on his neck. He hadn't shaved recently, but the blond whiskers on his cheeks were fine and very pale. They almost blended in with his complexion.

How could anyone have hurt him so badly?

Gabe rubbed at his stiffening cock with one hand, while balancing his computer with the other. He could probably get off just listening to Tristan talk about sex while licking his lower lip.

"Okay, cool," Tristan said as his attention returned to the screen. "Don't worry, Noel won't say no. Are you free this coming week?"

"I'm free until about four thirty. I swapped with someone to help cover the evening shift."

"That's cool, we can hang until then. We'll come into the city and pick you up."

Gabe wasn't thrilled with the idea of Tristan seeing the shithole he lived in, or the possibility of his mother making an appearance. "How about we meet someplace? You can let me know closer to the day."

"What? You don't want me to see Casa de—hell. What's your last name again?"

"Henson."

"Right." He wrote that down. "Henson. Gabe Henson. I like it. Mom's last name or dad's?"

"My bio dad's. My mother named me Gabriel, though."

"After the archangel?"

"After Gabriel Byrne."

"The actor?"

Gabe blinked, surprised someone else his age knew who Gabriel Byrne was. "Yeah, she was a little obsessed with the movie *Excalibur*, which led to an obsession with the King Arthur legend in general."

"I've never heard of *Excalibur*, but I've see a few Gabriel Byrne movies. I mean *The Usual Suspects* is the shit. And he really knew how to swing a sword in *The Man in the Iron Mask*."

Gabe blinked at the mention of one of his guilty pleasure movies. "You've seen that?"

"Sure. I mean, it's really nothing like the book, but who cares with all the eye candy. I mean, Peter Sarsgaard? Hello."

"I get what you mean. Who was your favorite Musketeer?"

Tristan made a *do you really have to ask?* face. "With his sexy-ass accent?"

"Aramis," they said in stereo.

"How did I know you'd get turned on by British accents?" Tristan said.

"It's the accent and the voice itself. I mean, it's Jeremy Irons. The only other Brit who comes close right now is Benedict Cumberbatch."

"Who?"

Shit, way to go and mention someone who's only gotten serious pop culture attention in the few years since Tristan's injury.

"Give me a second," Gabe said. He had to salvage this without drawing attention to it, so he searched for a video clip, then sent it to Tristan's email. "Check your inbox."

He waited while Tristan loaded and watched the clip. His blue eyes got wider with every passing minute. "Okay, yes," Tristan said. "I like him. What movie is this?"

"*Star Trek Into Darkness*."

"Really? They made a sequel? Noel and I saw the first one together in college. Are all the actors back?"

"Yep, same cast. Benedict plays the villain. It's pretty good."

"When my memory gets better, we'll have to watch it together."

Gabe grinned. "It's a date."

"There's probably a lot of movies I'll need to catch up on."

"No doubt. A bunch of really good animated films have come out. We'll have to have a marathon."

Tristan gave him a sly smile. "You do realize that I don't have a TV here, so in order to do that, you'll have to show me your house."

Gabe's stomach soured at the idea, but he kept that off his face. "We'll figure something out." Like use the den at his dads' house. They had a sixty-inch flat screen mounted on the wall. Although Gabe also liked the idea of cuddling with Tristan on his bed while they watched movies on his TV.

Not with Debbie around. No way.

Gabe told more stories about being a waiter until he inevitably had to end the call. He was already pushing it on being late to work. "Let's do this again, yeah?"

"Count on it."

They'd been chatting for more than forty minutes, and Gabe was curious. "Tristan, what's the first thing you remember us talking about?"

Tristan's brow scrunched up. "Um, we flirted a little, and then we talked about me remembering breakfast and dinner times."

A small burst of hope lit up inside of Gabe's heart. "That's our entire conversation. Almost forty-five minutes."

"Really? Damn." Tristan's baffled expression was ten kinds of adorable. "Damn."

"Don't sound so surprised."

"I guess part of me thought that the time thing was a fluke."

"Nope. Keep positive, okay? Believe this is working."

"I will. Thanks, Gabe. It really helps knowing I have someone to get better for."

Gabe shook his head. "No way. You get better for you. Us getting to know each other is a bonus."

"Okay. Have fun at work. Ogle some hot guys for me."

"I'll do my best. Bye, Tristan."

"Bye."

Gabe reluctantly ended the call and closed his computer. He knew he was doing exactly what Dad warned him not to do, which was get attached. But this was different than his constant struggle to fix Debbie and her addiction. Tristan wanted to get better, and he had a real shot at doing so. Gabe would do whatever he could to help make that happen.

9

Tristan was pretty sure he'd vibrate right through the car door before they ever made it to the Broad Street Market. He couldn't remember ever being this excited to meet someone for lunch. Then again, he couldn't remember most of the last three-plus years, so he didn't have the best frame of reference. Not that he cared because...Gabe.

Noel didn't have to remind him of their plans for their usual Thursday outing, because Tristan had spent most of the night and all morning staring at the note he'd made. Lunch with Gabe at the Broad Street Market, then bowling for a few hours. Actual time spent with Gabe that he would remember for longer periods.

Ever since Saturday's breakthrough, Tristan was noticing improvements with things every single day. He knew all of his meal times, and he was making it to them on a regular basis, which made Noel ecstatic. During his worst depressions, Tristan didn't even bother trying to eat, and he'd lost more weight than was healthy.

So far Tristan recalled everything from Noel and Shane walking into his room that morning, to Noel searching for a place to park near the Market. Shane's inclusion had become a regular thing, he was pretty sure. He'd still had to ask Shane's name, though, for the bazillionth time.

Maybe not for much longer.

Noel found a space, and Tristan practically bounced out of the car. The air had a cold November bite to it that tickled beautifully against his exposed skin. Tristan loved winter. He loved the snow and the cold and the way it made him feel alive.

I want to build a snowman with Gabe this year.

He wanted to do a lot with Gabe in the future, and he prayed Gabe felt the same way. He was pretty sure Gabe did. Just thinking his name made Tristan smile.

Shane led the way toward the brick market entrance. Tristan couldn't remember where they were meeting Gabe, so he followed them into a warm haven of wonderful scents. Roasting meat and baked bread, sweetness and bitter herbs and fryer oil. His mouth watered for all of the food in the various stalls they passed.

Near the Kabob House, a tall, muscled man with tan skin and black hair was grinning at them. Tristan knew right away. He knew.

"Gabe!" Tristan shouldered his way past Noel and threw his arms around Gabe. Strong arms circled his waist, and he melted into the kind of strong, full-bodied hug he loved. He breathed in deeply, inhaling Gabe's spicy aftershave.

"Hey you," Gabe said.

"I knew it was you." Tristan pulled back, suddenly wary of such a public display of affection. Not like he'd kissed Gabe on the mouth, but he'd been attacked once in this city. "I don't know the last time I looked at your photo, but I knew."

"You also know you have a photo of me."

He's right. "Yeah, I do. Ha!" He bounced on his toes, happier than he'd been in forever.

"Hey, man, how are you?" Gabe said, taking time to shake Noel's and Shane's hand.

Something kind of awkward seemed to linger between Gabe and Shane. Tristan needed to make a note to ask about that. He was pretty sure he never did.

"How's your day been so far?" Gabe asked.

"Well, I don't remember what I had for breakfast, but I know I ate," Tristan replied. "And I remember everything so far from when Noel and Shane picked me up. Plus you."

Gabe made a lovely rumbling sound that wasn't quite laughter. "That's great. Hungry for lunch?"

"Definitely." He glanced at Noel. "Have I eaten here?"

"Yep, twice," Noel replied.

"Did I order different things each time?"

"Yes, that hasn't changed." Noel looked at Gabe. "He doesn't like to order the same thing on a menu twice."

"He's a taster," Gabe said. "I like that. It means you're a fan of variety and exploration."

"He's also impulsive and quick tempered."

"Hey, standing right here," Tristan said, amused at being discussed like that. "Did I go down the menu like usual?"

"Yes, you tried the first two things."

Tristan stared at the board. "Okay, so lunch today is Honey Barbecue Chicken. Sounds good to me." Everything came with steamed vegetables and fried rice, and Tristan was pretty sure he wouldn't be able to manage his entire plate.

Gabe ordered the Polish sausage, which made Tristan think dirty thoughts while they went in search of an empty table. He didn't really care what Noel and Shane ordered, until something pungent tickled his nose. He stared at a bowl of red and tan that looked like spaghetti of some kind, but wasn't.

"Okay, what the hell is that?" he asked.

Shane plucked the bowl off the tray. "It's kimchi. Korean side dish. Spicy fermented cabbage."

"Gross."

"Don't knock it until you've tried it."

Never one to back down from a challenge, Tristan stuck his fork in the kimchi and brought back a healthy mouthful. The smell was kind of toxic, and he wasn't super fond of spicy shit, but what the hell. He put it in his mouth.

The texture reminded him of sauerkraut, but the explosion of spice and sour on his tongue made his eyes water. He chewed fast, then chugged from his soda to wash the rest down. Shane was laughing at him, the jerk, but Gabe was watching him with something like respect in his eyes. His very pretty, dark brown eyes.

"I have to admit," Gabe said, "I am not brave enough to try that."

"It's an acquired taste," Shane said.

"When did you acquire it?" Noel asked.

"Jason liked it. We'd buy it sometimes as a treat."

Noel squeezed Shane's shoulder, because Shane looked sad. The name Jason felt familiar, but Tristan simply couldn't place it. Gabe solved the mystery by leaning over and whispering, "Shane's brother. He died a few months ago."

"Oh." Such a sucky thing not to be able to remember about a person.

Tristan scraped his chicken off the bamboo skewer, because he was less likely to poke his eye out eating it that way. It was nicely sweet and tangy, and the rice was delicious. Noel started telling them about breaking up a bar fight the other night while on patrol, but Tristan let the words float idly by. All he could do was watch Gabe eat.

He studied the way Gabe cut his sausage into discs that he combined with a bit of the veggies and some of the rice. Every single bite was a combination. He chewed with care, his strong jaw flexing. A faint shadow suggested skin that never shaved down perfectly thanks to coarse, dark whiskers. He tried imagining Gabe with a full beard and the thought made his dick twitch. Back in college, he had his ass eaten by a guy with a beard, and the tickling whiskers had made him kind of nuts.

Stop that, or you'll end up walking around the market with a woody.

"How's the sausage?" Tristan asked.

For some reason, that made Shane choke on his mouthful of food.

"It's good," Gabe replied. "I've always loved Polish sausage, but this is so much better than what you buy in the store. Want to try some?"

Jesus, that sounds like a come-on.

"Definitely."

Gabe speared a disc of the meat with his own fork, then held it out. Tristan made the most of the moment by very slowly closing his lips around the fork and sliding back to capture the sausage. He watched Gabe closely, noting the way his eyes widened a fraction and his breathing seemed to quicken. Flavor and texture exploded on his tongue as he chewed. Swallowed.

"Delicious," Tristan said.

The corner of Gabe's mouth pulled up. "I know. You mind if I taste your meat?"

Shane choked again, this time on his soda.

Tristan forked a piece of his chicken and held it out for Gabe. Gabe wrapped his lips around the tines and slid back slowly, just like Tristan had, and dear God Tristan wanted that fork to be his cock.

"I'm never eating sausage again after this," Noel said.

"Say that when I get you alone later," Shane replied.

Noel kissed his cheek. "Okay, one exception."

"Taste good?" Tristan asked.

Gabe grinned. "Very good."

Tristan winked at Gabe, then glanced over at Noel. Noel's

expression was hard to read, caught somewhere between amusement and...annoyance? That couldn't be right. Tristan was usually able to read Noel's moods—at least he always used to be—so the look didn't make a lot of sense. And it seemed to be directed at Gabe.

So weird.

Noel's attention returned to his food.

Tristan mentally shrugged it off. He was having too much fun flirting with Gabe to pay too close attention to Noel. He could hash it out with his own boyfriend later. "I really like your sausage," he whispered to Gabe. "Can I try it again?"

Gabe's grin shifted into something downright sexy. "Of course." The intensity in his eyes when Gabe fed him a second piece of sausage made Tristan's heart flutter. He held eye contact while he chewed and swallowed, too entranced to look away.

Until someone jostled his chair hard from behind. "Dude." Tristan twisted around.

A guy his age, and with plenty of room to maneuver, paused to deliver a sneering, "Sorry."

Oh yeah, he's sorry. Not.

Gabe stood, all six-foot-plus of muscles. "You got a problem walking?"

The other guy scurried away.

"Sorry," Tristan said as Gabe sat back down.

"What are you sorry for?" Gabe asked.

"I probably shouldn't be so obvious in public." He glanced at Noel, who was watching him intently. "I keep forgetting that already got us hurt once."

"Hey, don't do that." Gabe grabbed his hand and squeezed, a comforting warmth that sent tingles up Tristan's arm. "It's not your fault that guy was an asshole. And it's not your fault that you and Noel got bashed."

Tristan wasn't entirely sure the second part was true. He had no memory of that night past going clubbing with Noel. Mostly he was glad he didn't remember. Once in a while, though, he really hated that Noel had to bear the burden alone.

Like right now.

"So if you two are done with your sausage fest," Shane said, "let's finish eating so we can walk the market a little while."

"Sounds like a plan," Gabe replied.

Gabe knew the basics of the night that Noel and Tristan were bashed, because Noel had explained it in greater detail before bringing Tristan to the club for his birthday. He knew they were heading for a bus stop, took a shortcut through an alley, and they were beaten by four guys who were never caught. Until Tristan said something, it hadn't occurred to him that Tristan might blame himself for calling attention to the pair.

He was watching Tristan blossom right before his eyes, so far gone from the terrified young man he'd first met back in July. Tristan was full of life, a huge flirt, and he had the kind of joyous laugh that could make someone smile simply by hearing it. Maybe Tristan had been carrying on with Noel that night, but that in no way made Tristan culpable for the beating.

And Tristan didn't see it, but Gabe did. He saw the flash in Noel's eyes the moment that Tristan said his carrying on "already got us hurt once". It pointed at some truth in the words. Or at least, Noel's idea of the truth. He was the only one who knew what happened that night. He knew who said or did what, and Tristan's entire perspective on the bashing was tied to Noel's word.

Gabe wasn't going to question it in front of Tristan, though. And the middle of the market wasn't the place. He finished his lunch and washed it down with a bottle of water. The sausage and fried rice had been a special treat, so he wasn't going to layer soda calories on top of that. He had a scene on Saturday and he had to look his best.

The conversation had reached an awkward stall by the time they threw away their trash and headed into the market. Noel and Shane led the way. Gabe hung back with Tristan, keeping close enough for their elbows to constantly brush together. Tristan tried to see everything at once, the way a kid in a toy store might.

They stopped in an Asian boutique full of handmade jewelry, silk clothing and potted lucky bamboo. Dad had lucky bamboo in his office at the club, and in both bathrooms at the house. Gabe didn't know if it was actually lucky, but his dads had been together a long time and their club was thriving.

Tristan moved past a display of figurines carved in jade to a jewelry case. He pointed at something and asked the clerk, "What's that?"

The woman walked over and peered down. "Silver phoenix over jade. You know the phoenix?"

"A mythical bird who is reborn from its own ashes. It's beautiful."

Gabe joined him at the counter so he could see the item in question. A silver pendant encased a piece of jade, which was mostly covered by a lovely silver phoenix. The pendant hung on a silver chain. "Dead and reborn," he said. "Sounds like someone I know."

Tristan looked at him, complete understanding in his eyes. "I guess it does."

"Would you like to try it on?" the clerk asked.

"No, thanks. I can't afford it, anyway."

Gabe glanced at the price, which was reasonable considering the exquisite detail, but a little beyond his own budget at the moment. He had a royalty check due from Chet at the end of next week, though. And Christmas was in a month and a half.

They wandered out of the shop and eventually found Shane

and Noel inside of a candy store. Wood bins of loose candy, plastic containers of pieced out candy, rows of fudge, candied apples and a glass case of chocolate-covered everything greeted them. The scents of chocolate and sugar made Gabe's mouth water right away.

"Holy crap, they have chocolate-covered bacon," Tristan said.

"We are so buying a piece of that to try," Gabe said. He forked over cash to one of the ladies working there, then handed the candy to Tristan. "You first."

Tristan put one end of the bacon in his mouth, then paused to meet Gabe's eyes. A very naughty gaze taunted him right before Tristan bit down. His eyes rolled back a bit while he chewed, expressing pure bliss with the food he was tasting. It buzzed in Gabe's dick. He'd never known anyone who made eating so fucking sexy.

Gabe took a bite. Sweet chocolate and salty bacon exploded in his mouth, the perfect combination. The chocolate melted fast, and the bacon was wonderfully crisp. He made a soft noise of appreciation, because it was the best thing he'd tasted in ages. They took turns until the treat was gone, and Gabe very nearly bought a dozen of them, except bacon was pure fat.

Besides, it wasn't a treat if you had it all the time.

"That was beyond amazing," Tristan said. "Wow."

"Anything else you want to try?"

"No way. Nothing else will ever top that, so why bother?"

Gabe chuckled, because yeah, he agreed. "Too true. What is your favorite candy, anyway? And you can't say chocolate-covered bacon."

"White chocolate with almonds. Usually candy places sell it all broken up, like bark. What about you?"

"Fireballs and Red Hots. Anything cinnamon like that."

"Ew, I can't stand Red Hots."

"Then remind me never to kiss you after eating some."

Tristan's eyes went wide, and Gabe could have kicked himself for letting that slip out. Gentle flirting over sausage was one thing, but outright admitting that he wanted to kiss Tristan—hell, do a lot more than that with him—raised the bar on expectations. And he didn't want to pressure Tristan into anything.

Except Tristan's surprise shifted right into something very seductive. Almost feral. He licked his lips, as if challenging Gabe to plant one on him right then and there. And he might have too, if they weren't surrounded by strangers and very nice Amish ladies. He didn't want to scorch their eyeballs.

Noel broke the spell by coming over, leading Shane by the sleeve of his jacket. "You guys ready to go bowling?"

"We're going bowling?" Tristan asked.

"Yep, that's part two of our plans for the day."

"Cool. What did you get?"

Noel held up a bag of assorted flavored Tootsie Rolls. "You get anything?"

"A religious experience."

"Huh?"

Tristan cracked up. Gabe didn't reveal their secret, either. He was too impressed by having spent close to an hour with Tristan and so far, the bowling thing seemed to be his first real memory lapse. "What did you have for lunch?" he asked when Tristan got a hold of himself.

"Um, honey barbecue chicken. And rice. Why?"

"Just checking."

"I'm getting better at this whole memory thing."

"Yes, you are."

Gabe rode over to the bowling lanes in Noel's car. It wasn't too far, and he wanted to spend every moment he could with Tristan. They sat in the backseat together, hands touching, keeping a connection that Gabe didn't quite know what to do with. He'd never been so insanely attracted to someone before, and not just because Tristan was beautiful. He had a kindness of spirit and a love of life that pulled Gabe in and wouldn't let go.

I'm falling for him.

He couldn't stop himself now if he wanted to—and he very much did not.

10

By the time they parked outside of the bowling alley, Tristan couldn't stand it any longer. He'd been half-hard since the bacon incident, and he fought against images of Gabe following up on the promise of that kiss, because he'd only go full wood. His coat wasn't long enough to hide a bulge.

At least he wasn't the only one struggling. Gabe sat with his legs tight together and one hand in his lap.

Fuck this, I am not some virgin wallflower.

The lanes were mostly empty. Not surprising for the middle of a Thursday in November—Tristan stopped walking so suddenly that someone crashed into him from behind.

"What's wrong?" Gabe asked. The warm body behind him.

"It's November."

"Yeah."

Noel turned, startled. "You recalled that?"

"Yep." A wiggle of excitement made him laugh. "It popped right into my head."

"Hearing you say stuff like that is never going to get old."

"Good, because chances are a lot more shit is going to start popping in there."

"That's what we all want," Gabe said.

No one more than me. Shit.

"Noel, why don't you and Shane get your shoes and bowl a frame." Tristan handed Noel his notebook, then turned to Gabe and put every ounce of obvious invitation into his expression that he could. "I need to use the restroom."

He went off in search of it without waiting for an answer. Six other people were bowling at the moment. Two pairs, and two people alone, and three of them female, so the chances of an interruption were slim. The bathrooms were at the far end of the lanes, and loud music was playing from hidden speakers.

Tristan pushed through the heavy wood door. Three stalls, all empty. He walked into the handicapped stall and waited.

Gabe wasn't thirty seconds behind him. He strode into the stall, pulled the lock in place, and then had Tristan pressed against the cement block wall with his body. Tristan's cock hummed with the thrill of it, with the proximity of someone who made his head spin with something as simple as a touch. The spice of Gabe's cologne filled his nose, and below it, he caught a subtle hint of sweat. Of Gabe.

He tilted his head, inviting Gabe to break that last barrier. To bend his neck and finally fucking kiss him.

Gabe pressed a firm thigh against his groin, and Tristan gasped. He clasped Gabe's ass through his jeans, inviting more pressure. Gabe slowly rubbed his own erection against Tristan's hip, and holy crap he was big. The moment seemed to last forever, imprinting itself on Tristan's heart, and maybe he wouldn't remember their first kiss tomorrow but holy shit he'd enjoy it today.

As Gabe continued to hesitate, Tristan made the first move. He pulled Gabe's head down. Closed his eyes and caught his lips in a firm press that gave way instantly. Gabe opened, allowing Tristan to thrust his tongue into his mouth, tasting Gabe for the first time. Something deep inside of Tristan came to life in that moment, awakening a part of himself he'd not known in a long time—genuine, physical connection with someone.

God yes, please.

Gabe's tongue danced with his, rolling and teasing, and then he forced Tristan's retreat. He relaxed into the kiss, enjoying the way Gabe licked at his teeth and the roof of his mouth, and it was everything. Nothing existed outside of them. One of Gabe's hands clenched his hair, while the other groped his ass. Tristan wanted Gabe naked so he could lick every inch of skin, but that couldn't happen here.

Not here but soon.

Gabe startled him by breaking the kiss. He pressed his forehead against Tristan's, warmth breath wafting across his cheeks in soft pants.

"What's wrong?" Tristan asked.

"I don't want to take advantage."

"Trust me, you aren't. I want you so bad, Gabe."

"I want you too, but I want you to remember the things we do. And to never regret them."

"I won't regret anything except stopping. Later you can help me write down every single detail so I can fantasize over my first time getting blown in public when I'm missing you. Please."

"You make a compelling argument."

"Did you notice I'm a stubborn person?"

Gabe stared at him for another beat, and then he did the sexiest thing ever by kneeling on the tile in front of Tristan. Memories of the way Gabe's lips slipped around his fork made Tristan's blood pulse with need. Gabe made quick work of his fly and pulled both jeans and underwear down just low enough to free his erection. They didn't have time for slow, and knowing someone could walk in at any second added to the thrill.

Warm lips closed over the head of his cock, and Tristan slapped a hand over his own mouth to cover his gasp. Gabe's tongue rubbed the underside of the crown, waking up nerves and sending pleasure signals zinging down Tristan's spine. His balls tingled with awareness, already drawing up, because yeah, this wasn't going to last. It had been so long and Gabe felt so amazing, sliding down, taking his cock right to the back of his throat.

Holy shit, that's hot.

He watched Gabe's lips stretch and his cheeks darken. So gorgeous. Gabe glanced up, meeting his gaze, and goddamn. Those dark eyes blazed with life and with want, and all of it was for Tristan. He threaded his fingers through Gabe's dark hair and held on while his world exploded on a rolling wave of bliss.

"Close."

Gabe sped up his efforts. He rolled Tristan's balls with one hand, and that was it. His orgasm hit hard and fast, and he couldn't warn Gabe to pull off. Everything went tight and hot and he shook with the force of it. Gabe swallowed his come, sucking him clean until Tristan couldn't stand it any longer.

"Oh my fucking God," Tristan gasped. He was hot and chilled all at once, with barely enough energy to tug Gabe to his feet and into his arms. His sensitive cock rubbed against denim and fueled those little sparks into a long, hard kiss.

He thrust into Gabe's mouth, tasting a bit of himself there and loving it. He reached between them and thumbed open Gabe's fly. Fished his impressive erection out of his boxers. Good grief, but he was going to love putting that in his mouth. And his ass? He'd probably come from the penetration alone.

Can't fucking wait.

Tristan slid into a squat, his back still against the wall, and licked a drop of bitter precome off the head of Gabe's cock. Gabe braced one hand on the wall, while his other slid behind Tristan's neck. A gentle hold, no demands. Tristan clasped the root of Gabe's thick cock and took the head into his mouth. The taste of Gabe exploded on his tongue, so perfectly masculine. Silky skin over so much heat. Gabe's width stretched his lips as Tristan took more in, as much as he could until his mouth met his hand.

Gabe made a strangled noise that made Tristan take just a little bit more, before pulling back on a gasp. He memorized every slide over his tongue and the roof of his mouth, each time the head hit the back of his throat. Every sound from Gabe. The way his hand tightened against Tristan's neck, like he wanted to hold him still and fuck into his mouth. Maybe one day Tristan would let Gabe, but right now this was what he wanted.

The sight of Tristan on the floor, his mouth wrapped around his cock, was like a scene out of a fantasy, and Gabe still couldn't believe it was happening. Tristan was sucking him down like a champ, and every pull and slide sent Gabe closer to the edge.

Nothing about this was like the sex he was used to having. Sex he was paid to have with hot guys. This was real in a way that went past the physical. He had actual feelings for Tristan, even though those exact feelings were undefined. This wasn't just a blowjob for either one of them.

It was only the first one Tristan had given or received in three years, and while Gabe trusted he was clean, Gabe was the one being paid to fuck other guys. He was tested regularly, and he never shot without condoms, but he would not risk Tristan's health. Not without Tristan being fully informed, and that wasn't happening with Tristan sucking his cock.

"Close," Gabe said. He felt it in his balls, and then in his gut as his belly got tight. He thrust once, which made Tristan gag, and then Gabe pulled back. Tristan's surprise became lust-filled. Gabe turned to stand over the toilet while he jacked himself hard, and then he came, shooting over the porcelain. Fine tremors ran across his shoulders and he gasped hard for air.

"Holy fuck," he said.

Tristan appeared behind him and rubbed a palm across his stomach. "You are so goddamn sexy."

"That was unbelievable." He spun so he could kiss Tristan,

putting everything he couldn't say into the action. Tristan melted against him, arms around his waist, and the moment would have been perfect if the bathroom door hadn't banged open.

They froze in place. Gabe's gut rolled. A belt buckle jangled, and then a zipper went down. Someone peeing at the urinal. Zipping up. Whoever it was left without washing, and Gabe let out a deep breath.

"That was close," Tristan said. "But worth it."

"Yes, it was." Gabe tucked himself back into his jeans, then cleaned off the toilet seat. Flushed away the evidence.

Except Tristan was wearing the evidence all over his face in the way his blue eyes shone and his cheeks remained flushed. He looked like a guy who'd gotten lucky, and Gabe imagined he didn't look any more innocent.

"Your friends are going to take one look and know exactly what we were doing in here," Gabe said.

"I don't care." Tristan pressed a hard kiss to his lips. "Come on. I want to go write down all the details while they're in my head."

"Lead the way."

They washed up before heading back. Shane walked down his lane and executed a perfect throw, leg sweep included. The ball zoomed toward the pins and crashed out an easy strike. As he turned back around, he spotted their return and smirked it up. Noel noticed. His expression was...flat. Not amused and not annoyed, and Gabe didn't know the guy well enough to guess what was going on his head. Probably some protective instinct kicking in because Tristan was actively seeking something he'd been missing for years—companionship.

Gabe could deal with an overprotective best friend, as long as it didn't downshift into outright jealousy. Tristan had the right to a life removed from Noel's.

Instead of joining them, Gabe directed Tristan to one of the booths set one level up from the lanes. Gabe fetched Tristan's notebook from one of the seats set in a semicircle behind the scoring machine. "Nice strike," he said to Shane.

Shane beamed. "Thanks. You're up, Carlson."

Gabe glanced at the terminal. Noel was losing by quite a lot. Something about that amused Gabe to no end. He returned to Tristan and they spent the next half hour recounting both their adventures at the market and their mutual blowjobs in the bathroom. Recalling every moment in whispered, glorious detail had Gabe fighting another erection.

Tristan had lost the details of lunch, which was okay. It had been roughly an hour and a half to two hours since that happened. The memory improvement made them both giggle like little boys when Gabe told Tristan about it.

"That's almost long enough to watch a whole movie," Tristan said.

"Yes it is."

"Maybe it's all of the endorphins today. I haven't felt this good in...I have no idea. Maybe never. Definitely not that I can remember, and I doubt any time that I can't."

"You should run that by your doctor. Ask him if regular sex is good for memory retention."

Tristan laughed again, his cheeks still adorably pink. "What if he says yes?"

Gabe pitched his voice low. "Then call me right away."

"Don't offer if you don't mean it."

"Oh I mean it. This was not a one-off, Tristan. Not even close."

Tristan stared at him, his eyes moving, taking something in. "Why do you like me?"

"Why wouldn't I like you? You're funny, you're easy to talk to, you're sexy as hell, and I'm attracted to you. Your memory impairments don't scare me. Very few things do."

"What is something that scares you?"

Coming home one day and finding Debbie dead. Getting a phone call that she did something awful to someone else while hammered. Her wandering out of the house and in front of a car. The bank seizing the house.

"I'm highly allergic to bee and wasp stings," Gabe said instead. "If one comes near me I scream like a girl."

"That's not a real fear, though, that's being smart and avoiding things that could hurt you."

"Then I guess that explains why I don't date."

"Someone broke your heart?"

"Yeah." Gabe wasn't going into the whole story yet, not in a bowling alley, but he could give Tristan a little bit more. "I let him hurt me twice. Kind of put me off of relationships. Until now."

Tristan's cheeks got a little pinker. "You aren't the one-off with a stranger guy, either, though. Long dry spell?"

"Not exactly." He was so not mentioning Mean Green and the regular sex he was having there. But he could use a version of the truth. "I have some friends in a similar boat. Not a fan of anonymous hookups, but we all have an itch to scratch, right?"

"That makes sense. Noel and I tried dating as freshmen, but it didn't really work out. We did hook up a few times, though, usually because we were drunk and horny."

"Those are the times you remember the most? College?"

"Yeah. It's so weird when the last really strong memories you have happened three years ago and involve guys your own age, and you keep waking up in a nursing home with old people all around."

"I can't imagine how frustrating this has been."

"Noel's been my touchstone, you know?" Tristan glanced over at the lanes, where Noel took a shot that brought down eight pins. "I'd have probably gone crazy or tried to kill myself before now if he hadn't stuck by me."

"Then I'm glad he did." Gabe couldn't imagine not knowing Tristan. For such a vibrant young man not to be part of his life. "Sometimes you have to stay close, even when it hurts, in order to see someone get better."

But unlike Debbie, Tristan wanted to get better.

"Besides, everything happens for a reason, right?" Tristan said. "I mean, if I hadn't been hurt, we never would have met."

"That's true. Of course, if we'd never met, you might have found another great guy a long time ago."

"I doubt it. Not a guy like you."

Yeah, I'm a great guy. So great I haven't told you about my other job.

His work in porn could contribute to the mixed signals he frequently received from Noel, and the outright weirdness he got from Shane. Seeing more of Tristan inevitably meant seeing more of Shane, and despite his once a week shift at Big Dick's, Gabe and Shane had never really discussed their porn history. Gabe had been doing porn long enough that he could compartmentalize Tony Ryder and the scenes he did. Separate them from his real life. He got the sense Shane was having a harder time with that.

It didn't explain Noel, though, and it would be pretty hypocritical for Noel to object to Gabe seeing Tristan based on the porn, since Noel had been regularly fucking Shane while Shane was actively filming. Gabe had no idea how the eventual reveal went down, but they were still together. They even bought a house and everything. "So you want to bowl a few frames?" Gabe asked.

Tristan blinked hard, probably thrown by the conversational curveball. "Um, sure."

"Then let's get some shoes."

Tristan held tight to Gabe's hand the entire ride back to where Gabe had left his car. He'd been fighting a headache since their last frame, but he didn't want their time together to end. The first few hours of the day had faded, but the emotions remained. He'd had an amazing time. He'd connected to another human being for the first time in years.

And dear God, Gabe knew how to suck a dick.

He was pretty sure he hadn't started the day with any sexual expectations, but he certainly wasn't going to complain. He didn't have a single thing to complain about, except maybe that he hadn't seen Gabe naked yet.

I will. I know I will.

Tristan had never figured out what he'd done so wrong in his life that God had seen fit to punish him like this. Whatever it was, he'd more than paid for it. He deserved to be happy. So did Gabe.

Too soon Noel pulled onto a metered side street and double-parked near a beat-up hatchback.

"Thanks for the ride," Gabe said. "I had a lot of fun today."

"Thanks for coming out," Noel said. Shane nodded at him from the front seat, that same awkwardness there.

"I'll walk you to your car," Tristan said. Didn't matter that it was five feet away. He wanted another moment. Standing up caused a flash of pain behind his eyes.

Fucking side effects.

Gabe met him by the bumper of his parked car. Tristan pressed up against him, enjoying the heat of his body, even through his jacket. The simple touch made his head hurt a little less. Gabe glanced around, then pressed his lips to Tristan's. The kiss was sweet, a gentle sweep of lips whispering a silent promise that this wasn't over. This beautiful thing they were exploring together had only just begun.

Tristan savored the taste of him, memorized the sensual way he licked along his lips, before pulling slowly back. "Thank you for today."

"No, thank you for today. It's the best time I've had in a while."

"Me too."

"We'll do it again soon."

The growled promise hit Tristan right in the balls and woke up his inner flirt. "Go bowling?"

"Among other things."

"Good." He leaned in closer to Gabe. "Although you're going to have to show me your house at some point. The staff at Benfield frowns on patients having sex in our rooms, and my door doesn't have a lock." Gabe tried to hide a flinch that made Tristan regret mentioning it. "Listen, I don't care if you live in a box or a mansion. I won't judge you. I promise."

Gabe's gentle smile settled him. "I know you won't. I think I judge myself more harshly than others."

"I'm pretty sure we all do that to ourselves."

"Probably so." Gabe kissed him again. "I have to go. Be safe."

"You too."

Tristan climbed back into Noel's car and put his head back, eyes closed to dim some of the headache throbbing behind his eyes. He hated leaving Gabe behind, but he knew in his soul that they'd talk again soon. Gabe was someone very special, and Tristan had somehow lucked into meeting him. He would do everything he could to keep him in his life as long as Gabe wanted him.

11

J on cornered Gabe upstairs the instant he walked into the Mean Green house for his Saturday shoot. "What the hell is wrong with you?" he asked.

Gabe stared. "What?" He wasn't late. He hadn't gotten the day wrong. He was there for a three-way shoot with Jon—they hung out so much off-hours that he had a hard time thinking of him as Boomer, even on set—and Dane. Gabe and Dane's last three-way with "Colby" had sold well, and fans were asking for another one. With Colby retired, Chet had enlisted Jon as the third.

An unexpectedly annoyed Jon. "You got an offer to work with Puppy Farm and you said you'd think about it? Are you insane?"

"It's a big decision."

"No, it's an easy yes. Dude, think of the exposure."

"That's all I've been thinking about." They were alone upstairs, so Gabe could be honest with his friend. "I don't want to do porn forever. Yeah, the extra money is always great, but the more times I'm seen, the harder it will be to find a good job after I'm done."

"Some guys use it to their advantage."

"Yeah, well, I'm not one of those guys. But I do need the

money, which is why I'm telling Chet yes." He'd figure out what to do about his mother later.

Jon's eyes widened. "I am so fucking jealous of you right now."

"Trust me, I'd let you go in my place if things worked that way."

"And I would totally go. Do you know who you'll work with?"

"No idea. Does it matter?"

"Well, yeah. The bigger the name, the more people will watch."

Please, God, give me one of their lesser-known models.

Only Gabe's luck wasn't that good.

"I'm topping, so I don't care," Gabe said. Only half a lie.

They went downstairs to the set, which featured a fake bedroom with a loveseat to the left, against a prop wall. Chet was chatting with Danny, the director of photography, over by the cameras, while the crew fiddled with the lights. Dane was leaning against the far right wall, eyes closed, quietly fluffing himself.

Dane was hot. Six feet of solid packed muscles, a waxed chest with the kind of pecs that made Gabe jealous, and thick brown hair he gelled back sixties greaser style. He always sported about two days' worth of stubble that he used to his advantage while eating ass. He was also one of the least chatty guys at Mean Green, rarely indulging in conversation that didn't revolve around the shoot.

Not that Gabe spilled his guts all over the set floor, either, but he tried to be polite with his fellow models. It was how he got Shane dancing once a week at Big Dick's.

"My boys," Chet said when he noticed them. "Right on time. Tony, love, do you have news for me?"

Gabe nodded as he closed the distance between them. His gut rolled with nerves. "I'll do it. I'll do the Puppy Farm shoot."

"I had a feeling you would. I'll call Stuart back and let him know. He's been haranguing me all week for an answer."

"Yeah, sorry about that."

"Excellent. That's a weight off my shoulders. Now let's get today started. Dane? Join us."

Dane took his hand out of his jeans and ambled over. He spared polite nods for Jon and Gabe, as well as a brief "hey."

"Straightforward shoot today, boys," Chet said. "No narrative. Boomer, you liked what you saw the last time Tony and Dane shot together, so you want in. Dane, you feel like taking one today? Just let Tony know."

Dane's lips twitched, but Gabe wouldn't call it a smile. The expression was almost sinister. He knew Dane was a switch. Dane had taken it beautifully from Shane a few months ago. And while Jon was more his type than Dane, Gabe never backed down from a challenge.

"Questions?" Chet asked. "No? Then let's get started."

The three of them piled onto the bed, making a sandwich of Jon. Gabe thought back to blowing Tristan in the bowling alley bathroom and his cock began to thicken. He'd already jacked off to the memory twice since Thursday. One of his favorite memories ever, and he hated that while Tristan had the words, he no longer had the pictures in his head.

Jon started off the prefuck chatting with his trademark "Boomer sass". He liked to play nelly bottom for the camera, even though he was anything but in real life. It worked for him, though, because of his muscles and blond hair—a great contrast that would make the scene that much hotter.

Gabe was already hard by the time Jon leaned over and unzipped his jeans. He'd done enough three-ways to automatically reach for Dane. He drew him closer by the neck, then landed a hard, demanding kiss. Starting out as the dominant one just in case Dane did want to get nailed. Chet gave direction a few times, and the two cameramen did their thing while the models stroked, sucked and kissed until they were all three naked. Gabe eventually shifted the action to the loveseat so Jon had a better angle to kiss and stroke Dane while Gabe first rimmed, and then fucked Jon.

Once Jon was in a proper, frenzied sweat, Gabe put him down on the loveseat, then arranged Dane kneeling over Jon so Jon could suck his dick. Going off Dane's signals, Gabe lined up behind him, one foot on the couch and one on the floor. Chet called a freeze so Gabe could put on a fresh condom and lube, and then got back to it.

Dane was crazy tight but he took it like a champ, fucking Jon's face with each thrust from Gabe. The synchronicity worked well, and Dane came first with Gabe's cock still in his ass. Dane moved off the couch so Gabe could reglove and fuck Jon into coming. Then Gabe thought of Tristan's beautiful blue eyes and came all over Jon's chest.

After Chet called cut, Gabe stood up and moved away, a strange feeling in his chest. He'd come and it had felt good, but it also felt...not good. He'd gone through the motions without really feeling anything. Not like in the bathroom with Tristan. They'd forged a connection, which had made the sex so incredibly moving and pleasurable. Instead of the energy he usually felt after a shoot, fucking Jon and Dane left him empty.

"Fantastic job, boys," Chet said. "And Tony, you fucked the come out of both of them. This is going to be scorching when it's edited."

"Awesome," Jon said. Someone tossed him a towel, which he used to wipe the various streaks of come off his chest. His cheeks were still red, his lips a bit puffy, but he looked like a well-satisfied, very fucked-out guy.

A pang of guilt surprised Gabe. He hadn't hurt either of his scene partners, and everyone came, so the guilt made no sense.

"Dibs on the shower," Dane said as he hustled off.

"When he's done, you want to share?" Jon asked.

"Sure," Gabe replied. They'd showered together plenty of times at the gym.

"Listen, Tony," Chet said, "I'm going to go give Stuart a call, okay? Bear with me. I might have some specifics for you before you leave."

"Yeah, okay."

Gabe went over to his gym bag to check his phone for messages. The email notification from Tristan filled up the part of his heart that was empty and confused.

–

11/08

2:19 pm _

G—

A funny thing happened on the way to my art class. Okay, so actually at the art class because when I walked in I remembered the name of the art teacher. I've been looking at my journals of those classes, and I have a list of names I want to remember. I didn't have a picture of her to associate, so maybe it was process of elimination since she was the only person in the room in her midthirties, but I knew Ms. Wendy Allen on sight. It was so cool! I got really excited, and I think I scared an old lady with big black glasses, because she gave me dirty looks the rest of the hour. Whatever. Ha!

Sometimes when I look at your picture I have these feelings. Not scary ones. Not really romantic ones, I don't think. But strong feelings of knowing you. Of having connected to you. It sucks that I can't remember the bathroom, but I have our notes, so it's like having porn to reread whenever I want. I can't wait for my evaluation on Monday. I really hope my doctors are impressed. I know I'm impressed.

I don't really have anything going on for the rest of the day (I know, I checked my calendar), so if you're free to Skype later, please call. I'd love to hear your voice. —T

"Okay, what's his name?" Jon asked.

"Whose name?" Gabe played dumb for the fun of it. Sooner or later he wouldn't be able to keep avoiding the conversation.

"You got that moon-eyed look again reading something on your phone. Same way you looked at the gym when you were checking messages. Are you seeing someone?"

"Not exactly."

Jon's pale eyebrows arched. "But you're admitting there is someone."

"Yes."

"Details. Why are you 'not exactly' seeing him?"

"Because it's complicated."

"Is he already with someone? Are you some guy's piece on the side?" For some reason the idea seemed to delight Jon.

"No. Christ." Gabe crossed his arms. "He's perfectly single."

"So are you not seeing him because you do porn?"

"Are you going to keep asking questions, or will you let me tell you?"

Jon mimed locking his lips with a key.

"A few years ago Tristan was hurt pretty badly." Gabe briefly ran down Tristan's limitations and how they first met.

"Tristan. That's very historical romance."

"Shut up. We met up again in September and had a really great time, so we started trading emails."

"Emails? What are you, forty?"

Gabe cuffed Jon across the back of his head for that one. "It's the best way for Tristan to communicate. Anyway, he got involved in a clinical drug trial that is actually improving his memory retention. I spent the day with him and his friends this past Thursday." He couldn't stop a broad smile simply from remembering that day.

"Holy shit, you're totally falling for this Tristan guy, aren't you?" Jon asked with a healthy amount of awe in his voice.

"Yeah. And I know he likes me too. It's just so..."

"Complicated?"

"Exactly."

Jon scrubbed a hand through his short hair. "But you said his memory is getting better, right?"

"It's getting better every day. He's remembering names and faces and different kinds of information. The brain is such a mystery, even to most neurologists, so his doctor isn't entirely sure what to expect in terms of improvement."

"That's pretty amazing, though, that the doctors might be able to fix him."

"I know. Noel has been by his side ever since he was hurt, but I know Tristan wants to be independent again. He doesn't want to be a burden to his friend anymore."

The set had mostly cleared and enough time had passed, so Gabe grabbed his gym bag and headed for the stairs. Jon followed. He even kept his mouth shut until they were both under the showerheads in the main bathroom upstairs.

"So are you going to introduce Tristan to Debbie?" Jon asked.

"I'll have to at some point, I guess." He hated the idea of Tristan meeting his dirty little secret. Debbie was unpredictable in her drinking and her moods, and the very last thing Gabe wanted was Tristan witnessing one of her tantrums. "Just like I'll have to tell him about this at some point."

Jon snatched the bottle of body wash. "Some guys think dating porn stars is hot."

"Is that what you tell yourself to fall asleep at night?"

"Fuck you, I'm not interested in dating."

"Every guy isn't going to be Rick."

Wrong tactic. Jon's eyes went cold and angry, and he turned away to finish washing up. Gabe sighed, then ducked under his own showerhead. He knew better than to bring up Jon's ex, but he needed to get it through Jon's thick head that controlling, verbally abusive assholes like Rick were not the norm. He could find a good guy if he allowed himself to look.

Jon would be mad at him for a while, so Gabe finished show-ering and got dressed. He didn't just want to Skype with Tristan. He wanted to touch him. He wanted to be near him. Except not at home. On a Saturday night, he knew exactly where they could hang out and be alone.

Once he got outside, he called Bear.

Tristan glanced at the clock on his wall. 5:10. Twenty minutes until dinnertime. A small part of him was sad that he hadn't heard from Gabe yet, but Gabe did have a life outside of their email conversations. He was probably busy working, which meant no Skype tonight.

After dinner he'd settle in and continue with season three of *Modern Family*. Now that he could remember things longer, he'd started catching up on sitcoms that Noel had recommended. So far he loved this one. Mostly because it starred the guy from *Married...With Children*, a show he'd once watched religiously in reruns.

Someone knocked on his half-closed door. Tristan twisted around on his bed. A drop-dead gorgeous—Gabe. His heart skipped.

"Hey!" Tristan scrambled off the bed and practically leapt into Gabe's arms. Gabe hauled him into a tight hug that made Tristan never want to let go. "I was just thinking about you."

"Good things, I hope."

"Oh definitely."

Gabe released his grip enough so they could look at each other. He was grinning like someone with a secret. "How are you?"

"I'm fine. Is this your first time at Benfield?"

"Yes. The nurse at the front desk seemed shocked someone else was here to visit you."

"I don't get many visitors. Mostly Noel and Shane. Sometimes my friends from college, Billy and Chris."

"Well, now you've got me. And if you're willing, I'd like to take you out for a few hours."

"Really?" Tristan's stomach flipped with excitement.

"Yes. I promised you a viewing of *Star Trek Into Darkness*."

"Do you think it's too long?"

"If you forget details of the beginning, I'll fill you in." Gabe's smile dimmed a bit. "But if you think going out just the two of us is a bad idea, you can say so. It won't hurt my feelings."

"No, I want to. It took me a few seconds to recognize you when you first got here but I know you. I want to go out with you, Gabe."

"Good." He glanced down. "You might want to put some pants on."

Tristan laughed. He tended to spend most days in pajama bottoms because they were more comfortable than jeans. "Do I need to know any kind of dress code?"

"Completely casual."

"Okay."

Tristan fished a pair of clean jeans and socks out of his dresser. Gabe amused him by turning his back while he switched from the pajama pants to the jeans. So gentlemanly. Once he had his socks and sneakers on, Tristan said, "Okay, I'm decent."

"Then let's go."

"Where to?"

"It's a surprise."

"You're going to surprise the guy with the memory problems?"

For a split second, Gabe faltered. Tristan laughed, then planted a kiss on his cheek.

"So joking," Tristan said. "Surprise away."

"Brat."

The affection in that one simple word made Tristan's blood hum. He grabbed his jacket, a notebook and a pen, then followed Gabe to the Admin desk so he could sign out. The nurse there, Caroline, smiled at him. "And who's this handsome fellow, Tristan?"

"My friend Gabe. We're going out for a while."

"Well, you have fun. And be safe."

"We will."

Once they were outside, Gabe took his hand. They walked to his car like that, the crisp air the only thing keeping him from combusting with joy. A small, perfect moment under the stars. Tristan didn't know how many—if any—other perfect moments he'd had, so he clung to this one as long as he could.

Eventually, they reached Gabe's car. Gabe opened the passenger door for him, which was one of the sexiest things Tristan had ever seen. Such a perfect gentleman. The car smelled like vanilla. He located a little scented clip thing on one of the vents.

Gabe got them on the road then took his hand again. Tristan contented himself with staring at Gabe's profile in the dim light. They were going out. They were going to watch a movie. If all went well, they were going to get naked too. Tristan really, really wanted that. He wanted to be with Gabe so badly he ached with it.

"What are you thinking about so hard?" Gabe asked.

Might as well be upfront.

"I want to have sex with you."

Gabe's hand jerked the wheel. "Jesus, Tristan. You're going to give me a hard-on before we even make it to dinner if you say stuff like that."

Tristan laughed. "Not sorry."

"I bet you aren't. And I didn't come out here simply to take you somewhere and fuck you. I want to spend time with you."

"I want to spend time with you too. And I wouldn't have

protested if you picked me up just to park us under a tree and fuck my brains out."

Gabe shifted in his seat. "Okay, those mental images are not helping."

"Good, because I would not object to said actions."

"As hot as that sounds, I'm not exactly prepared for it."

A tiny pang of disappointment was chased away by the bulge in Gabe's lap. "You don't keep a condom in your wallet?"

"Not for a while. Like I said, I'm not about casual hookups."

"Tell me you have supplies somewhere."

Gabe glanced at him, his intentions very clear in that brief moment of eye contact. "Oh I do. Trust me."

Tristan's own cock was half-hard from the conversation alone. He reached across their clasped hands to press his free hand against Gabe's erection. Gabe jumped then pushed toward the pressure. "You should find a dark spot so I can help you out with this."

"Christ. I didn't think you'd like public sex so much."

"Have we done this before?"

Gabe explained the bowling alley bathroom, and Tristan was fully hard by the time he was done. He also had Gabe humping against his hand.

The road to Benfield was mostly country, a winding two-lane through the forested hills of central Pennsylvania. They'd reached the stop sign and could only go right or left on the state road. One sign pointed toward the PA turnpike, the other toward a small town two miles away.

Gabe met his gaze, dark and seductive. Tristan slowly drew his tongue along his lower lip. Gabe's nostrils flared.

He turned toward the town. Maybe a mile down the road, he pulled off at a roadside produce stand boarded up for the winter. Gabe parked behind the shack, then turned off the lights and engine. He captured Tristan in a hard, claiming kiss, his tongue thrusting deeply into Tristan's mouth. Tristan savored the minty taste of him, the firm way he controlled the kiss.

So good. Oh my God.

Gabe pulled back, his eyes blazing. "Get in the backseat."

Tristan nearly came from the growled order alone. He climbed over the console and tumbled onto the rear bench seat. Gabe joined him and, in a dizzying move, had Tristan flat on his back, his legs hiked up over Gabe's hips. Their erections pressed together, a delicious friction Gabe intensified with brief thrusts.

He dragged Gabe down and into another tongue-lashing kiss. Everything about it felt right. Every sweep of tongue and clash of teeth. The heady taste of Gabe as the mint faded. The softness of his lips and light abrasion of his unshaven skin.

Gabe kissed his way along Tristan's neck, sending shivers down his spine that went straight to his cock. "Fuck, so good," Tristan gasped.

Tristan shoved a hand between them, making fast work of both of their flies. Gabe helped him get their jeans and under-wear down, out of the way. Tristan licked his palm then clasped their cocks together in his hand. Too much for him to manage with one, so Gabe used his hand not braced on the seat to help him out. They fucked their circle of fingers together, cocks pressing and sliding, somehow finding a rhythm that worked.

"Christ, that's good," Gabe said. He licked and sucked at Tristan's throat then moved back to his mouth.

Pleasure sailed through him on waves, and Tristan rode it. He closed his eyes and kissed Gabe, unwilling to sever any contact. He stroked Gabe's tongue with his, mimicking the thrusts of their cocks, until his balls drew up. Everything was hot and tight and so, so fucking good, and Gabe. All Gabe.

Gabe swallowed his cries when he came, a sharp burst of pleasure that seemed never-ending in its brilliance. Gabe followed a moment later, their combined release slicking their hands and bellies, and Gabe collapsed on top of him. Sealing them together. Hot breath puffed against the damp skin of his neck.

Tristan had never felt so alive or content than in that moment on the backseat of Gabe's car—Gabe a human blanket he wanted to cuddle with forever.

Eventually the cooling air and awkward position forced Gabe to sit up. His face was creased and his lips puffy, the very picture of satisfaction. Tristan had done that. Pride puffed his chest.

"Glad you pulled over?" Tristan asked.

Gabe chuckled. "Very glad. We should clean up. I still need to take you to dinner."

"And then more sex?"

With a wicked grin, Gabe leaned over and licked the tip of Tristan's softening cock. "Very definitely more sex."

12

Gabe wasn't entirely sure how he made it through dinner without touching Tristan all the time. After rubbing off together in the backseat of his car, he wanted contact. Way more contact than sitting across the booth from him at an Irish pub while they worked their way through two massive plates of food.

He'd ordered the Guinness beef stew and it was fantastic. Just enough beer flavor without overpowering the meat and vegetables. Tristan was packing away shepherd's pie. He'd opted out of the various Guinness-flavored items on the menu because of his medications. The dining room and bar were crowded, which didn't surprise Gabe. It was Saturday night.

He entertained Tristan with their exploits on Thursday. A few times Tristan reacted to something he said as though it was familiar. It gave Gabe hope that reinforcement and repetition would help Tristan's memory.

His cell rang. The screen lit up with Debbie's name. He almost didn't answer it, but she'd only call again until he did. "Hey, what's up?"

"I can't find my slippers. Where are my slippers?" she asked.

Fuck me.

"You threw them out two days ago because you said they smelled."

Tristan's eyebrows went up, asking a silent question, and Gabe hated her for doing this now.

"I did not," Debbie said. She slurred only a little bit, which hinted at tipsy rather than hammered. "Those slippers were brand new."

"They were brand new five years ago. Listen, I'll buy you slippers tomorrow. Wear socks for tonight."

"They were new slippers."

"I have to go." Gabe hung up then put the phone on silent.

"Who was that?" Tristan asked.

"My mother. And I know it sounded like a weird conversation, but can we not talk about it?"

"Sure." Tristan speared a piece of carrot. "We can, though, whenever you want. Talk about it, I mean."

"I know. But I don't want her crazy to interfere with tonight."

"I don't want my crazy to interfere with tonight."

"Hey, you aren't crazy." Gabe again resisted the urge to hold his hand in public, even to comfort him. Tristan had been hesitant with it at the market, and Gabe didn't want to make him uncomfortable. "And you're getting better."

"I know. So where are we going later in order to avoid your mother and her crazy?"

"My dads' house. They're both working until about two a.m., so we'll have plenty of privacy. And they have a sixty-inch flat screen in the den."

"Seriously? Damn."

"Yeah. They love watching old movies from the thirties and forties. Bear is a huge Humphrey Bogart fan. He swears *Casablanca* is the most perfect movie ever made."

"I've never seen it."

Gabe shrugged. "I watched it once. It was very good, but older movies aren't really my thing."

"What do you like?"

"Action and adventure. Screwball comedies. Anything that distracts me from real life."

"I hear you." Tristan sipped his iced tea. "That's why I like animation. It's a whole new world that can be imagined and drawn up. It's like magic."

"Creating something about of nothing is a little bit like magic, I agree. So have you done anything outside of art class?" Gabe was fishing with that question, hoping to jog some part of Tristan's slowly improving memory. "Don't check the notebook."

Tristan scrunched his eyebrows and stared at the table. "Yes? I feel like I have, but I don't know."

"Thursday after you guys dropped me off, Noel stopped at an art supply store."

"He did? Why?" His eyes went wide. "He bought me stuff with my debit card. My parents put money into a checking account every month in case I need anything. What did we buy?"

He seemed so excited by the idea of art supplies that Gabe had mercy. "A drawing pad, proper pencils and some pastels."

"Pastels are my favorite." Tristan blinked hard, his eyes too shiny. He studied his fingernails. "I've used them. My nails aren't clean. See?" He held out his right and, sure enough, bits of color were embedded beneath his short nails.

"I love seeing you this excited," Gabe said.

"It's been so long since I've been this happy."

Their waiter chose that moment to ask if either needed drink refills. Gabe asked for more water. Tristan was fine. He was still so overjoyed he didn't catch the waiter's dirty look. While Tristan wasn't exactly obvious, he had a way of talking when excited that got a little more noticeable. And the happy comment hadn't helped.

Fuck the waiter.

"Do you remember what you've been drawing?" Gabe asked. He knew the answer from their still frequent emails, but testing Tristan was like mental physical therapy.

Tristan poked at some mashed potatoes. "No...wait." He frowned. "Faces?"

Gabe grinned. "Yeah. Whose faces?"

"Um...." He looked all around the dining room, as if the answer was out there somewhere. "I don't know. I'm sorry."

"Hey, don't apologize for what you can't remember. Celebrate what you can."

"Okay." He didn't smile but he did seem less annoyed. "So whose faces am I drawing?"

"You're doing a drawing of Noel and Shane for them to hang in their new house."

Instead of being surprised by the new house comment, Tristan nodded. He'd retained that one. "That makes sense. It sounds like something I would do." A sly smile drew his lips back at one corner. "I'd like to draw you one day."

"You kind of already did in the weekend art class you take. You hung it on the wall in your room."

"Oh. Oh well, I want to draw you again. You have a great face."

A bit of heat rose in Gabe's cheeks. "Thank you. Yours is pretty great too."

"I know."

The flirty response made Gabe laugh. "I love seeing you so confident. Something tells me you lost a lot of that for a while."

"I'm positive I did. I know I was angry for a long time. And depressed. Even if this is the best my memory ever gets, it's leaps and bounds better than it was. And I am so grateful to know you, Gabe."

"Me too. I mean, I'm grateful to know you, Tristan."

Tristan grinned then attacked his meal. By the time he'd

finished his stew, Gabe was stuffed but he couldn't say no when Tristan asked to split a piece of chocolate cheesecake. It was ooey, gooey deliciousness with a wonderful strawberry sauce on top. Tristan ended up with a smear of it across his chin, and Gabe suppressed the very real urge to lean across the table and lick it off him.

The waiter dropped off the bill, and Tristan excused himself to use the bathroom. Gabe slid his debit card into the black sleeve, handed it back for processing and then took a moment to survey the dining room. So many pairs of men and women, most likely couples. A few families. Two men in suits by the far wall. A single woman with two tweens and an infant. Very much like the people he waited on every shift.

A different waiter brought his debit card and receipts back. He was young and was blushing. "I didn't want to impose in front of your boyfriend," he said. "But I love your work and was hoping to get an autograph."

"Your boyfriend." I'd be so lucky.

Gabe shifted into Tony for a moment and gave the waiter a sultry smile. "Sure thing." Inside the sleeve he found a blank slip of receipt paper. He signed Tony Ryder with a flourish, then added a tip and signed his receipt with a very scrawled, pretty much illegible version of his real name.

Thankfully, the waiter moved on before Tristan came back. Gabe slid out of the booth.

"Where to next?" Tristan asked.

"What do you feel like doing?"

"I'm pretty sure when you picked me up you mentioned a movie."

A blast of cold November air hit Gabe in the face when he pushed the restaurant door open. Next to him, Tristan shivered and wrapped his arms around his waist.

"I did mention a movie," Gabe said. "I'd planned to take you back to my dads' house, but would you rather see one in the theater? It's probably been a while."

Tristan glanced around them, then leaned closer to his ear. "Which option gets your dick in my ass faster?"

The sexy purr went straight to Gabe's cock. "Dads' house."

"Then let's go to their place."

Gabe wasn't about to object. Tristan knew what he wanted, and Gabe was certainly on board with the plan. He was a little nervous about it too. Tristan hadn't had penetrative sex in more than three years. Getting off before dinner would help both of them take things slow. The last thing in the world that Gabe wanted was to hurt Tristan.

On the ride through Harrisburg, Tristan clung hard to his memories of being with Gabe in the backseat as he wrote them down. Every touch of skin, every kiss and lick. The whole thing had him hard again by the time Gabe pulled into the driveway of a two-story, stone-front home in a residential neighborhood.

He hadn't paid attention to their route. "Where are we?"

"Paxtang," Gabe replied.

"Oh, okay. Cool." One of the better areas around Harrisburg.

"They have the money to move to a high-end neighborhood if they want, but this is the first house they bought together."

"No sense in moving if they're happy." Tristan had grown up in a ritzy, upscale neighborhood. Everyone in school had known he was one of the rich kids, and he'd hated it.

He loved the house the moment he stepped inside. Wood floors, thick throw rugs, simple furnishings. A warmth to the place that hit him right in the gut. It felt like a home. His childhood home had been ultramodern, stainless steel, every new gadget under the sun. His parents had loved him to the best of his scholastic abilities, but they valued their reputations more.

"Tristan?" Gabe squeezed his shoulder. "You okay?"

"Yeah. It's a great place. Very homey. Did you grow up here?"

"For the most part, yes. My mother and Bear divorced when I was five, but they had shared custody until I was eight. That's when she gave up her parental rights so Richard could legally adopt me, and I lived here full time until I was nineteen."

Tristan was pretty sure Gabe had never told him that about his parents. He was insanely curious why his mother gave Gabe up, but he had a feeling it was a painful story. Tonight had been a good night, and he didn't want Gabe upset over the past. "What was it like growing up with two dads?"

Gabe hung his coat on a wall hook, then took Tristan's and did the same. "I don't have much else to compare it to. They loved me, and that's the most important thing. I got bullied sometimes at school for it, which was part of the reason I stayed in the closet and denied who I was for so long."

That surprised Tristan. Gabe seemed like the kind of guy who'd always been confident and self-assured. "How old were you when you came out?"

"I figured out I was gay when I was fifteen, but I was nineteen when I came out. I'd been secretly in a relationship with an older man for about a year prior to that. When he dumped me I was heartbroken, and I told Bear everything. I don't know why I hid it for so long." He shook his head. "No, I do know. Debbie—my mother, she took it badly when she found out. But it wasn't me. It was old anger at Bear and how their relationship imploded because he was in the closet when they got married."

"Wow." Tristan kind of wanted to write all of that information down, but how would that look in front of Gabe?

Gabe shrugged. "My family is complicated."

"Most are."

"Do you want something to drink?"

"No." Tristan deposited his notebook on the floor then

invaded Gabe's personal space, hands sliding around to grip his very firm ass. "I want to see your room."

"That can definitely be arranged. One thing first."

"Yeah?"

Gabe's lips whispered over his, a kiss as gentle as their earlier kisses had been fiery. Soft brushes and light licks of his tongue. Just enough pressure to drive Tristan crazy with the need for harder, faster, right the hell now. Desire burned in his gut, and he pressed his erection against Gabe's hip. Gabe responded with a soft growl. A hand slipped into Tristan's hair, teasing and tickling, while another slid beneath his jeans to squeeze his ass cheek.

Tristan gasped, desperate for that hand to keep going, to touch him where he hadn't been touched in far too long. He reversed the kiss, plunging his tongue into Gabe's mouth, tasting him. Savoring every touch, every scent, every sound. They kissed for a long time standing inside the front door, until Tristan was drunk with it. Lost to sensation and no longer focused.

The world grayed out for the space of a heartbeat, and the instant confusion made him pull away. Away from a man he knew, who'd just been kissing him like a rock star. They were both hard. He blinked at the gorgeous man.

"Tristan? You with me?"

That voice soothed his confusion over why he was in a foyer making out with someone who wasn't Noel. "I know you."

"Yes. You've known me for months. We're on a date and this is my dads' house."

Recognition hit him. He found the name. "Gabe."

A stunning smile made Tristan's heart pound. "Yes."

Tristan tried to find other memories of tonight. They ghosted through his mind, intangible, but existing. He simply couldn't bring them into focus. "My memory is getting better." And he knew why. He did know. "Drug therapy, right?"

"Right."

Everything about them together felt right. He glanced down

at the erection outlined by Gabe's tight jeans. "And we're about to have sex?"

"As long as you still want to."

"Hell yes, I do." Maybe his mind wasn't giving him the clues about Gabe he needed, but his heart was completely on board with this man. He trusted Gabe.

Gabe took his hand and led him up a narrow staircase to the second floor. Down an ivory-painted hallway to the only shut door. A radiation warning sign had been hung on the outside, and Tristan laughed.

"I was going through a privacy phase," Gabe said. "Be warned. You're about to step back in time about six years."

"I am warned."

Gabe pushed open the door and flipped a light switch. The room had been painted a deep forest green, and the walls were covered with movie posters. *The Dark Knight, Iron Man, Tropic Thunder, Quantum of Solace, Transformers,* and *Death Proof*. A bed, a desk, a bookshelf filled with *Hardy Boys* and *Choose Your Own Adventure* books. A few baseball trophies. All very teenage boy.

"Where'd you get all the posters?" Tristan asked.

"A buddy of mine worked at a local theater. He'd get them for me."

"That's awesome. I loved *The Dark Knight*. Do you still put up posters where you live now?"

"No. I haven't gotten any new ones for a while." Gabe tilted his head. "Hey, you knew I don't live here."

"Yeah, well, this doesn't seem like you now."

"True. I still love comic book movies, but I outgrew hanging posters on the wall."

"So no posters of your favorite porn stars?"

Gabe laughed. "No."

"Good. Then I don't have to worry so much about living up to anyone else."

"You wouldn't have to worry about that anyway." Gabe cupped his cheeks with his palms. "You're perfect."

No, I'm not, but thanks for saying it.

"Hey, Gabe?"

"Yes?"

"Take your clothes off."

13

G abe slid his fingers beneath the hem of his shirt then hesitated.

This wouldn't do.

Tristan didn't want Gabe hesitating over anything. He snared Gabe's other hand and squeezed. "Look, I know it's been a long time for me, and from what I can see you've got, like, a porn star penis, but I'm not stupid. If it hurts, I'll tell you, and we'll slow down. Promise."

He wanted Gabe inside him so badly he ached with it, but he'd had a few regrettable fucks, and he didn't want any regrets with Gabe. Not a single one, and definitely not their first time.

His reassurances seemed to relax Gabe. He squeezed Tristan's hand in return, then let go and the shirt was gone.

Gabe's sculpted torso was a thing of beauty. Tan and waxed, perfectly defined pecs with dusky nipples, a six-pack that was teasing toward being eight, and a lovely V that disappeared into the top of his jeans. His broad shoulders were muscled without being obnoxious, and Tristan could not stop staring.

"Wow," was all he managed.

"Good wow?"

"Great wow."

Tristan ran his palms up the length of Gabe's arms, wrists to shoulders, exploring the hills and valleys of the body on display for him. Enjoying the soft, warm skin over taut muscle, attention drawn back to Gabe's nipples. He bent his head and swept his tongue over the left one. Gabe made a soft, happy noise, so Tristan did it again. The small bud hardened under his attention. He bit down gently. Gabe gasped. Fingers threaded into Tristan's hair, urging him to continue.

He licked his way to the other nipple and gave it equal attention, nipping with teeth and rolling it with his tongue. With his free hand, Tristan worked Gabe's belt and fly. He shoved jeans and briefs down, releasing his ultimate target. He stroked Gabe's cock while he worked his nipples, beyond turned on by the noises Gabe made. The hand not in Tristan's hair was yanking at his own belt and fly, and then that hand—someone else's hand—was on Tristan's cock.

Tristan bit down from the shock of it all, a little too hard, because Gabe shouted and wrested his head away. Up into a tongue-lashing kiss that nearly made Tristan come on the spot. So much sensation all at once. His entire body was alive in a way he couldn't remember it ever being before. Not with anyone.

He pulled away long enough to remove the rest of his clothes, while Gabe did the same. They were both naked and Tristan could only think of one thing. He pushed Gabe toward the bed, then down to sit so Tristan could kneel between his legs. Gabe's thick cock was a challenge for his hand, barely able to close his fingers completely around the base of it. He couldn't wait to get his mouth around it.

"Tristan, hold up a second," Gabe said.

He did, looking up without letting go of his prize. "You are not going to tell me you don't like blowjobs."

"No, I do. And I know this isn't the best timing for this conversation, but we haven't really had it."

"What conversation?"

Gabe tilted his head while he stroked Tristan's cheek with one hand. "About STDs. I mean, I know you've lived in a medical bubble for the last three years, but I haven't."

Unease slithered in his gut. "Why? Do you have something I should know about?"

"No."

Tristan's anxiety eased. "So what's the problem?"

"When you were in college, didn't you ever ask before you fucked a guy?"

"No. But I used condoms. That's like totally common sense."

"Good." Gabe cupped both cheeks and pressed his forehead to Tristan's. "I want you safe."

"I've never felt safer, Gabe. I know you won't hurt me."

Something flickered in Gabe's eyes, an emotion Tristan couldn't identify. Then Gabe kissed him, a slow and sensual slide of his mouth and tongue, reenergizing Tristan for the task literally in hand. Stomach quivering with anticipation and nerves, Tristan broke the kiss so he could flick out his tongue for a taste of Gabe's cock.

The bitter taste of precome was quickly followed by the musky flavor of Gabe himself. Tristan pressed his nose to the thick, neatly trimmed nest of black pubes around the base of his cock, inhaling Gabe's scent. It filled his nose and mouth and made his own cock pulse with need.

God, I have missed this.

He took the tip into his mouth and sucked around the crown, listening for Gabe's frequent gasps, pants and whispers of "oh fuck". Nothing mattered more in that moment than getting as much of Gabe into his mouth as he could. He inched down, velvet heat sliding against his tongue and the roof of his mouth, stretching his lips and jaw. He relaxed his throat with instinctive ease—something he'd learned and not forgotten despite lack of practice. Tristan held his breath and took Gabe in. All the way, until his lips hit his fist.

"Oh shit!"

Tristan held still until he needed air, popping off with a gasp, eyes watering. Gabe gaped at him with open admiration. So Tristan did it again, pride warming his chest, thrilled to be giving Gabe such pleasure, and Gabe wasn't shy with his words. Tristan deep-throated him once more then began sucking his cock with abandon. Memorizing the taste and texture of Gabe's cock, the way different licks and nips drew different sounds out of Gabe.

He held Gabe's cock out of the way and attacked his balls, sucking one, and then the other into his mouth. Gabe's gasps and pleas spurred him on, and he licked at Gabe's taint. Gabe lay back and hiked his feet up, clearly on board with Tristan's next destination. The waxed balls should have prepared him for a perfectly hairless asshole. Hairy guys or hairless guys, Tristan never cared as long as he was somewhat attracted to him. Something about every part of Gabe being smooth except for his head and pubes only made Tristan want him more.

Gabe's scent was even stronger now, everything more intense. More real. He pulled Gabe's cheeks apart and flicked his tongue against Gabe's hole.

"Fuck!"

Tristan licked harder, teasing the puckered opening with his tongue, pressing flat against it. A sharper musk joined the medley of tastes and scents, and Tristan existed in the pure pleasure of it, while Gabe writhed and cussed and gave Tristan exactly what he wanted—Gabe about to fall apart.

Gabe wrestled himself away with a breathless, "Fuck. Don't want to come yet."

Tristan laughed and wiped his mouth. "Enjoyed that?"

"You have no fucking idea how much. Get up here."

He climbed onto the bed. Gabe had him on his back, his knees hiked up around Gabe's hips, before he really registered the move, and the dizzying speed made him laugh again. His cock rubbed against Gabe's. So good. Gabe kissed him, tongue plunging into his mouth. God, he would never tire of kissing Gabe.

Gabe must have had similar thoughts, because he kissed his way down Tristan's throat. He paused to lave each nipple, but didn't stay long. Tristan's nipples weren't really an erogenous zone for him, and Gabe figured it out. He dipped his tongue into Tristan's navel, and Tristan squealed at how ticklish it was. Gabe explored his abdomen more, and Tristan kind of hated the way his hips jutted out and his belly was sort of concave. He was too skinny, but Gabe didn't seem to care.

"Please," Tristan said.

Gabe glanced up. "Please what?"

"Please suck me." He'd beg if he had to. It had been too damned long.

The sly smile his request produced made Tristan's stomach jump. "If you insist."

"Oh I do."

Tristan intended to watch, but the moment Gabe's lips closed around his cock, Tristan threw his head back and gave in to the wet heat slowly, insistently driving him mad. Gabe knew what he was doing. Long licks, hard sucking, using hands and mouth together in an orchestra of motions that had pleasure burning inside of Tristan so brightly he had to close his eyes. He couldn't do anything except feel.

And then his balls. Oh God, his balls were being sucked on and played with, and it was so fucking good. A finger rubbed his taint, a glorious buzz of sensation that went straight to his cock, and Tristan jerked his hips. Then he pressed down into it, because he loved that so much. He tried to tell Gabe so but all he could manage were sounds. Positive, joyful sounds, and he hoped it was enough. His body was a live wire, open and alive, and it was almost too much at once.

That wicked finger slid lower, pressing against Tristan's hole.

"Yes, please, God," he babbled.

Gabe rubbed at his entrance while he returned to sucking his cock, and little sparks of pure pleasure danced through his body. Tristan thrust his hips, needing more of both. Needing more pressure on his cock and in his ass, and Gabe teased just enough to drive him insane.

"Fuck me. Please, Gabe."

"Soon." No single word had ever sounded sexier to Tristan. Gabe gave his cock another lick, then sat up, away from Tristan. "Be right back. I need supplies."

Tristan didn't want him to leave. *What if he leaves and my memory has a hiccup? Please, not right now.* His entire body was coiled tight, ready for release, his cock hard and wet against his tight belly.

Gabe returned quickly with a couple of condoms and a pump bottle of lube. His tan skin glistened with perspiration, and he stood at the foot of the bed like Tristan's own personal sex god come to life. So beautiful.

He put the lube and condoms on the nightstand, then knee-walked his way across the bed to Tristan. "Hands and knees, sunshine," he said.

Sunshine. Yes.

Tristan had never changed positions faster in his life. His cock hung low, only air on it now, and he was desperate for Gabe to touch him. To get him off. Except he needed this first. He needed the stretch and burn, and then the oh so good. He needed Gabe inside of him with such an intensity that it might have scared him if he didn't feel so fucking good.

He cried out at the first press of a tongue against his hole. He loved getting rimmed, and Gabe knew what the fuck he was doing. Tristan closed his eyes, hands bunched in the duvet, and rode out the warring sensations of being licked, stabbed and swirled with a tongue, all colliding together to make him crazy.

Softening him, getting him wet and ready. He dropped a litany of "Please, please, please," that became one long word with no real ending. Gabe tugged on his cock and rolled his balls while he worshiped Tristan's ass.

A finger joined Gabe's tongue, followed soon by two, and it was too much and not enough and Tristan didn't know anymore what he wanted, except to come. He really wanted to come, only Gabe wasn't letting him.

Gabe kissed the small of his back. "How do you want me?"

"Like this. Please." He loved nothing more than a guy draped over his back, fucking him into the mattress. Except maybe standing up and getting fucked over a dining table. That was a good memory.

Gabe snagged the lube and a condom. Tristan listened to the foil packet tearing open. The pump of the lube bottle. The soft, sticky sound of Gabe rubbing it on the condom. More pumping. The cool lube against his ass made Tristan jump. Gabe pushed a finger inside, getting him ready. This part Tristan knew well—the prep. The actual fucking was always something brand new, different with every guy.

Every single thing about being with Gabe was amazing. This would be the same.

Gabe clutched his left hip. Blunt heat pressed against Tristan's entrance. The instant stretch, bordering on a burn, made him gasp. Perspiration prickled all along his shoulders and back. Gabe pushed in a bit, then pulled back. A little farther each time, taking it painfully, beautifully slow, filling Tristan more with each new thrust.

"Fuck, fuck, fuck." Tristan relaxed and bore down, fighting the need to impale himself and be done, because he didn't want anything about this to hurt. "Shit, so good."

Gabe gave a few shallow thrusts that made Tristan gasp hard. He loved this, and he'd missed this, and Christ, how much more was there? He braced himself on one elbow so he could reach behind. Gabe was only halfway in.

"More," Tristan said.

"I don't want to hurt you." The strain in Gabe's voice made Tristan's heart pound. He was holding so much back for Tristan's sake.

"You aren't. Please."

Gabe pressed in deeper. Tristan dipped his belly toward the bed, lifting his ass higher, giving Gabe a better angle. So much. So deep. So fucking good.

Tristan lost himself to the sensations bombarding his body. To the smell of musk and sex and sweat. To the heat emanating from the man behind him. To the glorious stretch and fullness in his ass. His cock and balls hummed with pleasure, warning him they wouldn't survive the onslaught much longer.

Not until Gabe really fucks me.

He pushed back, onto Gabe, earning a deep moan. Gabe squeezed both hips hard enough to bruise. "Fucking fuck me already," Tristan said.

Gabe slid one hand up to curl around Tristan's shoulder. "You sure?"

"Yes. You feel so good, Gabe, please."

He draped his broad body over Tristan's back and planted a hard, sideways kiss on him. The angle shifted his cock a little, and Tristan's balls tingled. He was rock hard and so close.

Gabe planted his hands on either side of Tristan's elbows and rocked his hips. Tristan held on, everything telescoping into the thick cock sliding in and out of his ass, the heat of Gabe's body, the slick of sweat and the pleasure pooling in his balls. Tingling at the base of his spine. Warning him of his own climax too damned soon. One touch to his cock and he'd be gone. He pressed his cheek against the duvet and existed in that perfect moment.

An arm wrapped around his waist, holding his back firmly to

Gabe's chest. Fingers splayed across his belly. Gabe nipped his shoulder, and Tristan felt that in his balls. He cried out, so desperate for release and unable to move to claim it. As if he knew, Gabe thrust deeper than ever, and then started jacking Tristan's cock.

Tristan shouted as his release rolled over him in waves, heating him all over, everything going hot and tight before relaxing again. His belly trembled and he couldn't get enough air to breathe. He barely stayed upright, but he did have the presence of mind to grab Gabe's hip before he could pull out.

"Come in me," he said.

Gabe stroked him once more before releasing his spent cock. "Are you sure?"

"Positive."

Tristan was ready for whatever Gabe needed, but after four hard thrusts, he groaned long and loud, then stilled. Gabe dropped soft kisses along Tristan's back and shoulders, reawakening already sensitized skin. He wanted the moment to last forever and hated that it would be gone in a few hours.

Gabe pulled out slowly, and yeah it kind of stung a little but it was the best kind of discomfort. Tristan flopped onto his stomach, his trembling limbs unable to support him. Gabe was gone a moment, probably to dump the condom on the floor. Then he turned Tristan onto his side and curled up behind him, arms around his waist, both palms flattening out over his heart, a shared pillow beneath their heads. Gabe kissed his neck again, breath puffing against his damp skin. Tristan knew deep down that he'd never been so happy, protected and safe in his life.

I could stay like this always.

"How are you?" Gabe whispered.

"Perfect."

He chuffed laughter. "That's a high compliment."

"Thank you for tonight. For this and whatever we did together before this."

"Thank you, Tristan. I know our lives can't be compared, but before I met you, I was alone too."

"We met by accident, right?"

"Sort of. Do you recall anything about it?"

Tristan closed his eyes and pictured Gabe's face. Backgrounds shifted. Walking outdoors. A tiled wall. A restaurant setting. Nothing specific or familiar. Then music. Dance music. "Did we meet at a party?"

"Close. A nightclub."

"Big Dick's?"

Gabe startled. "You remember?"

"Well, no, but it's the best known gay club in Harrisburg. So it was Big Dick's?"

"Yes. The first time we met, you went there alone and you got really confused so Noel came to get you. The second time, Noel and Shane brought you for your birthday and we spent all night dancing."

Warmth settled in Tristan's belly. "Good. I love dancing." And because teasing Gabe was fun, he added, "Were you any good?"

Gabe laughed and kissed his shoulder. "Not as good as you."

"Good answer." Tristan twisted around to his other side, because he wanted every single memory he could make of Gabe's face. Especially his blissed out, postsex face of rosy cheeks, puffy lips and sleepy eyes. "Hi."

"Hey." Gabe stroked his cheek with the tip of his finger. "As much as I'd love to take a nap with you, I'm scared you'll forget me when you wake up."

Tristan's heart fluttered. "Me too. But my memory is getting better. I know that."

"It is. You're part of a clinical drug trial, and you're getting better every day. You're retaining things longer, and you're able to recall things."

"Want to know something ironic? For my sophomore psychology class, I did a paper on improving memory loss. No one really knows for sure how our memories work, so it's hard to know how to fix faulty ones. One school of thought is that our brain retains everything it's exposed to, from images to sensations to sounds, but the functionality of our memory limits the amount of information that we can actually recall once the moment has passed."

Gabe stared at him, and yeah, not very sexy pillow talk, but still relevant. "Is that what you think?"

"It makes the most sense. It means that the accident severely limited my recollection ability, but it also means the information is there. It's possible that I could start to remember things from days, months, maybe years ago. I like believing that one day I'll remember all of the time we've spent together."

"Then I'll believe that too."

He kissed Gabe for that. A soft press of lips because it felt like the right thing.

Gabe grinned, but it dimmed quickly. "I hate that I have to take you back to Benfield."

"Me too. But not for a while, right?"

"No, not for a while."

Tristan snuggled up closer and tucked his head under Gabe's chin, enjoying every moment of togetherness that they had. The shift also reminded him of his sore, still lubey ass. No way was he going back to Benfield in that state. Not that he wasn't proud of Gabe, but some of the more conservative nurses might freak out.

"You want to take a shower together?" Gabe asked. "The one in my dads' room is big enough for two."

"In a bit. Can you just...hold me for a while?"

Gabe's arms tightened around his waist. "As long as you want."

14

Tristan dozed off halfway through their viewing of *Star Trek Into Darkness*, his head in Gabe's lap, his lean body stretched out across the plush den couch. After a long, playful shower, they'd come downstairs to watch the promised film with popcorn and sodas. The popcorn was gone before anyone in the movie said the name Khan, and then Tristan turned Gabe into a pillow.

He didn't mind. The entire scene was so domestic that Gabe's chest hurt. He'd never had this simplicity, not even in the year he was with Andrew. He'd been Andrew's dirty little secret, not a real boyfriend, even though Gabe had felt differently.

He was eighteen when he met Andrew, and they bonded over the one thing they actually had in common—they were both in the closet. Andrew was thirty-three, a lawyer with a string of ex-girlfriends, and they each found in the other a body to fuck. Gabe could see it as that through the clear lens of time, no longer skewed by the lust of a confused teenager. And Gabe fucked him as often as Andrew would allow it for over a year, usually at Andrew's house—after Gabe parked a block away and went in through the side yard.

That should have been his first clue that they'd never be more than fuck buddies, but Gabe had fallen for him. And when Andrew discovered just how fucked up Gabe's family life was, Andrew dumped him via email. Heartbroken and scared, Gabe finally came out to Bear. Both his dads were great about it, even though they knew all too well the rough road he had ahead of him.

So no, he'd never had tender moments with Andrew like right then with Tristan, a lover falling asleep with his head in Gabe's lap. He hated knowing Tristan might have forgotten their night together when he finally woke up, but he did know Gabe. He'd recognized him when Gabe picked him up at Benfield, and he'd put it together very quickly during his moment in the foyer earlier.

Baby steps.

Gabe half watched the rest of the movie, but mostly he watched Tristan. The sharp planes of his too-thin face. The way his blond hair curled around his ears. The long leanness of a body he could worship for hours. Sex with Tristan was something truly special. He'd never had a partner so responsive, so perfectly in the moment. Every touch, every caress, every kiss was something Tristan treasured, because he might not remember it in a few hours. Gabe couldn't imagine walking in Tristan's shoes. He couldn't fathom how differently Tristan saw the world and the people in it.

The movie credits rolled. It was past eleven, and Gabe was tired. A long day shooting, and then his amazing time with Tristan had worn him out, and he still had at least forty minutes of round-trip driving. As much as he wanted to carry Tristan upstairs and fall asleep together, he didn't want to risk freaking Tristan out if he woke up in the dark.

He rubbed Tristan's shoulder. "Hey, sleepyhead. Time to head home."

Tristan mumbled something then turned his face into Gabe's lap.

Stubborn.

"If I have to carry you to the car, it will be over my shoulder like a sack of potatoes," Gabe said.

Tristan stirred then came fully awake. He blinked up at Gabe, his initial confusion disappearing quickly. "Gabe."

"Yes."

"Where are we?" He eased up, one hand pressing against his left temple. He took in the den, with its dark furniture and big sofa. "Is this your place?"

"No, it's my dads' house. Does your head hurt?"

"A little bit." His eyes widened. "I fell asleep during the movie, didn't I? Crap, what did we watch?"

"The newest *Star Trek* movie."

"They made another one?"

Gabe smiled. "Yeah. It's okay. We can try again some other time."

"I didn't mean to fall asleep." Tristan shifted his weight. His entire face lit up with his grin. "We totally had sex, didn't we?"

"Yes, we did, and it was amazing."

"Of course it was. You must have a big dick, because I can still kind of feel you. Not that I'm complaining, or anything."

Gabe didn't know if he should be proud or concerned. "Are you in pain?"

"Nah, only my head but that's nothing new." He glanced around until he found the giant pocket watch-shaped clock on the wall. "I don't suppose we have time for another round? Isn't there research or something that sex cures headaches?"

Gabe had already come three times today. He was exhausted and didn't have much left in terms of sexual energy, despite Tristan's proximity and big, begging blue eyes. Still, he wasn't opposed to giving Tristan a nightcap. "I don't think I can manage a repeat of earlier, but I wouldn't mind testing your headache theory another way."

"Oh yeah?"

He slid off the couch and knelt between Tristan's legs. Tristan figured it out fast and helped Gabe remove his jeans and briefs. Gabe had loved sucking Tristan off earlier, almost as much as he'd loved rimming him. The sounds Tristan had made were imprinted in his mind. So genuine. So very much Tristan.

Gabe took Tristan's soft cock in his mouth. He was rewarded with a sharp, slightly soapy taste he adored, and a gasp that sent a tingle down his spine. He loved the sensation of a cock slowly hardening in his mouth. Growing and thickening to fullness under his ministrations.

Tristan's fingers curled in his hair, urging him. Encouraging him. Gabe took him deep and worked his throat muscles. Tristan gasped and cursed. He rolled Tristan's nuts in his hand, and Tristan jerked his hips. Gabe held still, allowing Tristan to take control. To fuck up into his mouth, to stretch his lips and throat, and it was fantastic. Tristan had a big enough cock that Gabe felt it. Saliva dribbled down his chin but he didn't care. This was all for Tristan.

His thrusts stuttered, so Gabe retook control, sucking him with long, firm strokes. Allowing the silky skin to slide across his tongue. His senses were full of Tristan's taste and scent. Tristan's thighs trembled, and his gasped "Fuck, fuck, fuck," warned Gabe he was close. Time to amp it up.

He wetted a finger with spit, then worked it down to press against Tristan's entrance.

Tristan shouted and came, pumping his release into Gabe's mouth. Gabe savored the salty tang of him, sucking hard until Tristan flopped over sideways, and then he licked him clean. Not a drop spilled.

"Holy fuck that was good," Tristan said. "Dude."

Gabe chuckled. "Glad to be of assistance. How's the headache?"

"A very, very dull roar." Tristan's head lolled to the side, his eyes sparkling. "You are really good at that."

I've had a hell of a lot of practice. "Thanks."

"Want me to return the favor?"

While Gabe felt great for having given Tristan so much pleasure, his cock hadn't gotten into the game. "I'm good. Rain check?"

"Definitely." He heaved a deep sigh. "I hate that I can't stay over like a normal adult."

"One day you will."

"Here or at your place?"

Gabe didn't know how to answer. His dads wouldn't care if he and Tristan stayed over. Hell, they'd probably cook up a crazy brunch for the four of them the next morning to celebrate Gabe getting a life. But he didn't live here anymore, and he couldn't hide his ailing mother forever.

"I don't know," Gabe said, because that was honest. "My place is complicated." *And the last time I told a guy the truth about my mother, he dumped my ass.*

"I get complicated, believe me. You must be the most patient person on the planet to put up with me."

"I am patient but you make it easy. I want you in my life, Tristan. I feel good when I'm with you." Gabe's cheeks warmed. He hadn't meant to be quite that honest.

Tristan sat up slowly. He put his jeans back on then joined him on the floor. "I feel good when I'm with you too. Really good. Like nothing bad can happen as long as you're here."

Gabe's heart thumped hard against his ribs. *I am so falling for him.* "What are you doing for Thanksgiving?" he blurted out. Smooth, very smooth.

"I have no idea." He glanced at the closed notebook on the coffee table. "I probably do something with Noel. He never went home for it in college because his family was too far away. One year he couldn't even afford to go home for Christmas."

"That bites. Do you want to come here? My dads always do a big dinner and invite friends. Noel and Shane can come too, if it makes you more comfortable."

"Sure. That sounds like fun. A real turkey dinner."

"Bear makes a really good cornbread dressing. And every year he swears he's going to rig up a way to deep fry the turkey, but Dad is always afraid he'll burn the house down."

Tristan laughed. "I'd worry about that too. Should I bring anything? I mean, I don't have a kitchen to cook in, and I can't really do anything except boil ramen, but—"

"Nope, it will be covered."

"Cool. How far away is Thanksgiving?"

"About three weeks."

"Okay."

Gabe helped him stand then held on, reluctant to let go of his hand. Tristan held his gaze, so full of understanding. Brimming with unspoken emotion.

Tristan blinked first. He grabbed his notebook. "I guess we should go."

"Yeah."

Tristan spent the entire ride back to Benfield staring at Gabe. He couldn't help himself. His body ached with exhaustion and the release of really good sex, and even though he couldn't remember the details, he hadn't lost the emotions. The connection he felt to Gabe was scarily intense and also amazingly wonderful. He didn't understand it, but he'd fight to keep it.

One of the radio stations was already playing Christmas music, even though it was only November, and they both often sang along. Tristan didn't have much of a voice, but Gabe could carry a decent tune, especially matched up with a singer like Harry Connick, Jr.

At Benfield, Gabe walked him inside. The nurse at the desk tossed them both a grim look, but Tristan didn't care. He didn't know her name without the name tag, but he knew he didn't like her. She always gave him a bad feeling when she was around, so he ignored the look and held tight to Gabe's hand all the way to his room.

He tossed the notebook onto his desk. "Did I write down everything from tonight?"

"No," Gabe replied. "But I'll email you the sordid details in the morning. How's that sound?"

"Sounds perfect. Lots of sordid details."

Gabe looped his arms around his waist. "Like what your ass tastes like?"

Tristan shivered. "Did I know you're this dirty?"

"I haven't gotten started with the dirty, trust me."

"Oh? Do tell."

"I'd rather show you. Next time."

He's trying to kill me. "Tease."

"A tease doesn't follow through. I will definitely follow through."

"Soon?"

Gabe chuckled. "Miss my cock already?"

"Hey, I've got three years of celibacy to make up for." He reached between them to cup Gabe's groin. "Besides, I really like your cock."

Gabe pressed his forehead to Tristan's, his warm breath fanning over Tristan's mouth. "I really like yours too."

"Can I ask you something I might have already asked you?"

"Of course."

"Are you exclusively a top?"

"Pretty much. I've tried bottoming twice, but it doesn't work for me."

"It doesn't work for everyone. Me? There are few things I love more than a guy with a big dick pounding me through the floor."

Gabe made a very sexy noise. He reached down to squeeze Tristan's ass. "You are making it very hard for me to say good night."

"So stay. Ever had bathroom sex?"

"You're trouble, which is exactly why I didn't bring any condoms."

"Spoilsport."

Gabe kissed him, his tongue sweeping into Tristan's mouth to claim him. Making a promise of more in the future. Tristan clung to him, thrusting his own tongue against Gabe's, pretending for a moment they were naked in bed. That they were a regular couple who did normal things like sleeping and waking up together.

Then Gabe pulled back, and the fantasy was gone.

"Good night, Tristan," he said.

"Good night."

He watched from his doorway until Gabe disappeared. Melancholy settled over him as he closed his door, shutting out the world for a while. He sat at his desk and checked the last notebook entry. Scribbles about parking with Gabe and rubbing off together in the backseat. More about eating in an Irish restaurant.

Nothing else. A blank space that Gabe had promised to fill in for him in great detail. Tristan left an empty page so he could staple in the eventual email, then snagged a pen.

I may not remember having sex with Gabe, but hot damn I did. And I know deep down it was amazing. I'm pretty sure everything I do with Gabe is amazing and wonderful and fun. I fell asleep while watching a movie, and when I woke up I wasn't scared. Probably because I was with him. It took me a few seconds to remember his name, but I did. All on my own. My heart knows him. Maybe my heart is telling my brain who he is for me.

He gave me a wonderful blowjob on the couch. He's got an amazing mouth, and I came so fucking hard. He's funny about compliments too. He gets all shy and it's adorable. He didn't want me to blow him back, but I got a rain check. I can't wait. I can't wait to see him again. He drove me home and walked me inside, and then he made promises about dirty things, and I can't fucking wait. I didn't want him to leave. I hate that he's gone. And not just because I want to wrap up in his hugs and stay there forever. Something about him draws me there. Makes me feel safe.

I'm sitting at my desk writing this, and it's a little scary, but here goes: I think I'm falling in love with Gabe.

Holy shit.

15

Shattering glass roused Gabe from a deep sleep, and he floundered a moment. His room. Monday. What the hell—? Shit, Debbie.

He tripped over a pair of sneakers in his haste to get out of his room and down the hall to Debbie's. She stood in the midst of a sea of broken glass, staring down like she didn't know how it had gotten there. Gabe identified the shards as the remains of a blue vase that used to sit on her dresser. One of many things she'd ordered off QVC and one of the few she'd ever actually used.

"Debbie, don't move," he said. "Are you cut?"

"No." The bland reply held no emotion whatsoever. She also wasn't very stable on her feet.

"Okay, hold still for one minute."

He dashed back to his room for a pair of shoes then returned to her. He gently stepped over the glass so he could pick her up. She was tiny compared to him, and he deposited her on the messy bed.

"Hang out while I get the vacuum cleaner," he said. No response. "Debbie?"

"Okay."

Miraculously, she stayed put while he lugged the ancient vacuum upstairs and cleaned up the mess. The biggest shards went into the bathroom trash can, and he sucked up the smaller bits. Debbie watched him with a blank expression, unaffected by the entire thing while Gabe was barely keeping a lid on his frustration. He was exhausted of cleaning up after her, but he didn't know what else to do.

"Did you knock it off the dresser?" he asked.

"Dropped it."

"Why?"

"Don't like it anymore. It's ugly."

"So you broke a forty dollar art glass vase?"

"Yes."

Goddamn her.

She had no concept of money, never had, but this was beyond idiotic. She could have given it away, traded it, hell, tried to sell it on Craigslist. But no. She gave no thought to how hard Gabe worked to keep the mortgage paid and the electricity on and the credit card minimums up to date. Debbie didn't want the vase anymore, so she trashed it. She trashed whatever she didn't like at any given moment, including him, and he was done.

"We can't keep doing this," he said. "I can't keep doing this."

"I could have cleaned it up."

"You'd have shredded your hands and feet to ribbons."

"I can clean up after myself. I'm a grown woman."

"Yeah, and you're a fucking alcoholic."

The blankness lifted, replaced by a deadly glare he knew too well. The anger that came before the attack. "Don't you call me that, boy. I am your mother."

His own frustration boiled out of control. "You haven't been a mother to me since I was a child. I am living here taking care of you, not the other way around."

She launched off the bed, her small hands beating at his

forearm and shoulder. "Don't talk to me like that, you ungrateful brat!"

"I'm ungrateful?" He shoved her back, hard enough for her to stumble against the far wall. "I pay for everything around here. I clean this house. I clean you up when you drink so much you vomit everywhere except the john. I watch to make sure you don't drink yourself to death, and sometimes I wonder why I bother because you don't seem to care if you live or die!"

Debbie gaped at him with teary eyes. He'd never gone off on her like that before, but maybe it was past due. He was tired of their merry-go-round of drinking and depression, and he wanted off. He wanted a life, damn it.

"Get out," she snapped.

"Debbie—"

"Get out!" She grabbed a book off her nightstand and threw it at him.

Gabe ducked and darted out the door, in no mood to deal with her anymore today. She slammed the bedroom door, and that was just as well.

He returned to his room, got dressed, grabbed his phone and locked up. He had no real destination in mind when he got in the car, but it didn't surprise him when he found himself heading toward Paxtang. Dad would still be asleep, but Bear was an early riser no matter how late he stayed up the night before.

He let himself in. Bear was at the kitchen counter drinking coffee and reading on his tablet. He looked up and instantly knew.

"What did she do?" Bear asked.

"Doesn't matter. I can't keep doing this."

"Never should have been on you to do it." Bear pulled out the stool next to his, and Gabe sank down into it. "I'm so sorry, son."

"Not your fault. I thought I could help her. I can't."

"Some people don't want to be fixed. I know me and Richard hurt her a lot of years ago, carrying on while Debbie and me were still married, but we can't fix the past. If she wants to hold on to it, that's on her. Not you."

Gabe hadn't found out the whole story of the end of Bear's marriage to Debbie and the start of his relationship with Richard until Gabe was in high school. He'd learned that Bear had cheated on Debbie with Richard, but even after she found out she wouldn't divorce him. She wanted their family intact for Gabe's sake, but she was drinking more heavily and becoming more and more unstable.

He only vaguely remembered the incident, but when he was four he'd somehow fallen down the stairs and broken his arm. He learned later that he'd lain there for hours because Debbie was passed out on the sofa, dead drunk. When Bear found them like that, he'd begun divorce proceedings and forced Debbie into rehab. They shared custody for a few years, but she began drinking again. Gabe was eight years old when she passed out in her own vomit, and he was so scared he went out to find a neighbor to help. He was hit by a car and sustained several broken bones and a concussion.

A month later, Debbie signed away her parental rights and Richard officially adopted him. He had limited contact with Debbie for years until she sobered up again. She stayed clean through most of high school, so he'd visit her once a week. He kept her house in good repair. He learned about the cheating, and he began to understand her alcoholism. Their relationship was the best it had ever been.

Until she started drinking again right before his high school graduation. And she hadn't stopped since.

"I don't know what to do," Gabe said.

"Not much else you can do. You're a good kid, though, trying so hard when she doesn't really want to get better."

"I may have to go out of town for a few days for work, and I'm scared to leave her alone."

"Work, huh?"

Bear had always been super supportive of his work in porn, so Gabe told him about the Puppy Farm offer. "There are some good-looking boys on that site," Bear replied with a big old grin. "You know who you're nailing yet?"

Gabe rolled his eyes. "No, and I don't care as long as the money comes through."

"I didn't think you wanted to expand that career too far."

"I don't, but I can't really afford not to."

"You can if you unload your mother."

"Unload her how? Get my own place? The house is in my name. I pay the mortgage every month to keep a roof over our heads."

"Give her an ultimatum. Rehab and zero tolerance, or she's out."

Gabe shook his head. "Even if she goes to rehab, the day she falls off the wagon I won't have the balls to kick her out on the street. She's got no money that isn't mine, and as hateful as she can be, she is still my mother. I won't make her homeless."

"Debbie doesn't deserve you, you know."

"Maybe, but I'm all she's got."

"She could have still had me and Richard, but she chose bitterness and anger over forgiveness and friendship. There's only so far you can go for someone like that."

"I guess."

Bear tapped the side of his coffee mug. "Move back in with us for a while then."

Gabe startled. "Here?"

"Sure. We'd both love to see you more."

"You see me several nights a week at the club."

Bear waved a hand in the air. "Seeing you at work's not like seeing you at home."

"Debbie will be pissed if I leave her for you."

"Don't tell her then. You tell her you're gone until she gets herself together. Pay the mortgage but the rest is on her. Everything that she does after you leave isn't your fault. She's a grown-ass woman and she's been taking advantage of your generous spirit for years."

Bear's voice went up at the end, some hidden anger peeking through. Bear had never been shy about his hatred of Gabe moving in to take care of Debbie, instead of going to college full-time and having a life. Richard pretended he had no opinion, but Gabe knew he felt the same as Bear.

Bear also had a point. Gabe wasn't his mother's keeper. She needed to clean up or risk losing her son's support, period. He wouldn't kick her out onto the streets, but he could cut her out of his life.

"Adult Protective Services would check on her, right?" Gabe asked.

"Probably. We'll make sure someone does so you don't have to make contact."

"How long can I stay?"

Bear grinned. "As long as you need, my boy."

"Okay. But I won't tell her what I'm doing until my stuff is here."

"Good idea."

Debbie would pitch a fit and then some. He didn't need to spend the next couple of days waiting for her to attack him in a drunken, pity-filled rage.

"Besides," Bear said, "me and Richard will be able to spend time with your Tristan."

My Tristan.

"That's going well?"

"Oh yeah." Memories from Saturday night replayed in vivid detail. "We Skype every day and email all the time. His memory keeps getting better, and I really enjoy the time we spend together. I've never known anyone like him."

"He having any side effects from the drug trial?"

"Some issues with constipation, so he's taking a fiber supplement. But he said his doctor thinks it's his system resetting now that he's remembering to eat regular meals again. Other than that, he's only mentioned a few bad headaches."

"That boy's been blessed."

"So have I."

Bear's bushy eyebrows arched. "That so?"

"Just thinking about him makes me smile. I'm constantly wondering how he is and what he's doing."

"How's the sex?"

Gabe didn't even pretend to be surprised by the nosy question. "It's intense. I know it sounds kind of Bella Swan of me, but I feel connected to him."

"Sounds like a man in love to me."

"I think I might be." His heart thumped harder. "He's the best thing in my life."

"That's how I feel about Richard. Always have. Had to give some of that to you when you were born, but I love my two men, even if I don't say it much."

"I love you too, old man."

"Watch it, kid. I may be old, but I can still thump your ass."

Gabe laughed. Bear had never laid a finger on him, not even a childhood spanking. Probably because Debbie had smacked him around enough behind closed doors, and Bear still harbored some guilt over that. Little boys fell down, roughhoused and got bruises. Gabe never spoke up because Bear and Debbie were always mad at each other, and little Gabe hated seeing his parents fight.

Those early years often felt more like a nightmare than actual memories, and Gabe was more than happy to forget them.

"Since I'm moving back in and will be turning twenty-five in a few weeks," Gabe said, "do I need permission to bring my boyfriend over?"

"Hell no. Tell him he's welcome any time, so long as the sound of two old farts fucking doesn't bother him."

Gabe snorted. "Well, hopefully the sound of two hot, young guys fucking doesn't burn your ancient ears."

"Son, I will be listening with my ear pressed to the door."

He laughed out loud along with Bear, because he knew Bear would never do that. Bear and Richard respected the decisions he made, both personally and in his sex life, and they'd always given him his privacy.

"So Tristan's officially your boyfriend?" Bear asked.

Gabe realized what he'd said before. "We haven't actually talked about it, but I want him to be. If he'll have me."

Bear's expression shifted from amused to serious. "Can I ask you something? It's more personal than you usually get from me."

"Sure."

"Say this drug stops working, or the effects aren't permanent like they hope for, and he goes back short bursts of memory like before."

Gabe hated thinking about Tristan's progress reversing, and he saw the question coming before Bear asked, "Would you stay with him?"

"I hope so. I mean, I was interested before he began the drug trial. I'd like to believe that if Tristan stopped improving, he'd remember enough of me to move forward. That we'd find a way to work it out."

"Well, that's honest."

"It's all I've got. Right now all Tristan and I can do is live one day at a time and treasure every moment."

"That's all any of us can do. No one's guaranteed tomorrow, after all."

"Gee, that's a happy thought. Thanks."

"Keeping it real, kiddo. Richard and me? We've been blessed with our time together. I'm grateful every day that he's not been sick once in the last twelve years."

"Me too."

Being twelve years old and trying to understand his dad's

pneumonia could kill him because his immune system was compromised by HIV had been seriously fucking scary. Until that day in the hospital he'd had no idea Richard was positive and had been since before he and Bear met.

Bear leaned back in his chair, grinning like a fool. "So the pup's coming home."

"Only until I can get Debbie sorted out." He was sick of supporting someone who rewarded his efforts by throwing shit at him.

"So should I book your room for one year or five?"

"Fuck you very much. It won't be that long."

It had better not be.

Gabe's last email said he'd Skype at three o'clock, and at 2:59 Tristan's laptop chimed. His stomach rolled with a familiar sense of excitement and longing as he hit the key to answer. Gabe's face filled his screen with a smile that didn't quite reach his eyes. He almost seemed...timid.

"What's wrong?" Tristan asked.

"Nothing now," Gabe said. "I missed you."

"Me too." He wasn't letting Gabe off the hook by virtue of being adorable. "Seriously, what's going on?"

"Just more drama with my mother."

"Oh." He glanced at his Gabe Henson crib sheet. Nothing on his mother except "doesn't like to talk about".

"I'm moving out of the house I share with her and back in with Bear and Dad. I need space from her for a while."

"Do you need help packing? Believe it or not, I'm actually really good at organizing things."

"No, thanks, though. I'm only taking personal stuff, and I don't have a lot of it at Debbie's. Mostly clothes and video games."

Tristan had a vague sense of being in a house with Gabe. "I've been there, right? At your dads' house?"

This time Gabe's smile brightened his eyes. "Yes. Two nights ago. We had dinner out, and then we went to their house to—"

"Watch a movie."

"That too."

Tristan studied the smugness that crept into Gabe's expression. "We had sex."

"We had amazing sex."

"Only once?"

Tristan listened with rapt attention as Gabe described their entire evening in vivid detail. So vivid that his dick started to thicken by the time Gabe was describing their first kisses in Gabe's bedroom. Bits and pieces seemed familiar, but he didn't know if it was because he'd read the details so often, or because he was remembering the actual event. By the time Gabe finished with the blowjob on the couch, Tristan had a hand in his pajama pants and was firmly stroking his erection.

Even Gabe seemed worked up over the retelling.

"You're someplace private, right?" Tristan asked.

"Yes."

His own door was shut, so he fished out his cock, spat on his palm and got to work for real.

"Shit, Tristan, are you jerking off?" Gabe asked, a sharp edge to his voice.

"Hell yes, I am. Ever had Skype sex?"

"First time for everything."

Gabe was sitting in a chair, probably at a desk, but Tristan could see his arm moving. He watched Gabe's face, and Gabe looked right back. Pleasure rolled gently through Tristan, as much for the friction below as the man in front of him. He imagined Gabe sucking him, stroking him, fingering him—all of the things Gabe had described doing to his body two nights ago. All things Tristan loved.

Gabe came first, with a muffled groan, and the way he tried to be quiet took Tristan over the edge. He made a mess of his T-shirt, but he didn't care. He could change. All he cared about was the satisfied smile on Gabe's face.

"Can we do that every time we Skype?" Tristan asked.

Gabe laughed out loud. "Works for me. Listen, I want to see you again. In person. Are you free tonight?"

"Um." Tristan glanced at his calendar. "No, actually. Noel had to cancel yesterday, so he's coming by to visit this afternoon at"— he saw the time—"shit, in like twenty minutes. I need to get cleaned up."

"Yeah, of course." Some of Gabe's smile had dimmed, and Tristan hated seeing that. "Tomorrow? I get off work at seven. I can pick you up."

"Tomorrow works. Will your dads be home?"

"Dad won't but it's Bear's night off, so maybe."

"Cool. I'd like to meet them. Again?"

"Yes, you've met them both before, but only briefly."

"Okay." Something a little off the wall occurred to him. "Who's your best friend?"

Gabe blinked hard. "What?"

"Well, you know Noel, right? He's been my best friend since college. But if you've ever told me about your friends, I didn't write it down."

"We've never really talked about my friends. I mean, I have friends at the restaurant where I work, and people I know at Big Dick's. But I've always been kind of a drifter, I guess. I drift in and out of social circles." He stared off in the distance for a moment. "I guess my best friend at the moment, other than you, is Jon."

Other than you. "Jon who?"

"Jon Buchanan. We met at the gym a few years ago, and we've worked out together at least once a week since. We hang out sometimes, and we vent to each other about the crazy shit in our lives."

"You guys ever fuck?" Tristan was being nosy, but he didn't care. He was also taking notes.

Gabe shrugged. "A few times when we had an itch to scratch. It was never more than sex, though. And before you ask, we haven't hooked up since I met you."

"It's cool. I mean, I'm sure I told you Noel and I hooked up for a while in college, but we couldn't figure out the relationship part of it." Tristan had fallen for Noel back then, and he'd fallen hard. But he was young, had a very active sex drive and wasn't ready to settle down with one guy. Partying and sowing his metaphorical oats was a bigger priority.

At least he'd never lost Noel's friendship. And because of Noel, he'd met Gabe.

"You and Noel never got together after the, uh, accident?" Gabe asked.

"No. I'm positive we didn't, although I'm sure I threw myself at him a few times out of needy desperation." Tristan hated knowing he'd done it. He knew himself, and he knew how easy it had been to lose all sense of time and think he was back in college again.

Noel had been blessed with the kind of patience that Tristan would never comprehend.

"I'm sure Noel understands," Gabe said. His tone was flat, kind of off.

He's jealous.

"He does. But I don't have any reason to do it again now that I have you." That got Gabe smiling again, so Tristan figured he might as well go for broke. "This might sound goofy, but are we boyfriends? Or is this like a casual thing for you?"

"It's not casual for me." Gabe reached out, then stopped, like he forgot Tristan wasn't actually in the same room. "I'd like to be your boyfriend, officially, if that's what you want."

"Hell yes, it is." Something bright and warm and joyous burst in Tristan's chest. "I've never had an actual boyfriend before."

"Well, I'm very happy to be your first. I care about you, Tristan. A lot. And the good news in me moving in with my dads is we'll have a lot more opportunities to spend time together."

"Time in bed?"

Gabe laughed. "You are insatiable."

"Three year dry spell, remember?"

"Yes, lots of opportunities in bed. But please tell me we'll do some things with our clothes on once in a while."

"Once in a while. Cross my heart."

"Good. Because I want to take you to an art museum. I want to take you to a movie. I want to go to a Senators game in the spring."

Tristan adored him for making plans that far out. "Okay. Can we go to Hershey Park too?"

"Anywhere you want."

"Awesome."

Gabe reached out again, and this time Tristan was positive he was touching the computer screen. "Have fun with Noel, okay?"

"I will. I'll see you tomorrow night."

"Definitely."

Tristan closed his laptop then practically bounced into the bathroom for a quick shower. His shirt went into the hamper. He took a second to study his reflection in the wide mirror. His cheeks seemed fuller, his hips less narrow. He was gaining weight, which wasn't something he'd ever imagined wanting to do back in college.

I'm getting healthy.

He was getting better every single day, and even though his visits with Noel were what he used to look forward to the most, he couldn't wait for it to be over so he'd be that much closer to his date with Gabe.

16

"I wish I had a car," Tristan said. "Then you wouldn't have to pick me up all the time."

Noel shrugged from his spot in the driver's seat. "I don't mind."

"Yeah, you do, you're just too polite to admit it."

"I really don't mind. It's not like you're an hour away from Stratton."

"I know, but still."

"Don't 'but still' me, pal. Besides, your allowance is nowhere near enough to use for a car payment."

Tristan watched the rolling hills and homes along the turnpike blur past. "Not right now. But one day maybe I can get an actual, you know, job or something. Make my own money."

"I think that's a good goal to set for yourself." Something in Noel's tone was off. Almost patronizing.

"I don't want to live off my parents forever." Tristan hated that the most about his situation. Hated that he relied on parents who'd written him off for being gay, but he still took their money every single month because what choice did he have? None.

Not yet.

"I know you don't," Noel said. "But let's see how this drug keeps affecting you before you make too many grand plans for the future."

Tristan grumped and sank down in his seat. He didn't want to be reasonable about his future. He wanted to plan. He hadn't been able to plan for years. He'd missed out on so much sitting in his room at Benfield, and as much as Noel wanted to understand, he simply didn't get this. He didn't get how freeing his life was now, or how much he needed to hope for new things.

"Who knows?" Tristan said, mostly to mess with Noel. "Maybe in a few months I'll be living with Gabe."

Noel's hand jerked the wheel. Thankfully they stayed in their lane. "Why would you do that?"

"Seriously?"

"Yes, seriously. You guys barely know each other."

"Dude, we know each other way better than you think. We email every single day. We Skype. We even had a real, official date Saturday night."

"You did?"

"Yup." More than forty minutes had passed since his call with Gabe, but Gabe's recitation of their date was still fresh in his mind. "And holy shit, does he have a dick he knows how to use."

Noel didn't react to that at all, which was weird. He stared at the road ahead, his jaw a little tight.

Maybe he's jealous because Shane's been holding out on him.

"You two had sex?" Noel asked after a few minutes of awkwardly silent driving.

"Oh yeah. He picked me up, we went out to dinner, and then we went back to his dads' house and spent some very quality time naked in his room." Noel wasn't big on sharing details of his sex life, but Tristan had never, ever been shy about it. "You should see his abs, Noel. Oh-em-gee. And the man knows how to suck cock."

"He should," Noel said, quiet and growly like he hadn't meant to say it out loud.

Tristan frowned. "What does that mean?"

"Nothing. Just, you know, he's gay and he hangs out at Big Dick's. He probably has experience."

"He's not a slut, Noel. What gives? You're not usually so judgy about people."

"Sorry. I don't want to fight over Gabe, okay?"

"Good, because I'm going to keep seeing him and keep fucking him, thank you very much. I really like him. I mean, really like him."

"Do you think he feels as strongly about you?"

"Yes." He knew it in his gut. "We made it official today."

"Made what official?"

"We're boyfriends."

Noel glanced his way, both blond eyebrows arched high. "Okay, I have to admit that I never thought I'd hear you say that. You were so commitment-phobic in college."

"I know. But that me is gone. I can't be him again, all free to be me and fuck everyone else if they don't like it. I understand what I have to lose."

"I hear that. I came face-to-face with it the night we were bashed."

He means the accident. He was there. He was hurt too. And he's the one burdened with the memories of that night.

Tristan squeezed Noel's shoulder. "I'm sorry."

"None of it was your fault, Tris. All you can do is fight to get better and to have the life you deserve."

"That's what I'm doing."

Noel took the turnpike exit for Stratton, and in less than ten minutes they were pulling into the driveway of a small, single story home, painted white with blue shutters. A car was parked in the driveway, along with a blue van.

"This your house?" Tristan said. Noel had told him that was

their destination when he picked Tristan up. Asking was more for Tristan, so he could cement that fact into his brain. "It's nice."

"Thanks."

"What's with the van? Having some work done?"

"Something like that."

The front door opened, and two very familiar faces popped out onto the stoop. Billy Meeks and Chris Sherman were a little older and dressed in paint-splattered gym clothes, but they both ran toward Tristan with big old smiles.

"You guys!" Tristan squealed. He had no idea when he'd last seen his old college roommates, and he buzzed with the excitement of seeing them again. The three of them ended up in a group hug.

Billy, who'd played basketball and was six foot four, lifted Tristan right up off the ground. "Dude, it's good to see you."

"You too." Tristan laughed with utter delight. "You guys look exactly the same. Well, Chris's hair is longer, but whatever."

"You haven't changed," Chris said. "Except for the guyliner. You were the only guy I know, gay or straight, who could pull that off."

"That was totally a phase, and I am very over it."

"Good."

"So what are you guys doing here?"

"Helping Noel and Shane paint," Billy replied. "It was the only day where our schedules all worked, so we made Noel promise to kidnap you for a few hours so we could all hang."

Tristan shuddered. "And do manual labor?"

"I'll feed you pizza and chips," Noel said.

"Deal." For free food and time with his friends, Tristan could paint a wall or two.

"Come on, slacker," Billy said. He cuffed the back of Tristan's neck. "I wanna hear about this miracle drug that's fixing your crazy brain."

God, I've missed my friends.

While Debbie was mostly comatose on the couch watching game show reruns, Gabe moved around upstairs as quietly as he could. He packed his clothes in the only suitcase he owned, and in his assorted gym bags. He went through his room and set aside the things he wanted to keep, leaving the things he didn't really care about. If Debbie started drinking early enough, he could take his bags down to the car before he went to sleep.

Alone.

He'd spent most of his life sleeping alone, but it was bothering him more and more recently. He wanted to wake up with Tristan in his bed, preferably naked in his arms, and that hadn't even happened for real yet.

Reliving Saturday's date on Skype and then jerking off with Tristan had been beyond sexy. Hearing that he had plans with Noel had hurt a little, but he couldn't begrudge Tristan time with his best friend. It gave him something to look forward to tomorrow. Today had sucked enough, and all he wanted was to get through it and get to their next date.

A few minutes after nine p.m., Debbie had passed out in her room, which gave him a window to move some crap downstairs. Naturally, that's when his phone rang.

Noel's name on the screen sent his heart right into his throat. "Is Tristan okay?"

"He's fine so far," Noel replied.

"What do you mean so far? Did something happen?"

"Look, Gabe, I don't want to be the asshole here, but I need to know what it is you're doing with Tristan."

Gabe stared at his own reflection in his dresser mirror, unsure how to take the question. "What do you mean?"

"He told me about Saturday."

"Okay." If Noel was waiting for some kind of explanation as to why two consenting adults had had sex, he wasn't getting it from Gabe. His sexual relationship with Tristan was not Noel's business.

"Okay? Tristan has been locked inside of his own head for over three years. And now that he's starting to get out from under that, now that he's starting to have a life again, there's you."

"Yes, there's me." Gabe still wasn't seeing the problem. "I'm part of the life that he's having again, and I really like him. We get along great, and we have fun together."

"Yeah, Tristan said something similar."

"So what's your deal?"

"My deal is you. Yes, Tristan is better now, but what if the drugs stop working? What if he has bad side effects and has to stop them? If things get bad again, and you can't handle it, and you decide to bail, it will destroy him." Noel's voice cracked a bit. "You weren't there with him those first six months after the bashing. You didn't get him through severe depression and crying fits. You didn't cry for his pain. You didn't see his face every single time I had to tell him his parents had written him off, because he kept forgetting."

Gabe's throat closed and his eyes stung. He had no idea the depth of pain Noel had suffered while watching his best friend adapt to a new, much more difficult life. He did understand Noel's protectiveness, though, and his need to keep protecting Tristan.

He also couldn't shut off his feelings for Tristan over a what-if.

"I'm sorry," Gabe said. "I know you guys went through hell, and believe me, I know there's a chance Tristan could regress. I talked this out with one of my dads this morning."

Noel cleared his throat. "And?"

"And I can't promise you anything. I know it isn't what you want to hear, but it's all I've got. No one can say for sure what we'll do five days or five years down the road. Circumstances can change in an instant. You know that."

"Yeah, I do."

"The only thing I can promise is that I will always be a part of his life, whether as a friend or a lover. I'd never abandon him." And for someone who didn't make close friends easily, Gabe treasured the promise he'd just made. Because he treasured Tristan.

Christ, I am so whipped.

"For whatever it's worth," Gabe added, "I am so sorry for the pain you two have gone through. And I'm even sorrier they never caught the bastards who did it."

"Thanks."

"So are you done playing the overprotective parent?"

Noel snorted. "Just one other question. Have you told him about your side job yet?"

Some people had issues saying porn. "Not yet."

"When will you?"

"When it feels right. I'd rather not have to explain it multiple times, if I can avoid it." And because Noel was Tristan's best friend, it felt okay to ask, "How do you think he'll react?"

"Honestly? Knowing Tristan, he'll probably be really excited by the idea at first."

"At first?"

Gabe swore he heard Noel shrug. "Yeah. Tristan doesn't judge people very harshly, unless they do something to directly hurt him or the people he loves. But how he'll feel about you doing porn? No idea."

"How did you take it when Shane told you?"

"I was shocked as hell. He had it in his head that I was going to think he was a horrible person and dump him on the spot, but I didn't. I asked questions and I listened. Eventually I figured out how to separate his character of Colby from the Jody McShane I know and love. Hopefully Tristan will do the same with you and Tony."

Tony. Noel knew his screen name. "Did Shane show you our scenes?"

"I kind of found them on my own after he told me. I was curious."

Normally being recognized for his videos didn't bother Gabe, but knowing that Tristan's best friend had seen filmed evidence of Gabe having sex with Shane made Gabe's insides squirm. People really shouldn't know that much about their best friend's boyfriend.

Gabe didn't care if Tristan eventually wanted to see his videos, but no way in hell was Shane ever seeing Tristan naked.

Tristan's mine.

"The real difference," Noel said, "is that Jo wanted out. You're still in."

"Yes, I am. It wasn't what I'd have picked on Career Day but I enjoy the people I work with, and it pays the bills. I won't do porn forever, though."

"Whether you're working or not, Tristan deserves to know that you're fucking other guys."

Gabe hated it when people phrased his scenes that way, like he was going out and hooking up with random strangers for sexual thrills. Porn was work. Did he get off? Sure. But Chet kept a clean house, and Gabe wasn't fucking anyone else off set. "Is that how you saw Shane's scenes? He's out fucking other guys?"

"At first, a little, but not now. And Jo never promised to be exclusive until he got out of porn."

He hadn't made that promise to Tristan, either. Boyfriends, yes, but not exclusivity. It was a dangerous loophole. "Look, Noel, I get that you want to protect Tristan, and I swear the last thing I ever want to do is hurt him. But none of this is your business. It's between me and Tristan, and we'll work it out."

"Fine. Just maybe do it sooner rather than later."

"Nice talking to you too."

Gabe hung up, and then tossed his phone onto the bed. Good thing Noel had done that over the phone, rather than in person, because Gabe kind of wanted to throttle the man. His patience and understanding only stretched so far, and Noel was pushing the limit.

He'd tell Tristan about doing porn when the time was right for them.

First he had to get the hell out of Debbie's house.

17

Tristan had already signed out and was bouncing around the Benfield lobby when tall, dark and handsome strode inside. His heart fluttered. He'd been staring at Gabe's picture before leaving his room, and he practically threw himself at Gabe.

Gabe laughed and lifted him up in a tight hug. "Someone missed me."

"All the time." Tristan kissed his cheek, then his mouth, because he didn't give a shit what the nurses thought. "Hi."

"Hi yourself. I take it you're ready to go?"

"Definitely."

"Prepare yourself. I think our warm autumn is over. It's freezing outside."

"That's okay." Tristan zipped up his coat then snagged his notebook off a chair. "I grew up in upstate New York, so I'm used to cold winters."

"Really? I got the impression you were from around here."

"My parents moved us to Chambersburg when I was thirteen."

"Got it."

"But you've always lived in Harrisburg, right?"

"In and around it my whole life."

The shock of cold air on his face woke Tristan right up. The temperature difference from only a week ago was staggering, but that was November in the mid-Atlantic. "So did we make plans?"

"I was hoping you wouldn't mind a late dinner with my dads," Gabe replied.

"Really?" Tristan knew he'd met Gabe's dads, even if he didn't remember the interactions.

"Sure. Bear especially wants to get to know you. They know how important you are to me, so you're important to them."

That's one of the sweetest things I've ever heard. "Okay."

"Excellent."

Gabe further proved his adorableness by holding Tristan's car door open—an act that Tristan was pretty sure Gabe had done before. Once they were both inside the still warm car, Tristan tugged him across the console so he could kiss his boyfriend properly. Gabe tasted like cinnamon gum.

"I don't suppose we could put off dinner until after you've properly fucked me, could we?" Tristan asked.

"You really want your dessert before dinner?"

"Always."

Gabe chuckled, then kissed him again. "Patience, babe. When I get you in bed, I want you there for at least a couple of hours."

"Oh yeah?"

"Oh yes."

Tristan squirmed, but gave in. He tried to think of anything except sex on the drive, so he didn't arrive for dinner sporting wood. That would be embarrassing, despite his sense that Gabe's dads would understand.

Gabe told him a few stories about his day waiting tables. He kind of admired Gabe for being able to do that kind of work. Tristan didn't have the patience to deal with stupid people on a day-to-day basis.

Gabe drove them through a residential neighborhood for a while before parking on the street in front of a two-story home. A sense of familiarity washed over Tristan. He might not have picked it out from the other dozen homes lining the street, but pulling up in front of that particular house told him he'd absolutely been here before.

"We're not going out to eat?" Tristan asked.

"Bear is a decent cook, so he volunteered."

"Shit, should I have brought something? Like a bottle of wine?"

"Don't worry about it. They just want a chance to get to know you. Be yourself. It'll be fun."

"Okay." Tristan hated showing up for a home-cooked meal without a gift for the host. His parents had drilled that one into him throughout his teen years. Then again, they lived in a world where appearances meant more than their kids' emotional well-being.

His heart ached for Alex. Sometimes he missed his brother so much it hurt.

"Hey, you okay?" Gabe asked.

Tristan had stopped halfway up the driveway. He rolled his shoulders and pushed away the macabre thoughts. "Yeah, sorry. Unfortunate train of thought."

"Want to tell me about it?"

"Maybe later." He didn't want to bring Gabe down with a conversation about his brother who committed suicide because he couldn't handle the pressure their parents had put him under. "Come on, let's go eat."

Before Gabe could open the front door, it swung open. A barrel of a man in a black band T-shirt and bare feet filled the entryway, grinning at both of them. "Come on in, boys. Richard is setting the table now," he said.

Once they'd been hustled inside and their coats taken, the big man held out his hand for Tristan. "Bernard Henson, but everyone calls me Bear."

No kidding. "Tristan Lavalle." He expected a bone-breaking handshake, but Bear was gentle. "Nice to meet you again."

"You too. Gabe doesn't stop talking about you."

Gabe, bless him, actually blushed.

"Well, I am pretty amazing," Tristan said.

Bear's deep laughter made Tristan smile. "I like you already. Confidence is a good thing to have, son."

"Gabe's been helping me find mine again."

"Good. Gabe's a good kid."

"Are you going to share, or keep him all to yourself?" a new voice asked. A second man waltzed down the hall. He was shorter than Tristan, with silver hair and the sparkliest green sequined vest he'd ever seen outside of a music video.

"I'm keeping him to myself," Bear replied. "Go away."

The newcomer laughed then swatted Bear's ass. "I'm Richard Brightman, this one's husband."

"Pleasure to meet you," Tristan said. Seeing the pair standing side by side had Tristan a little bit boggled. They were so completely opposite in every physical way that he couldn't figure it out until Bear leaned down and kissed his husband's cheek. Richard grinned, and the love was so obvious that it socked Tristan right in the feels.

Gabe had been lucky to grow up with them.

"So what's for dinner?" Gabe asked. He sniffed the air. "Italian?"

Tristan noted the hints of tomato and spices, and his stomach growled. He'd skipped dinner in anticipation of seeing Gabe tonight.

"I made my five-meat lasagna," Bear said.

Gabe slapped a hand over his heart. "Say it isn't so. You only break that out for birthdays."

"I figured you could have your birthday lasagna a month early."

"Your birthday is next month?" Tristan asked.

"December eighth," Gabe said. "I'm a winter baby."

"How was that, having a birthday so close to Christmas? Did you always get presents wrapped in Santa paper?"

"Not really. Bear always hit up the party stores for summer decorations when they went super-cheap clearance, so I'd have luau parties, or Mexican fiesta parties. A little bit of summer in the middle of winter."

"That's really cool."

"I have awesome dads."

Tristan followed the small family unit into a cozy dining room. Walnut table and chairs, and a matching sideboard. Four place settings. A basket of bread, a large pan of lasagna and a big bowl of mixed salad. Tristan couldn't remember the last time he'd sat down for a meal like this.

Gabe pulled a chair out for Tristan, then sat down opposite. Richard fetched drinks for everyone while Bear pieced out big chunks of lasagna. Tristan helped himself to salad and a breadstick. Everything looked and smelled amazing. No one paused to say grace, so Tristan dug into the pasta.

So many different flavors burst on his tongue. The sauce was deliciously spiced, the cheese perfectly gooey, and the different meats played havoc with his senses. "Holy crap that's good," he said.

Bear chuckled. "Glad you like it."

"What meats do you use?"

"I only ever tell four of them. Ground beef, ground pork, pepperoni and Italian sausage."

"So the fifth is a mystery?"

"Always has been," Richard said. "Somehow he manages to hide all evidence of it, and we've never been able to correctly guess."

"There are only so many meat products in the world, though."

"Searching too hard for the mystery ingredient takes some of the fun out," Gabe said. "Plus, Bear warned us that if we did figure it out, he'd stop making it."

"Good reason not to think too hard."

"Exactly."

Tristan watched his portions as he ate, not wanting to overdo it on the delicious food and make himself sick. Even the salad had a homemade lemon vinaigrette that made every ingredient pop in his mouth. Bear and Richard chatted with Gabe about everyday things, including his progress with moving out of his mother's house.

It seemed familiar, so Tristan paid attention.

"I have a load of stuff in the trunk of my car," Gabe said. "I'll bring it in later. One more load should do it. I'll probably tell Debbie I'm moving out on Friday."

"It's about time you put your foot down with that woman," Richard said.

Gabe glanced at Tristan, an odd look on his face. Anxiety, maybe? They all knew something about Gabe's mother that Tristan didn't, and they were dancing around the topic. Tristan hated being left out, but family business was family business. He wasn't going to pry.

Bear caught the look on Gabe's face. "So Tristan, Gabe tells us you'll be joining us for Thanksgiving dinner."

"Yes," Tristan said. Apparently he'd agreed to that. "Should I bring anything? I don't have any place to cook, but I could bring sodas or something."

"It's taken care of. You just show up with Gabe on your arm."

"I can do that." So far he liked both of Gabe's dads very much.

"So I'm the eye candy date?" Gabe asked.

"Yes," Tristan said in stereo with Bear.

Gabe shrugged. "Just making sure I know my place."

Your place is with me.

Gabe's cell rang. He frowned at the screen then ignored the call.

"That work?" Richard asked.

"No one who can't leave a message," Gabe replied. "Besides, you don't like when I take calls during meals."

"You're right. We never answered the house phone when you were a kid, and we don't answer our cells now."

"Unless the club calls," Bear said.

"Mario knows to send a text too, if it's an emergency." To Tristan, Richard said, "Mario is my assistant general manager at Big Dick's."

"So he's in charge when you're not there?" Tristan said.

"Precisely."

"Mario keeps Richard's head from exploding," Bear said.

"I'm also too old to be there seven nights a week." Richard faked a big yawn. "Old and tired, that's what I am."

"And still a closet drama queen."

"Oh hush, you."

Tristan smiled at the gentle banter. Their history was woven around them like an invisible net. He couldn't imagine having been with a partner for so long that he knew them better than he knew himself. But he wanted that, and he truly hoped he could have it with Gabe.

Across the table, Gabe was grinning at him in a way that made Tristan's heart flip, as if silently confirming he wanted it too.

"Will you two be joining us for dessert later?" Richard asked. "We've got an ice cream cake in the freezer."

Gabe's eyebrows rose in silent question.

"We'll see," Tristan replied. He loved ice cream cake, but he'd much rather spend as much time possible having a different kind of dessert.

"Don't plan on seeing us," Gabe said with a soft growl.

Oh boy.

Gabe collapsed on the bed next to Tristan, a giant sweaty mess, and fighting for air. Goddamn, but that had been better than the first time he'd fucked Tristan. Next to him, Tristan squirmed around so he could drape himself across Gabe's chest, head on his shoulder. Gabe stripped off the condom and dropped it over the side of the bed.

"That was fucking amazing," Tristan said. "Fuck."

"It's all you, sunshine."

"It's definitely not all me. I thought you were going to eat my ass all night."

"I probably could have just to hear those noises you make."

Tristan traced a finger around Gabe's right nipple. "Same for when I play with these."

Gabe slid his hand down Tristan's damp back and squeezed his cheek, concern overriding some of his endorphin high. "How do you feel? Sore?"

"Not really. Not enough that I don't want a second round before I leave."

"A second round?" Tristan's cock was still semihard against his thigh, but Gabe's was down for now. Not that it would take much coaxing to get him back in the game, but Tristan didn't know that. "You might have to work for it."

Tristan rose up on one elbow. "That a challenge?"

"Definitely." It wouldn't take much, but Gabe loved the way Tristan's entire demeanor changed now that he'd been goaded.

Tristan slid atop Gabe's body and straddled his waist, their cocks pressed together between their bellies. The simple touch had blood reversing direction. Gabe clasped his waist, eager and curious to see where Tristan was going with this. Tristan ducked his head and bit Gabe's left nipple hard enough to sting. But it was a fantastic kind of sting that made Gabe's hips jerk. Tristan laughed then did it to his other nipple.

"Fuck, that feels good," Gabe said.

"I can tell." He thrust against Gabe, doing great things for Gabe's refraction time. "I don't think I'll need to work too hard for it after all."

"Can't help it with you."

"I bet you say that to all the boys."

"I don't." Gabe dumped Tristan onto his back and knelt between his spread legs, their cocks still rubbing together. He braced himself on his elbows so he could thread his fingers into Tristan's soft, thick hair. "This thing with us? It's special for me, Tristan. Don't ever doubt that."

"It's special for me too. I couldn't have kept going like I was."

"With the memory loss?"

"Alone. I had Noel, and I had the people at Benfield, but this is different."

He seemed to struggle for the rest, so Gabe had mercy and kissed him. Long, slow licks into his mouth. Gentle caresses against Tristan's tongue. He savored the taste of this man he'd come to care for so much in only a few short months. They rocked their hips at a steady rate, riding the soft waves of pleasure without tilting too close to the edge.

Fingers skated across his back, up and down his spine, and finally came to rest on his ass. Tristan squeezed his cheeks, then hiked his legs up around Gabe's hips. The angle changed, giving more room for their balls to rub together, and that made Gabe's entire body tingle with need. With the urge to claim Tristan again.

Gabe reached between them to move his dick to a downward angle so he could rub against Tristan's crease. The head of his cock dragged against his hole, and that felt amazing. Gabe thrust more insistently, Tristan's entrance still wet with lube. It would be so easy to slide inside of him. Too easy.

"You can," Tristan whispered, as if reading his mind. "I trust you."

Gabe froze as the enormity of what Tristan was offering hit him. His breathing stuttered and he stopped moving. Tristan gazed up, his blue eyes reflecting that absolute trust, and Gabe wanted to so badly.

Not while I'm doing porn. Not while there's the slightest chance of exposing him to something. No.

"Thank you for that," Gabe said, "but not yet."

He grabbed a condom and more lube, and then he slid home. Deep into Tristan's welcoming body. Tristan let out a long, breathy moan. Gabe pulled Tristan's legs up over his shoulders so he could lean down close enough to kiss Tristan if he wanted. Gabe loved fucking like this, with his partner nearly bent in half, but sometimes it got too intense for the other guy, so he took his time. Long, slow strokes, memorizing each slide in and out of Tristan's body. Cataloging the sounds Tristan made, the way he panted and trembled. His fingers clenched and unclenched the sheets by Gabe's knees.

And his face. Tristan held nothing back, allowing his experience to play out in the way he licked his lips. In the splotches of color on his cheeks and neck. With every emotion shining in his eyes.

So beautiful.

He captured Tristan's mouth for an explorative kiss, deepening the angle of his penetration. Tristan cried out, the sound lost in Gabe's mouth. He worked a hand between them, and in a few short strokes was coming on both of their chests.

"Oh fuck," Tristan said. "Wanna see you come."

The request sent a tingle down Gabe's spine. He gently pulled out and dumped the condom. He stayed between Tristan's spread legs, the sexy sight of him almost more than he could stand. Tristan's chest glistened with sweat and semen, and he watched Gabe like a starving man seeing food for the first time.

Gabe jerked himself with firm pulls, focusing on Tristan and how great it felt to be inside of him, fucking him. Making love to him.

His release shot through him, and he forced his eyes to stay open so he could watch his come spray onto Tristan's abs. Marking him. Pleasure danced through him, waking him up and telling him to collapse already. He bent down and licked up every drop, cleaning Tristan's chest off maybe a little too thoroughly.

So fucking good.

He tugged Tristan into his arms and stuffed a pillow beneath their heads. Tristan burrowed as close as he could get to Gabe without actually climbing inside of him. Cuddling with Tristan after sex was almost as fun as the sex itself, and he wanted this part to last for as long as possible, before Tristan inevitably had to leave.

Fatigue crept in and settled in Gabe's bones. Every part of him began to relax. He drifted a while, content to hold Tristan close, until a soft whisper woke him back up. The words had been mumbled against his chest, but he swore he'd heard them clear as a bell.

He kissed Tristan's temple, which prompted him to look up. Tristan's cheeks blazed, and he seemed cautious. "What did you say?" Gabe asked.

"I said, I love you." Tristan ducked his head, hiding his face in the crook of Gabe's shoulder.

"Hey, look at me." Gabe caressed the back of Tristan's neck until he finally turned his head enough to meet Gabe's gaze. "I love you too."

"Yeah?"

"Yes. I think I have for a while."

Tristan raised his head, his smile a thing of beauty. "Really?"

"Yes."

"Say it again."

Gabe grinned. "I love you."

"I've never been in love before. Not like this."

"I've never been in love like this before, either." His love for Andrew had been real, but it had also been born out of stress and need. He'd found acceptance in Andrew that had helped him cope with being gay, and it was never really more than that. Loving Tristan was everything he'd ever wanted and more.

"Can I stay tonight?" Tristan asked. "Please?"

Gabe didn't know how to deny him anything in that moment. "Are you sure it's a good idea?"

"Yes. I might be confused when I wake up but I know you now. I want to wake up with you in the morning, and to have breakfast together. Please?"

"Okay."

Tristan rewarded him with a firm kiss. "Then let's clean up. I hate waking up with dried come stuck to my pubes."

Gabe laughed. Dried come anywhere was not fun. "Or stomach. Or your chest hair."

"Says the guy with none. Why do you wax, anyway?"

Because Chet likes the look. "To better show off my muscles at the gym."

"I think you'd look pretty hot with a dark carpet over these." Tristan traced a finger around Gabe's pecs, then down to his abs. "And here."

"Behave or you may get a third round before bed."

Tristan's hand snaked lower and stroked his cock. "And that would be a bad thing why?"

Challenge accepted.

18

A ringing cell phone jolted Tristan awake. Next to him, someone snuffled and grumbled. He sat up, taking in the unfamiliar bedroom walls covered in movie posters.

Shit, I'm naked.

His bedmate rolled over and grabbed a phone off the night-stand, hit something, then put it back. Tan. Muscles. Familiar. He turned toward Tristan, face creased from the pillow and still half asleep.

Gabe.

Relief rolled over him. "Morning. I think." Bits of sunlight were peeking through the navy blue curtains.

"It's early. Come here."

Tristan let Gabe wrap him up in a full-body hug. His legs ached a little from what he could only imagine had been a very active night before. He clenched his hole, and yeah, active night. "How many times did we go at it?"

"Three. Twice in bed, and one time that started in bed and finished in the shower."

"Ooh, shower sex. Fun."

"Do you remember any of it?"

Tristan pressed his nose into the hollow of Gabe's neck and inhaled. He loved the way Gabe smelled, especially with the scent of his soap lingering on his skin. Shadows of the night before lingered, knowledge of having sex with Gabe without real memory of their time. "Yes and no. It's kind of how déjà vu feels. It's like you know something is familiar, but you aren't sure if it's because you did it or you read about it or saw it on TV."

"That makes sense. How about I send you the details in a very sexy email later?"

"Works for me. It will give me something fun to jerk off to."

Gabe dropped kisses on his forehead and cheeks. "I hate that this can't last."

"No one gets to stay in bed forever."

"True."

Tristan's stomach rumbled. "Feel like breakfast?"

"Definitely. I don't have to be at the restaurant until eleven, so I have some time."

"Cool." Tristan rolled out of bed, amused to find his clothes all over the place. "Guess we got down to it pretty fast last night."

"You were a tad eager." Gabe leaned against the dresser, arms folded, his soft cock still an impressive thing to see. Tristan wanted to take a photo of him like that so he could always remember it.

"I don't know how you are not a model," Tristan said. "Seriously. Have you looked at yourself in a mirror?"

Gabe shrugged. "Fashion model is not my thing."

"That's okay. It means your hunky body is all mine to enjoy."

Instead of agreeing with him, Gabe opened a drawer and pulled out a pair of briefs. The ungraceful ending to the conversation stuck with Tristan while he got dressed. He couldn't put his finger on why it bothered him. Okay, sure, other guys got to enjoy Gabe's body at the gym, but only Tristan was having sex with him.

Did we have that conversation?

"Gabe?"

"Yeah?" He paused in putting on a pair of socks and looked up.

Tristan bit his lip, unsure why he was nervous about asking. "We're exclusive, right?"

"Of course." Gabe's lips twisted briefly, almost into a frown, as if he realized he was wrong about something.

"What?" Tristan sat on the bed next to him, a funny feeling in the pit of his stomach. "You do want to be exclusive, right?"

"I do. I don't want to be with anyone other than you, Tristan, I swear. I meant it last night when I said I love you."

The familiarity of the words made Tristan's heart flutter, even though the buildup had his gut in a knot. "I love you too. Did I say it back? I think I did."

"Yes, you did."

"Then what's wrong?"

Gabe shifted to face him more directly. His brown eyes were full of something Tristan didn't like seeing—anxiety. "There is one thing I haven't told you about myself, and now that we're at a place where I see a future for us, I need to tell you. Because it affects you, and I should have been honest after the first time we had sex."

Tristan's heart nearly stopped. "Are you positive?"

"What? No. No, it's not that."

"Then what?"

"Waiting tables and working at the club bar aren't my only jobs."

The dancing around was making Tristan sick to his stomach. He preferred people being direct with him. It saved stress and aggravation. "Just fucking tell me already."

Gabe blinked. "About twice a month I film gay porn scenes for a local filmmaker who posts them on his Internet site."

Tristan allowed those words to roll through his head for a few moments, while he struggled to understand them. Gabe watched him closely, as if he expected Tristan to spontaneously combust or something. Tristan couldn't imagine the look on his own face, because he couldn't get his thoughts to latch onto any one thing other than confusion.

"You're serious?" he asked.

"Perfectly. I wouldn't lie to you, Tristan. I promise."

"Why? I mean, not why wouldn't you lie to me, but why do you do porn?"

"I like sex, and I like the guys I work with. The money is good, and I need it. My mother is...not well." Gabe closed his eyes for a moment, and when he opened them again, they were glistening. Real grief settled around him, slumping his shoulders and drooping his mouth.

Tristan grabbed his hands and held tight. "Tell me."

"She's an alcoholic. Has been most of my life. We had some really good years when I was in high school, but then she started deteriorating. She was drinking again. She started...well, hoarding, I guess. Buying all kinds of shit she didn't need and never used. She maxed out her credit cards and took out unsecured loans. I moved in with her to help her out and try to control her bills."

"Shit, that sucks so much, Gabe." Tristan ached for Gabe's obvious pain. He wanted to take it away from him, but he didn't know how. "Is it okay to say I'm sorry?"

"Sure. I'm sorry every single day, because she doesn't want to get better. I'm moving back here, away from her, because I can't do it anymore. I can't watch her kill herself."

"I don't blame you. There's only so much you can do before you have to put yourself first."

"I know. And it's time I do that, because I have you now, and you are the best thing I've ever had. I don't want her to hurt you too."

"So you work two jobs and do porn to support her."

"Yes."

The whole thing was just weird to Tristan. "How do you even get into porn? Is there like an open casting call or something?"

"I met a guy at the gym who models for them too. He got me an interview with the producer."

"How long?"

"A little over two years."

"Damn. You've been getting laid twice a month for two years?"

Gabe blinked. "I guess you could put it like that. There is work involved. It can take four or five hours to put together a twenty-minute video."

"Really?"

"Chet's a good director. He makes high quality stuff. It's a small house, but he's building a reputation for solid work and sexy videos."

Tristan had seen enough porn in his lifetime to know some of it was really good, and some of it was just plain awful. "You don't do, like, whips and leather and being tied up, do you?"

"No, that's not my thing and Chet knows it. He's been experimenting with harder stuff, but only with models who want to go there. He's a decent guy, respects our limits."

"What's your limit?"

"Bottoming." He flinched. "Well, except once."

"Really?" The idea of someone bending big, bulky Gabe over and fucking him sent happy signals to his cock and balls.

"Deb—my mother had just taken out another unsecured loan, and I knew it would sell well. I picked someone I trusted to be careful with me."

"But you didn't like it."

"No."

"I'm sorry."

"Don't be. I made the decision, and I can't believe we're sitting here talking about this like it's perfectly normal."

Tristan grinned. "Will you think I'm crazy if I say it's kind of a turn on?"

Gabe's lips parted. "Really? The idea of me having sex with other guys is turning you on?"

"A little bit. I mean, you don't love them, right? And you're safe, right? Shit, please tell me—"

"Yes, I've always used condoms, and everyone is tested regularly. But that's also why I wouldn't go bare with you last night. I can't take that risk while I'm still working, because there will always be a risk."

Tristan's heart skipped a beat. They'd almost gone bare. Holy hell, it must have been some night.

He also loved Gabe even more for being so thoughtful when the lure of no condom had to have messed with his head a little. "Is porn something you want to keep doing?"

"Not forever. Honestly? Besides the money, I got into it as a way to get off without risking a casual hookup. And the guys I work with are mostly really cool. But I don't want to do it until I'm thirty, and I also don't want to wait tables forever."

"What do you want to do?"

"I have no idea. So much of my focus is on keeping Debbie under control, and now that I'm getting away from her, I'll be able to focus on myself. Maybe find a career that lets me keep my clothes on."

Tristan wiggled his eyebrows. "I like you with your clothes off."

"I know you do. One day I want you to be the only person I'm having sex with for any reason." Gabe kissed him. "I really can't believe this doesn't bother you more."

"Honestly? Yes, it's a little weird. But if it's something you need to keep doing, I understand. And maybe it isn't sinking in because it's all words and I haven't seen actual proof that you've done it. I don't know. I can't promise not to become jealous at some point in the future, though."

"I know, and I'm not asking you to promise anything. You're taking it all way better than I expected or probably deserve."

"Hey." He curled his fingers around the back of Gabe's neck. "You deserve the world."

"I've got everything in the world I need right here."

If Tristan could have melted into a pile of goo, he would have in that moment. Instead, he hugged Gabe because, yeah, porn was kind of a weird career choice in central Pennsylvania, but Gabe had good reasons. And he loved Gabe too much to judge him for it.

"Do your parents know?" Tristan asked.

"My dads do. They support me like they always have. I can't tell my mother. She'll have a fit."

"Do you think knowing you're doing porn to pay her bills might prompt her to get help?"

"No. Probably the opposite. She'll wonder where she went wrong, how she failed me, how she'll look if other people find out. It won't be about me at all."

"That sucks."

"I don't care. She doesn't need to know. It's not as if it's a career I tweet about."

"Do you ever get recognized?"

Gabe's cheeks pinked up. "Once in a while. I've even signed a few autographs."

"Really?" Tristan wasn't sure why he loved that so much. It was kind of like dating a celebrity. "What site do you work for?"

"Uh-uh, not today."

"Why not?"

"Because if I tell you, you'll go back to Benfield and look me up, and I want us to be together when we look at my work."

"So let's look now."

Gabe seemed to consider it for a moment. "Not today. I have to be at work in a few hours, we still need to eat, and if we watch porn together I'm going to end up fucking you again."

Tristan's dick twitched. "And that's a bad thing?"

"It is when I'd have to sneak into my dads' bathroom to get

more condoms. I need to invest in my own now that this is going to be a thing."

"Your dads still use condoms?" He couldn't remember how long they'd been together, but he knew it was a long time.

"Yes." Sadness flickered in Gabe's eyes. "Richard is positive."

Tristan's stomach churned. "Shit, really?"

"Has been my whole life."

"He's your non-bio dad, right?"

"Right. Bear's my bio dad."

"That can't be easy on them."

"It isn't sometimes, but they love each other. They've overcome a lot and they've never given up on each other."

"Now I see where you get your strength from." Tristan startled. "Is it okay that you told me? I don't want to say the wrong thing by accident."

"It's fine. Richard doesn't wear a sign, but he doesn't hide it. Every year my dads hold a fundraiser at Big Dick's to support HIV awareness, especially for young people."

"When's the fundraiser held?"

"February."

"I'll help." Tristan wanted to get involved in something that was important to Gabe. He wanted to be part of something again.

Gabe grinned. "We're always looking for volunteers."

"Awesome. Porn site?"

"No." Gabe kissed his nose. "Just think of the anticipation."

"For a few hours, until it's gone. Poof."

"I'll remind you. Besides, you need to write all this down. Why don't you do that while I go downstairs and see what we've got for breakfast. Bear should be up."

"Your other dad sleeps in?"

"Oh yeah. He considers noon to be early."

Tristan laughed. After Gabe left, he took his time recounting every detail he could remember since he woke up, including

Gabe's references to the previous night. He couldn't wait for Gabe's inevitable email detailing the three times they'd had sex.

I wonder if we can break that record next time I stay over.

It hit him that he'd spent the night somewhere other than Benfield for the first time since the accident, and he hadn't freaked out. Sure, he'd had a brief moment when he woke up, but he'd known Gabe immediately. Some of the details had come back. He didn't know if it was his brain getting better, or Gabe being there, and he didn't care. He was overjoyed to have slept all night with another guy for the first time in more than three years.

He wanted to do it as often as possible.

And then there was the fact that Gabe was a porn star. Okay, so maybe not a star-star, but he got recognized. He probably had fans. He got to fuck other hot guys on a regular basis. Hot guys with muscles and perfect memories and a lot less baggage than Tristan. Guys who were way less complicated. Gabe had no reason to have chosen Tristan over any one of them, but he had. For whatever reason, Gabe loved *him*.

For now, that simple fact mattered more than anything.

Bear occupied his usual spot at the counter when Gabe hit the kitchen. He helped himself to coffee before scouting the fridge.

"Didn't think you boys were staying the night," Bear said.

"We didn't plan to."

"Tristan okay this morning?"

Gabe grabbed eggs, mushrooms and butter, then closed the fridge door. "Yep. I think he was startled at first, because my phone woke us up. But he acclimated really fast. He recognizes me almost immediately now, which is fantastic."

"That is good news."

He grabbed a frying pan and scooped some butter into it.

"Yeah. I also told him about the porn, and he barely blinked. He wants to watch it."

Bear's startled expression was priceless. "Yeah?"

"I know. I mean, I didn't think he'd freak out and dump me, but I thought he'd react more strongly than he did."

"Did you tell him about Debbie?"

"Yes. Not too many details, but he understands why I need the extra money."

Gabe chopped up mushrooms then added them to the melted butter to sauté. As soon as they began to sizzle, it occurred to him he had no idea if Tristan had food allergies. He'd never asked. But mushrooms had been in the sauce Dad used in the lasagna last night, so that soothed his fears. He'd hate himself if he accidentally poisoned Tristan.

"He joining you for breakfast?" Bear asked.

"In a little while. He wanted to write everything down to remind himself later. He still uses the notebooks, but he refers to them less and less."

"Good to hear."

Tristan came downstairs right as the mushrooms were soft enough to add four eggs and scramble it all together. "Good morning," he said to Bear. "That smells good."

"I guess I should have asked if you liked mushrooms before I started cooking," Gabe replied.

"I love mushrooms. Never had them with eggs."

"It's my favorite way to eat scrambled eggs."

Tristan joined him by the stove and watched with his chin on Gabe's shoulder. So easy and domestic. "This might become my favorite way to eat scrambled eggs too."

"Help yourself to coffee."

"I don't really drink it. Caffeine messes with my meds."

"The trial meds?"

"No, the ones I take for depression."

Gabe scraped his spatula on the bottom of the pan. He'd

forgotten that Tristan took medication for depression and anxiety.

"It was the absolute worst for the first six months," Tristan continued. "I've reread those notebook entries enough for that to have stuck pretty hard in my brain. I probably spent more days doped up than otherwise. Noel told me I tried to hurt myself a couple of times."

"I can't imagine how hard that was for you, losing everything that you were."

"I didn't really lose me, though. I know that now. I went away for a while, but you've helped me come back out and play. So thanks for that."

"You don't ever have to thank me for making you happy." Gabe grabbed two plates and divided the mushrooms and eggs. "You like ketchup on your eggs?"

"Ew, no. You have any mayo?"

Gabe blinked.

Tristan started laughing. "I'm kidding. Gross."

"Something to drink, Tristan?" Bear asked. "We've got cranberry juice and sweet tea."

"Juice is fine. Thanks."

They occupied the other two stools at the counter. Gabe blew over his black coffee, desperate for it to cool enough to gulp. He wasn't quite awake yet, and he still had Debbie's missed call to deal with. She'd woken them, probably screaming to know where he'd been all night. He didn't want to go back, but he'd left his work apron there and needed it for his shift.

Fun times.

Tristan yum-noised his way through his eggs. Gabe loved watching him eat, because he truly seemed to enjoy the experience of tasting food. The eggs weren't exactly fine dining but he was glad to make Tristan smile. Tristan had spent too many years locked away, existing in small pockets of time without really taking pleasure in anything.

"Might as well say it so you know it," Bear said. "You're welcome over anytime, Tristan. Haven't seen my boy smile so much in a long while, so you keep making each other happy."

Tristan flushed bright red. "Thank you."

"You boys enjoy the day." Bear put his coffee mug in the sink, then shuffled out of the kitchen.

"I agree with Bear," Gabe said. "You can visit anytime, as long as I'm free to come get you."

Tristan moved his arm so their elbows touched. "You know I'll be taking you up on that as often as possible."

"Good. Because the more you're here, the more this will be familiar to you."

"I want that." Tristan speared a piece of mushroom but didn't eat it. "Did we talk about your birthday last night?"

Gabe made a mental fist pump for that question. "Yes, we did. It's December eighth."

"Are you having a party?"

"Don't usually. Bear's trying to trick me into coming to Big Dick's that night, because it's a Monday this year. He's already planning a tiki theme night with dancers in grass skirts and everything."

"That sounds like fun."

"Yeah, but Richard will inevitably find a way to embarrass me."

"How?"

"Goading me into getting up on the risers with the dancers, usually. He'll dare me, and I'll do it, because he knows I hate failing a dare."

"Oh yeah?" Something wicked danced in Tristan's eyes. "I dare you to take me to Big Dick's on your birthday. I want to go to a tiki party."

Gabe laughed out loud. He'd walked right into that one. "Fine, we'll go. And you'll get to see Shane dance. He's our newest Monday night draw."

He watched Tristan's eyebrows scrunch, then smooth out as he placed the name. "Right, Noel's boyfriend. They live together."

"Yes. Do you remember where?"

"Um, Stratton? I think I've been to their place. It makes me think of blue."

"The trim is blue. It's a single-story house."

"Right. Yes." Tristan finished off his eggs, then chugged his juice. "So when can we do this again?"

Gabe mentally went through his schedule for the rest of the week. Wednesdays he usually worked eleven to seven shifts. Tomorrow was the same. Friday he had two to ten, then straight over to the club to help behind the bar. Saturday he had off—his boss was good about trying to give everyone at least one Saturday a month, and they had the staff to manage it—and he hadn't promised to bartend. He also didn't want to wait that long to see Tristan.

"How about tomorrow night?" Gabe asked. "I work until seven, so it won't be until late that I can pick you up."

"What if Noel and I hang out in the city until then? We can meet where you work, and it will save you both a trip to Benfield."

"If Noel's down for that, so am I."

"I'll make sure he is. So can we watch a scene of yours tomorrow?"

"We'll see." Gabe glanced at the clock on the stove. "As much as I hate to say it, we have to go."

"Already?"

"Yeah. I'm sorry." He really, truly was sorry to have to take Tristan back to Benfield. He'd much rather leave him here, so he'd be waiting when Gabe came home. Only that wasn't how it worked.

Not yet.

And as reluctant as he was to leave Tristan behind, he was even more reluctant to return home to face Debbie's wrath.

Picking up his work uniform from home had been a nightmare for Gabe. More accusations from his mother, more guilt trips over not being there last night. It stuck with Gabe all during his work shift, like a sliver of glass he couldn't get out from under his skin. The need to end this cycle with his mother once and for all was what had him knocking on Chet Green's door at nine thirty on a Wednesday morning.

Chet answered with a glass of something amber in his hand. "Well, this is a surprise."

"I'm sorry for not calling first," Gabe said. Now that he was there, the idea felt idiotic. Chet had no good reason to help him.

"Well, it's obviously important. Come in, please."

Gabe was used to heading straight downstairs to the set. Following Chet down a short hallway and into his living room felt a little strange.

"Would you like something to drink?" Chet asked.

"No, I'm good."

Chet relaxed into a wide-armed chair, so Gabe perched on the edge of the sofa across from him. "Is this about the Puppy Farm shoot?"

"No, it's not." Gabe really wished he hadn't come here. He hated asking anyone for favors, and this one was huge. But he didn't see any other way to make sure Debbie got the treatment she needed to get and stay sober. "It's actually pretty personal."

"All right."

"My mother's an alcoholic." Gabe launched into a brief retelling of the last ten or so years of his life, up to that morning's battle. "I need to be able to give her an ultimatum when I move out, but rehab is expensive, and I don't have enough to cover all of it."

Chet's expression was both sad and sympathetic, not a hint of judgment. "You want to put her in the best position possible to get better."

"Exactly. I hate coming to you about this, but I don't have any credit, so I doubt I'd qualify for a bank loan."

"How much do you need?"

Chet didn't even blink at the figure Gabe quoted. "It's yours."

"Seriously? That's a lot of money, Chet. I mean, I'll obviously pay you back when we start selling some of the crap she's hoarded away, but it might take time."

"We'll work out the details of repayment, but the money is yours."

Gabe was still too stunned by the easy yes to say anything else.

"I'm actually very flattered that you trusted me enough to come to me," Chet continued. "So I'll tell you something not many of the boys know. I didn't create Mean Green to pay me. I created it to pay the models."

"To pay us?"

"I know what it's like to grow up being told your sexuality is something sinful and gross. I know what it's like to live on the streets with nothing but the clothes on your back and a few dollars in your pocket. I built Green Enterprises from nothing, and now I live quite comfortably off my investments.

"Mean Green was my way of creating something that would give young gay men a way to embrace and celebrate their sexuality in a safe, healthy way, and get paid well to do it. It's why I set up the royalty program. You're the ones doing the work, so you get the bulk of the profits. I keep enough to pay the crew and maintain the website."

"Wow." Gabe wasn't sure what else to say.

"Every young man who comes to me for work comes for a different reason." Chet swirled the liquid in his glass around. "I try not to judge anyone for their past mistakes, because I've made a boatload of my own. I do what I can to give them steady employment and to never exploit the trust given to me. I am more than able and willing to help you with your mother's sobriety, Gabriel."

Chet so very rarely said his given name that Gabe thought he was speaking to someone else. "Thank you. I can't begin to tell you how much this means. If she can get sober and finally stay that way..."

"I know."

Gabe's entire life would change for the better.

And that was everything.

19

After an artery-clogging dinner of burgers and fries at Five
Guys, Tristan was more than ready to burn off some calories walking to Gabe's workplace. Not that he'd ever complain
about treating himself to Five Guys, because they had the very
best burgers on the planet. Didn't stop him from feeling like a
bloated beast afterward, though. Add nervous anticipation on top
of that and his stomach was a hot mess.

Noel hadn't seemed entirely thrilled about handing him off to
Gabe, instead of hand-delivering him back to Benfield, but whatever. He'd been weird when Tristan told him about the incredible
sex he and Gabe had had the other night, so Tristan left out the
sleeping over part. The first time—that he could remember—that
he'd kept something from Noel. He usually told Noel everything,
but Noel didn't seem to want to hear about this stuff.

Gabe had given them an address to an Italian bistro called
Ristorante Totaro, which was in midtown, a few blocks from the
nearest public parking garage. Noel hated parallel parking, so
they were hoofing it to the drop off spot. They'd left Noel's car at
about five minutes to seven, which put them on time to be there
when Gabe was leaving.

Unless he got stuck with a table or something. Tristan wasn't sure how that worked. He'd never waited tables.

"Are you mad at me?" he asked Noel after a few minutes of walking in silence.

"No," Noel said, not missing a beat. "Why would I be mad at you?"

"I don't know, but you're being weird."

"How am I being weird?"

"Well, for starters, Mister Policeman, you keep answering my questions with a question."

Noel stopped walking, and Tristan nearly hit a stranger in passing. "I'm not mad at you."

"Then what's wrong?"

"I just worry about you spending all of this time with Gabe, because I'm not used to you like this, and I want to be sure that you're being careful."

"Careful like how? Using condoms? That's kind of a duh, isn't it?"

A strange kind of relief settled around Noel, relaxing some of his tension.

So weird.

"Have you seriously been worrying about that?" Tristan asked.

Noel ducked his head. "A little, I guess."

"Why? I mean, yeah, I was kind of a slut in college, but I'm not stupid."

"I know you aren't stupid, Tris. I don't want you to put yourself at risk."

"With Gabe?" Something dinged in the back of his mind. Something about Gabe. Tristan checked the Gabe Crib Sheet he'd stapled into the front of his notebook.

Porn star, that's it. But how could Noel know?

"What do you know about what Gabe does for a living?"

Tristan asked. He didn't care that they were having this conversation on a public street.

Noel swallowed hard, a sure sign that he was stalling. He had to know. "What has he told you about what he does for a living?"

Another question. Two could play that game. "What has he told *you* about what he does for a living?"

"Gabe didn't tell me anything."

He knew Noel well enough to see the word play. "Then who did?"

"Tris—"

"Who told you?"

Noel glanced around, then tugged Tristan closer to a building and out of direct foot traffic. "Who told me that Gabe shoots gay porn?"

"Yes."

Tristan's lack of reaction made Noel do a double take. "You know?"

"Of course I know. Gabe told me. We do talk to each other, Noel, in between the fucking. How did you find out?"

Noel's face pinched. "Shane told me."

Shane. Boyfriend. That didn't make much sense, unless— "Is Shane a fan who recognized him or something?"

"No."

"So then what?"

Noel's expression went from uncomfortable to completely mortified, which only piqued Tristan's curiosity. "For a few weeks this summer, while Shane and I were kind of on-again, off-again, Shane filmed with the same company," Noel said.

"Really?"

Me and Noel are both dating porn stars?

"He needed the money," Noel added. "And he quit once he didn't need it anymore. He quit before we committed to each other. Neither one of us wants anyone else."

"Gabe doesn't want anyone but me."

"So he quit?"

"No. But porn sex isn't the same as what we do. We're real, Noel, we aren't some illusion of intimacy created for an audience. We love each other."

Noel flinched, and the simple action pissed Tristan the hell off. Who the fuck was Noel to judge who Tristan chose to love, or who chose to love him back? Nothing about Tristan's relationship with Gabe was Noel's to scrutinize or to judge. "What is your deal with me and Gabe? Seriously."

"I don't have a problem with Gabe."

"No? Because you're acting like you do. If it doesn't bother me that he does porn, then there's no reason it should bother you."

"You're right."

"Good. Because I'm happy. So fucking happy I can't breathe sometimes."

"I know you are, and that's what worries me."

Tristan was absolutely baffled. What was so worrisome about someone being happy? And maybe a public street wasn't the best place to hash this out, but he had to know. "Why?"

"Because Gabe is the first guy you've been with since college. He's the first one who's shown you attention and affection, and I worry that you're latching on this tight. You've been hurt so much, Tristan. More than anyone deserves, and I can't stand to see you get hurt again."

The grief in Noel's voice made Tristan's heart give a little twist. Noel had been the only constant in his life since the accident. The only person who never gave up on him, no matter how angry or depressed he got. Noel would always worry. Tristan loved him for it as much as it frustrated him.

"I know these past few years have been hard on you too," Tristan said. "But I'm not an idiot."

"I don't think—"

Tristan held up a staying hand. "I'm talking." He put his hand down when Noel kept quiet. "I'm not an idiot. Yes, Gabe is the first person I've been with in a long time, but I'm not going into this blind and neither is he. He was interested in me before I began the trial, and maybe he can't promise me a long, happy life together, but who can? No one is certain of the future. You could get shot on the job tomorrow and be gone and fuck all the promises you made to Shane."

Noel flinched back like he'd been slapped.

"My point," Tristan continued, ignoring a pang of guilt for the look on Noel's face, "is that I don't know if this drug will keep working. I don't know if this is the best I'll be, or if it will stop working and I'll go back to before. I don't know if Gabe will one day decide to hell with all my drama and dump me for some hot, hung scene partner. But no matter what happens tomorrow, I want to enjoy every single moment I have today. I don't want to lose any more time. And if for some reason Gabe ends up being a mistake, he was my mistake to make."

He hated being so harsh with Noel. He hated seeing his best friend so upset.

Then something surprising happened. Noel smiled. Not a fake *I'm humoring you* smile. A genuine *I hear you* smile.

"You always were smarter than you gave yourself credit for," Noel said. "I guess I deserved that."

"I love Gabe, and while I don't need your blessing, so to speak, I'd like to have it."

"You've got it. Sorry I've been an ass about this."

"Forgotten. Just don't do it again."

"I'll do my best."

The decision to try was better than a promise he couldn't keep.

Tristan was about to suggest they haul ass to the restaurant when something Noel said earlier came back and pinged his curiosity. "You said Gabe and Shane worked for the same company. Did they ever film a scene together?"

The instant frown on Noel's face answered his question.

"Okay, never mind," Tristan said. "Awkward subject."

"Come on." Noel cuffed the back of his head. "Let's go meet your boyfriend."

They walked the rest of the two blocks in a comfortable silence. Tristan held his head a little higher, proud of standing up for what he wanted, instead of what someone else thought he needed. He wanted Gabe, goddamn it, and he'd fight for him if he had to.

Ristorante Totaro had a red stone exterior that wanted to mimic something Old World Italian and came across kind of cheesy. But the place seemed busy, and Gabe was standing outside, leaning against the building with a foam soda cup in his hand. Tristan knew it was him without thinking about it, and the grin on Gabe's face when he spotted them cemented the conclusion as fact.

"Hey, handsome," Tristan said as he practically skipped over. He resisted throwing his arms around Gabe and kissing him silly. They were in a pretty big city, yeah, but it was the same city where he'd lost his fucking memory, so caution was his new default mode.

"Hey yourself," Gabe said. "Hi Noel."

Noel shook his hand in a very straight-guy-greeting kind of way that made Tristan do a mental eye-roll.

"You guys have any plans?" Noel asked.

Gabe gave a lazy, one-shouldered shrug. "I thought maybe we could try our hand at seeing a movie."

"Really?" Tristan bounced up on his toes. "What movie?"

"I don't know. I'll pull up the theater app and see what's playing."

"Yes, can we? I haven't been to see a movie in forever."

Gabe grinned. "I know. Thought we could find something not too long and give it a shot."

"That sounds like a good plan," Noel said. No sarcasm. He meant it.

"You want to join us?" Gabe asked. So polite.

"No, thanks. You two enjoy your date."

Tristan tried to reply but his mouth wouldn't work. Everything seemed to tunnel away, like the volume being turned down on a television. He was hot all over, despite the chilly air, and then his entire body went numb.

Gabe saw the change in Tristan, from aware to blank in the blink of an eye, and a sharp knife stabbed him in the heart. He knew what was happening. He'd seen it before, and he couldn't stop it.

He reached out as Tristan's eyes rolled back. The tremors began in his shoulders and radiated down his arms. Then his back arched, and his legs gave out. Gabe caught him around the waist before he could collapse and hit his head. Noel supported his other side, and together they lowered Tristan's trembling body to the sidewalk.

"Shit, Tristan?" Noel said. The terror in his voice cut through Gabe like a knife.

"He's having a seizure," Gabe said. He shrugged out of his coat, folded it, and eased it under Tristan's head to cushion him from the cold sidewalk.

"Should we hold him still?"

"No, you're not supposed to do that." Gabe had researched seizures years ago thanks to Debbie. Holding a seizing person down or putting something in their mouth was not the thing to do, no matter what they did on television.

They'd amassed a small crowd of gawkers. Gabe glared up at the nearest young woman who had her phone in hand and was simply staring at them. "Be fucking useful and call an ambulance."

She jerked into action.

"Shit, shit, shit." Noel was panicking and stuck on repeat.

Gabe focused on Tristan, willing him to stop. Hating that this was happening, and that he couldn't do anything to stop the seizing. All he could do was pay attention and not panic. And pray.

Please, God, he doesn't deserve this.

"What's happening?"

"You think it's drugs?"

"Is he dying?"

"Did someone hit him?"

Gabe tried to ignore the voices all around them, asking ignorant, if innocent, questions. "It's his new medication," he said, mostly to shut them up. "Can we have some room please?"

That got Noel to pay attention. He raised his head, his face red and his eyes blazing. "Everyone back the hell up," he snarled. Probably the voice he used for crowd control on the job. "We don't know it's the meds," Noel said to him.

"What else could it be? Dr. Fischer told Tristan seizures were a possible side effect."

Tristan's muscles began to settle, until only his head gave the occasional shake. His eyelids fluttered.

"Tristan?" Gabe said. "Come back to me, sunshine."

He struggled to wake up.

"You're going to be okay, you hear me? An ambulance is coming, and some doctors are going to check you out."

Tristan's lips moved. No words came out.

Gabe swallowed hard against rising bile. He wasn't going to lose it here. Not until Tristan was safe. Not until he knew for sure Tristan was going to be okay. Then he'd let it all sink in.

"Gabe, you okay?"

He jerked his head up. The owner of the ristorante, Paulo, was standing behind him with a towel in his hands. "Hey, I'm fine. A friend had a seizure just now."

"Shit, you need anything?"

"We've already called an ambulance, but thanks."

"How about a coat, man? It's freezing."

Gabe couldn't really feel his body. "I'm fine."

"You need anything, you call me."

"Will do."

Paulo disappeared into the crowd to the tune of distant sirens. Gabe caught Noel's gaze. The anger there surprised him. Redirected anger over Tristan's situation? Because Gabe hadn't done anything wrong.

"Shouldn't you call Tristan's doctors?" Gabe asked.

"I'll call them once I know which hospital we're going to," Noel replied. Tight and pissed.

Whatever. He can take this out on me if he wants.

Gabe didn't care. All he wanted was for someone to tell him Tristan was okay.

The ambulance arrived in a flurry of noise and flashing lights. Gabe let Noel explain what had happened while the paramedics checked Tristan's vitals. He was still struggling to wake up. Gabe didn't know if that was better than being unconscious or worse. They lifted Tristan onto the gurney. Gabe faltered a moment before remembering to grab his coat and follow.

"Family only," the paramedic said as they loaded him into the back.

"I have power of attorney over Tristan's medical care," Noel said.

"Fine, you can ride with us."

Gabe blinked hard, surprised to know Noel had the power to make medical decisions for Tristan. And angry at being left behind. "Which hospital are you taking him to?" Gabe asked.

"PinnacleHealth on South Front Street."

"Thank you. I'll meet you there," he said to Noel.

Noel didn't reply.

Asshole.

He waited until the ambulance was pulling out into the street, and then he sprinted the two blocks to where he'd parked his car. Panic seeped into his veins like ice water, squeezing his heart and constricting his chest. His hands shook so badly he dropped his keys twice, and then he had trouble getting the damned right key into the ignition.

He's fine, he'll be fine. He has to be fine.

Traffic wasn't terrible for seven thirty on a Thursday, but it irritated him enough that he was cussing at every car that got in front of him. Every red light impeded his progress. His cell phone rang.

Debbie.

He ignored the call. He could not handle her drama tonight.

Gabe had been to PinnacleHealth a handful of times, usually because of Debbie, so he found the visitor parking garage with little fuss. The ER was a brief hike across the medical center's campus, and then he was finally there.

Noel paced in one corner of the waiting area, phone to his ear, speaking softly to someone. Gabe hung back until Noel hung up and noticed him.

"They took him back a few minutes ago," Noel said, icy anger still in place. "Dr. Fischer is in Gettysburg, but he's driving up soon, and I called Benfield so they know what's happening and can contact Dr. Coolidge and his GP."

He'd made a lot of calls in a brief amount of time. "I didn't know you had power of attorney."

Noel shrugged. "It's only been for a few months. I guess his parents wanted to forget they have a son. They still pay his bills and give him an allowance, but they want no part in his medical care."

"So they put it all on you?"

"At least they chose someone who loves him."

"Good point."

Noel still looked like he wanted to take a swing at him. Gabe got fear, but this was something else.

"Did I do something to piss you off?" Gabe asked.

"A friend?"

"What?"

"When that guy on the sidewalk asked what was going on, you said your friend was having a seizure."

Gabe thought back, but he genuinely couldn't remember what he'd said to Paulo. The entire sidewalk encounter was a blur. "I might have, I don't know. I was a little busy worrying about Tristan."

Noel took a step closer. "If you say you love Tristan, you can at least acknowledge his fucking existence."

"What are you—?"

"Friend, Gabe, not boyfriend."

He stared at Noel until it all sank in. "Are you serious right now? You're pissed at me over something I said during a moment of extreme stress? I do love him, and fuck you for doubting that."

Someone nearby cleared their throat. Gabe didn't really give a shit if their conversation was making someone else uncomfortable. It was an emergency room. No one was comfortable in an emergency room, and everyone there was worried about someone else.

Noel didn't apologize, but he let the conversation drop. Gabe wanted to call Bear and tell him what was happening, only he didn't really know what was happening. No sense in getting his parents worried until he had some good news to go along with the bad.

More than forty minutes of no news passed before the nurse who occasionally called out names finally said, "Tristan Lavalle?"

He and Noel both barreled toward the petite woman in blue scrubs.

"You can come back with me," she said with a bright smile.

"Is he okay?" Noel asked. They followed her through automatic doors and into a maze of hallways and cubicles.

"He's stable and awake."

Gabe's heart gave a happy little lurch.

She led them to a small room with a single bed. Tristan was sitting up, pale but otherwise alert. And he looked pissed as hell.

Noel beat him to the bed for a hug, but Tristan untangled quickly and reached out for Gabe. Gabe silently cheered and hauled Tristan into his arms. He hated how cool Tristan's skin was, and how he shook against his chest. Gabe wanted to do more to make this all okay, but the only thing he could do was comfort his boyfriend.

"Has the doctor been in to see you?" Noel asked.

"Just for an exam. They did some tests too, but no one's been back."

"Doesn't surprise me," Gabe said. "Hospitals like to take their damned time unless you're bleeding all over their floors."

"Nurse Johnson said I had a seizure?"

"You did."

"Fuck."

Gabe pulled away long enough to kiss his forehead. "It wasn't a severe one, but it was still pretty damned scary to watch."

"I'm so sorry."

"It's not your fault. None of this is, so don't be sorry."

"Can't help it. I hate worrying both of you."

Noel sat on the opposite side of the bed. "What would I do with my free time if I didn't spend it worrying about you?"

Tristan smiled, but the joke felt flat to Gabe. "How do you feel?" Gabe asked.

"Exhausted," Tristan said. "Like I just worked out at the gym for ten hours straight. Everything feels like jelly, and I don't really remember what happened."

"That's actually not uncommon with seizures."

"How do you know?" Noel asked.

Gabe glanced at Noel, whose surprise bordered on being impressed that he knew about more than waiting tables and porn. "My mother has had seizures before because of her drinking. I studied up a few years ago. She never remembered them either."

"Oh. Sorry."

Tristan's eyes went wide. "You don't think I'll have to stop the clinical trial, do you? I can't. Not when everything is so great."

"Let's not guess, okay?" Gabe said. "Let's wait for Dr. Fischer to get here and look at your tests."

"I knew there was a risk but—" His voice broke. "Shit."

"Hey." Gabe cupped his cheek and made those big, teary eyes meet his. "I am right here, okay? I'm not leaving."

Tristan inhaled long and hard, then swallowed down his tears. "Thanks. Some date, huh?"

"We're together, aren't we?"

He laughed. "I guess so." To Noel he said, "Did you call Shane? He'll wonder why you're late."

Noel checked his phone. "Shit, it is late. I'll be right back."

"I'm not going anywhere."

Once they were alone, Gabe hugged Tristan again, for nothing else except to try and calm his suddenly racing heart. Tristan rubbed his back, a touch he barely felt through the bulk of his winter coat. They existed like that for a while, even after Noel returned to the room. Eventually Gabe let go so Tristan could lie back and relax.

"Since Shane's about as stubborn as you are," Noel said to Tristan, "he's on his way here."

"Good," Tristan said. "You look like hell. You need him."

"Yeah, I kind of do."

"Besides, who knows how long all of this will take. If I have to stay overnight, he can drive you back to your car."

Gabe nearly said he could have done that, but then he caught on. Tristan was subtly saying Noel didn't have to stay. Gabe would be there.

I love him so much.

More time ticked by. Shane arrived before any of the doctors. At a quarter to ten Gabe was ready to storm the front desk and demand someone talk to them. He was saved the trouble by a knock at the half-shut door. Two men strode in, one of them in a white lab coat and the other in a blue sweater.

"Dr. Fischer," Noel said. He shook the hand of the younger man in the sweater.

"Noel," Dr. Fischer said. He introduced the ER doctor as Dr. Matthews before turning his attention to the bed. "Tristan, how are you feeling?"

"Okay," Tristan replied. "Tired mostly."

"That is absolutely to be expected after a tonic-clonic seizure."

"A what?"

"We used to refer to them as grand mal seizures. From your tests and from Noel's description, that's what you had this evening."

"Because of the drug trial?" Gabe asked.

"I'm sorry, you must be Gabe?" Dr. Fischer shook his hand too. "Tristan's spoken about you several times."

"Yes, I am."

"It's very likely, yes, that the trial medication caused the seizure, seeing as Tristan's never had a history of them before this."

"We knew this could happen," Tristan said. "Especially with how I've been improving."

"Yes we did."

"Can you treat it with something so it doesn't happen again?" Gabe asked.

"Unfortunately many of the commonly used antiseizure medications have side effects that negatively affect memory."

"I've got enough problems there, thanks," Tristan said.

"Phenobarbital is an option not known to affect memory. However, I hesitate in using it because it could still interfere with how the trial meds are working. One seizure doesn't always guarantee a second. In some cases, a patient has a single seizure and never has another occurrence, even without the assistance of medication."

"So this could be a one-off?"

"It's possible, yes. It's also possible you'll have another, and that you'll need to take the phenobarbital for the rest of the trial. Maybe longer."

"What are the side effects?" Noel asked.

"The most common is sedation. So you may feel sleepy or lack energy while taking it. Dizziness, involuntary eye movement and ataxia are much less common. Ataxia is loss of control over various muscles in your body."

Tristan made a face. "Sounds like fun, and no thanks. I don't want to sleep through the life I'm just getting back. Plus I would have known going into the trial that this could happen, right?"

"We knew," Noel said.

Dr. Fischer smiled. "The good news, Tristan, is that you've had a single seizure and, as I said, there is a chance it won't reoccur. For now, I won't prescribe anything new."

"Thank God."

"So we're supposed to sit back and hope he doesn't have another one?" Noel asked.

"Tristan has an evaluation on Monday," Dr. Fischer said. "We can compare those tests to today's to see if there has been improvement or degradation."

Noel frowned. Gabe kind of wanted to shove him out of the room for a while. Power of attorney or not, Tristan was of sound fucking mind, and he was the one who got to decide his medical care.

"So I don't have to stay in the hospital?" Tristan asked.

"No, you don't," Dr. Matthews said, adding to the conversation for the first time. "The staff at Benfield will be informed, so they can keep a close watch on you over the weekend. We'll have you signed out as soon as we can get the paperwork together."

"Oh thank God." Tristan looked at Gabe. "You'll take me home, right?"

"Absolutely," Gabe replied.

"Good. Now that I'm sorted out, everyone can stop panicking and go home." He grabbed Gabe's hand. "Except you."

"I'm not going anywhere without you."

"Tristan, I will see you again on Monday," Dr. Fischer said. "And if you have any other side effects over the weekend, let me know immediately."

"Will do," Tristan said. To Gabe he added, "Make sure I do that."

"No more seizures for you, young man," Gabe replied with a smile.

Gabe moved over a bit so Shane and Noel could hug Tristan. Noel clung for a little while, and Gabe couldn't blame him for it. They were best friends, and tonight had freaked everyone the fuck out.

"Call me if you need anything," Noel said. "I mean it."

"I know you do. Thank you."

"Take care of him," Noel said to Gabe.

"I will," Gabe said.

Once the room was empty, Gabe curled up next to Tristan and held him tight. Tristan rested his head over Gabe's heart, and they lay together, waiting for Tristan's release.

"I love you," Tristan whispered.

"Love you too."

No matter what.

20

"Your silence is scaring me," Shane said.

They'd been in the car less than two minutes, but they'd spent the entire walk to the parking garage in perfect silence. Noel didn't trust himself to speak. He'd run the gamut tonight on emotions, from terror to anger to confusion and back again.

Watching Tristan collapse had given Noel a brief flashback to the night of their bashing. To seeing a bruised and bloodied Tristan hit on the back of the head with a bottle hard enough to shatter it, and hard enough to send Tristan crashing to the pavement. Unlike tonight, he'd been so still that Noel thought he was dead. Even while their asshole attackers sliced up Noel's chest, all he could do was grieve over Tristan.

He hadn't been able to voice all of that to Gabe, so he'd allowed himself to get angry at the other guy. Nothing that had happened tonight was Gabe's fault, but Noel had needed a target. Fair or unfair, Gabe briefly became the enemy.

"I know you're worried about Tristan," Shane added. "I mean, you're always worried about Tristan, but this is fucking huge.

Please don't keep it inside. I know better than anyone that's never a good idea."

Shane used to be the king of bottling up his emotions and keeping secrets, until everything came crashing down. They both knew it was better to vent and be honest. It saved angry fights later on.

"Tonight made me think about the bashing," Noel said, unsurprised that his voice was rough. "The way Tristan went down. For just a second, I was back there, positive he was dead."

Shane reached across the console to squeeze his thigh.

Noel covered that hand with his. "I took it out on Gabe, and that wasn't fair."

"Emotional reactions usually aren't. Gabe's a decent guy. He gets it."

"Still, I should have apologized."

"So text him later. Get it off your chest."

"I think I'm a little bit jealous too."

"Of Gabe?"

"Yeah." Noel picked for the right words, so he didn't make Shane mad. "I guess I'm used to having Tristan's undivided attention, being the one who cares the most about him. It's strange seeing him reach for someone else when he's upset."

"That makes sense," Shane said. "It isn't just Tristan's life that's changing, babe. You have to adapt too."

"I know. So much has happened in the last six months." From meeting and falling for Shane, to buying a house together, to Tristan's memory improvement and Gabe's addition to their lives. So much change.

"Good news is human beings were made to adapt."

"True. Some of us just take more time than others."

"You'll get there." Shane squeezed his thigh once more, then returned his hand to the wheel to negotiate a turn. "Eventually we all get to where we're supposed to be."

Noel desperately wanted to believe that was true—not only

for his and Shane's sake, but also for Tristan's.

Gabe jerked awake and blinked sleepily around the dark, unfamiliar room. Photos, pages and sticky notes all over the walls. A single window. Narrow bed that had a lean body pressed close to his.

Tristan's room at Benfield. They'd fallen asleep together.

He'd brought Tristan back here, rather than to Bear's house, because it felt safer having Tristan close to medical professionals. Tristan had tried to protest, but he'd been worn out from the seizure and hadn't put up much of a fight. Gabe explained what was happening to Debra, the night nurse on duty. She complained that it was a little late for visiting a patient—granted, it was after midnight by the time they got back—but he walked Tristan to his room anyway.

Somehow a long cuddle turned into them sleeping together.

But the oddness of that wasn't what woke him up.

A sliver of light on the floor traced back to the open door—a door Gabe remembered closing. Someone had come inside. Or peeked in to check on them. Either way, it disconcerted Gabe. Sure, Tristan lived in an assisted living center but he deserved privacy. He wasn't an elderly patient who could have a heart attack at any moment and die.

He could have another seizure, maybe worse than the first one.

He hugged Tristan tighter, glad he hadn't woken up. Tristan looked so peaceful when he slept. Nothing hurt and nothing scared him. He could get out of his own head for a while and dream of something nicer.

Gabe should have gone home, but since no one was kicking him out, he didn't. He stayed right where he wanted to be, which was with Tristan. Debbie would be on the warpath in the morning, but he didn't care. He was giving her his ultimatum tomorrow and officially moving in with his dads. She'd pitched a solid fit the previous morning when he finally got home. He said he'd had wine at dinner and fallen asleep there—only half a lie. She'd bought it and calmed down.

Telling her he was leaving after being out all night again was not high on his Friday to-do list, but he had to do it. No more taking her abuse. No more enabling.

He closed his eyes and let himself drift back into a restless sleep, marred by dreams of Debbie and her verbal onslaughts, and memories of the different ways she knew how to smack and slap. He woke later with arms around his waist and a warm mouth pressing kisses on the side of his neck.

Tristan was holding him.

"Morning," Gabe said. He rolled onto his back so he could kiss Tristan's mouth.

"Hey." Tristan's sleepy smile also held a touch of worry. "Did you sleep okay? You were mumbling a lot."

"Less than nice dreams. But this is a wonderful thing to wake up to."

"I can't believe none of the night nurses kicked you out."

"You must have them all tied around your little finger."

"Or they see how happy you make me. I bet I was a shitty patient for a lot of years."

"Resident."

Tristan tilted his head. "What?"

"You aren't a patient here. That implies you're sick, and you're not. You're a resident." Even if it had been a slip of the tongue, Gabe didn't ever want Tristan thinking he was sick or broken. Not ever again.

"Okay." He glanced down at their fully clothed bodies and laughed. "We didn't even take our shoes off."

"Well, falling asleep wasn't exactly the plan, but I'm not going to complain."

"Me either. Do you work today?"

"Later tonight at the club. I have something I need to do today, though, so I can't hang around too long this morning."

Tristan sucked at hiding his disappointment. "Okay."

"I can come back this afternoon. We'll hang out for a few hours."

"Awesome." He frowned. "Wait, do I have something to do in the afternoon?"

"No, your painting class is tomorrow. Saturday. It's Friday."

"Oh, okay. Then yes, let's totally hang out this afternoon. I can do something to pass the time." Tristan looked around until his gaze landed on the far corner of his room. "I'm drawing again. That's right. I can do that. Hey!"

Tristan rolled out of bed and scrambled over to a desk littered with notebooks and art supplies. He picked up a wide drawing pad, then turned with the pad facing his chest. "You want to see what I'm drawing Noel for a housewarming present? It's almost finished."

"Definitely." Gabe sat up. He rolled his shoulders because the bed wasn't very comfortable. He didn't know how Tristan stood it.

Tristan turned the pad around to present the drawing. Noel's finished image took up the bottom left of the page, just his head and shoulders. In the top right, Shane was about half finished, details missing and his coloring un-shaded. The likenesses were amazing.

"I'm going to draw their house into the background once I'm done with Shane," Tristan said. "I had Noel send me some photos, but I didn't tell him why."

"It's beautiful." Gabe envied him his talent. The only thing Gabe seemed to be good at was smiling at rude customers and fucking.

"What is it?"

Gabe blinked. "What do you mean?"

"You looked really sad for a second." Tristan put the pad

down. "What were you thinking about?"

"Wishing I had some kind of amazing talent like you. You're a super gifted artist, Tristan. Seems like not very many people are really, genuinely good at something."

Tristan wrapped his arms around Gabe's waist. "Maybe you haven't found your talent yet. I'm sure you haven't tried doing everything there is to do."

"That's true. At least I know what I'm not good at."

"And what's that?"

"Musical instruments. I wanted to play something so badly in middle school. I tried a dozen different instruments. Piano, percussion, string, wood, brass. Nothing. I have zero musical talent."

"You have a decent singing voice." Tristan paused with his mouth open, like his thought process has simply stopped. "Hey, how do I know that? Did we do karaoke or something?"

Gabe chuckled at that mental image. "No. I was probably singing along to Christmas carols in the car one of the times I drove you."

"Oh. Well that makes sense." A wicked smile slunk across his lips. "So then we definitely have to do karaoke. I've never done it sober, but I'd give up my dignity for you. Do you ever do it at your dads' club?"

"First and third Tuesday every month."

"When's the next one?"

"Next week. Only I have to work in the restaurant that night."

The epic disappointment on Tristan's face completely broke Gabe's No Karaoke Ever rule. "I can try to switch with someone."

Tristan planted a hard kiss on his cheek. "Please?"

"I said I'll try, I promise." Shouldn't be too difficult to swap an evening shift for a day shift. Evenings always brought in better tips.

"Thank you. I think it would be really, really fun. Anything we do together is fun." He nuzzled at Gabe's earlobe. "I'm sorry we didn't get to do really fun things last night. You're here, so something weird happened, right?"

"Can you remember?"

Tristan stuck the tip of his tongue out like he often did while thinking. "I was with Noel because it was Thursday, but it was late and we were still out. But no, nothing."

"That's not a surprise." Gabe explained the seizure and the hospital, and how it wasn't unusual for someone to be groggy and not remember what had happened afterward. He hated the way Tristan's eyes got wet and his mouth twisted into something upset and ugly.

"It was just one, though, right?" Tristan asked. Panic pitched his voice higher. "I don't have to stop the trial, right?"

"No, you don't have to stop the trial. Dr. Fischer said sometimes people had one and never had another, so he didn't even want to give you medicine for it yet."

Tristan calmed a little, but not enough for Gabe, so he hauled Tristan into a proper hug. Chests and arms and chins on shoulders. Tristan's heart thumped wildly in his chest, hard enough for Gabe to feel it.

"I know it's scary, but you're okay," Gabe said. "You're okay."

Maybe if I say that enough, it will always be true.

"Sorry to be such a wimp about this," Tristan said as he pulled back.

"Hey, you're allowed to have feelings. This is scary, but I've got your back. I promise."

"It helps. Knowing that helps."

"I'm glad." Gabe checked the time on his phone. "Shit, I should go. You've got breakfast soon anyway."

"Okay. Email me later about coming over?"

"Definitely." He caught Tristan's soft lips in a gentle kiss, just enough to put the taste of him back where it belonged. "See you later."

Every time he dropped Tristan off, he walked out of Benfield like he was abandoning something important. Tristan wasn't alone. He was cared for at Benfield. But he thrived with Gabe. And Gabe wanted him around as often as possible, not locked away in an assisted living center, surrounded by great-grandparents and sleeping alone at night.

He hated leaving Tristan behind, and he silently vowed one day to pick Tristan up for the last time—the time when he'd come to live with Gabe for good.

Debbie was asleep on the couch when Gabe got home. He stood in the doorway, hand still on the knob, a sense of wrongness slamming down over him. No evidence of a takeout binge, no wine box or random bottle on the coffee table. The downstairs didn't reek.

He hadn't walked into the wrong house. That was definitely his mother stretched out on the couch, dressed in her yellow bathrobe and floral slippers. She'd fall asleep like that when he was in high school and stayed out late with his friends. She always waited up to make sure he got home safely.

She hadn't waited up for him in years.

Nervous now, Gabe went about making coffee as quietly as possible. He only had one bag left upstairs, as well as his laptop. Getting them and getting out while she was asleep was probably the safest, sanest plan. Except he'd have to come back. Giving her the ultimatum over the phone wouldn't have the same effect as handing it over, and then walking out.

So he made toast and ate that while his coffee cooled to a not-scorching temperature. He drank two mugs at the kitchen table while playing Tetris on his phone, sound down low. Finally a freakishly loud yawn bounced in from the living room. Acid splashed in his stomach.

Debbie shuffled into the kitchen, her usually frizzy hair

smoothed out and only slightly tangled. She went straight for the coffee pot and poured herself a mug. Black. She blew across the top as she turned, then almost dropped the mug when she saw Gabe.

"Figured you'd be up in your room," she said. "You don't usually eat down here."

"I was waiting for you to wake up."

She took a step toward the table, then stopped. Uncertain. She seemed more aware than usual during a morning-after, and it made him wonder how much she drank last night. "What time did you get in?"

"About forty-five minutes ago."

He waited for the anger, only none came. She nodded, her expression difficult to discern. A little sad, a lot exhausted.

"Fall asleep at your father's again?" she asked.

"No, with my boyfriend."

She almost dropped her mug again. "Your what? You have a boyfriend?"

He'd never mentioned Tristan, because Tristan was too special. Too precious to be exposed to her. Only Tristan was never going to meet the drunk her. Not if he had any say in it. And in that moment, he wanted her to know that he was happy. That he had something in his life worth fighting for.

"I do," he said. "We haven't been together long, but I love him very much."

"Well, I...that's good."

So not the reaction he'd expected. She should be angry. Screaming about him having someone when she was all alone. He didn't know what to do with this calm, rational Debbie. Might as well take his chances now, rather than wait.

"It is good. He's an amazing man, and he loves me back."

"I should hope so. You're too special to be wasting time with someone who doesn't love you back."

He blinked. This was the Debbie he remembered from high

school. The aware, loving mother who'd been on the wagon, attentive, and who cared about his life. This Debbie had been absent for the last six years. "I know I am. That's why I'm leaving."

"You just got home."

"I don't mean for the day. I've already taken most of my stuff out of here. I'm not living here anymore as of today."

Her eyes went wide. "Where are you going?"

"I have a place. Everything is arranged."

"But this is your home."

"This is a house. It's a house you live in because I allow it. It's a house I pay for because you can't. You won't. You lose every job you get because of your drinking. You spend my money on shit you don't need."

"I can't help myself."

"Yes you fucking well can, but you choose not to."

She flinched like he'd smacked her for a change.

"I can't do this anymore, Mom. I'm done."

She put the coffee mug down on the counter then pressed her palms flat. "I haven't had a drink since yesterday morning."

Gabe wasn't entirely sure he'd heard that correctly. "You what?"

"You've been acting different lately, and it worried me. I don't want to lose you, Gabriel, you're all I have. So I stopped. It's been twenty-four hours."

"Bullshit. You'd be shaking all over the floor by now."

Her shoulders hunched. "I maybe had a shot or two last night to stop the tremors. I had to!"

"No you didn't." He stood up so fast his chair fell over backward, and she jumped from the noise. "You could have stayed sober, but you took the easy way out. You can't stay dry, not even for one day, can you?"

"I'm trying."

"It's not enough. We've played this game, and I won't be duped by you again." His chest ached, but he had to get it all out.

"I'm moving out today. I'll pay the mortgage but nothing else. You have three weeks."

"Three weeks to do what?"

Gabe wished he had the pamphlet in front of him, but it was upstairs in his room. "There's an alcohol rehab and treatment center in New Jersey that I've spoken with. They have a slot for you. Four weeks, intensive rehab. I've also got a lead on a community outreach program that will help train you to get back into the workforce."

Debbie's eyes filled with tears. Her cheeks reddened. "You want to send me away?"

"No. I want you to send yourself away." He swallowed hard against rising bile, ready for the onslaught if she decided to unleash her wrath. "You have three weeks to either get yourself together and get out of this house, or to willingly go to this rehab program."

"And if I don't?"

"I'll begin eviction proceedings." His skin crawled with the cruelty of his words, even though he knew it was for the best. "I won't do this anymore, Mom. This is it. And I think three weeks is damned generous."

"You'll kick your own mother out onto the street?"

Her overwhelming indignation pissed him off a little. "No, you'll be kicking yourself out if you choose to continue drinking and rotting away, instead of taking this chance. If I'm going to keep pissing my hard-earned money away, I'd rather put it toward getting you better. I'm done enabling you."

Her face went scarlet. "You ungrateful little shit."

"I'm ungrateful? The other day I cleaned up a sea of broken glass, and you thanked me by throwing a book at my head. I keep you fed and a roof over your head, and you thank me by screaming at me, calling me names and breaking shit."

"I have bad days, you know that. I'd work if I could."

"Bullshit. You lose every job you get because you either stop going, or you show up hammered. You don't want to work. You want to feel sorry for yourself."

"After what your father did to me—"

"It was twenty years ago!" Gabe's voice kept rising to match Debbie's. "You could have found someone else, remarried and been happy. Instead, you dove into a bottle and you chose to stay there and be miserable. I'm sick of being miserable with you. I have someone who loves me, and I choose him."

"Gabriel—"

"No. I'm going upstairs for my last few things, and then I'm out. If you haven't left for rehab by the time twenty-one days pass, you're out."

He stalked from the kitchen before he really lost his temper—something he'd definitely inherited from her. Gabe unlocked his bedroom door for the last time for a while. Let her destroy the furniture and carpet in a fit of rage. He'd replace it. Whatever. He shoved his laptop and charger into his gym bag with a few final sets of clothes, then slung it over his shoulder. He wouldn't miss the room. It had been a place to hide from his mother, nothing more.

Debbie was standing in the middle of the living room, arms clasped around her middle. "Please, Gabriel, don't go. I'll change, I promise, but I need you here."

"No."

"I can't do this alone."

"You couldn't do it while I was here." He dropped the pamphlet on the coffee table. "I'm going."

"If it's about money, we can sell some of the stuff I bought. We can have a yard sale."

"It's November."

"What about a pawn shop?"

"Go for it, if that's your choice. Then you'll have money to buy food when what's here runs out."

Her face went slack. "You aren't giving me anything?"

"Hell no. Besides, you have a basement and bedroom closet full of brand new shit that you can pawn. Make your own money for a change."

"You can't do this."

"I've already done it. All I need to do is walk out that door."

"You won't. You're too good a boy to your mother. You've got too big a heart to do this to me."

"I'm doing this *for* you, Mom. You can't see that, but I want you to get better. I want to be proud to introduce you to my boyfriend. I want us to do normal things like go grocery shopping without you falling down drunk. You can do this if you want to. You're the most stubborn person I know."

Nothing he said made a difference. Tears streaked down her red cheeks, and she stomped one foot on the floor. "You're abandoning me just like your father did. Leaving me for another man!"

Gabe's chest blazed with anger. "You can frame this however you want, but the result is the same. Three weeks. Rehab or you're gone."

He stormed past her and out the front door. The moment it slammed shut, something inside the house shattered. His hands started shaking, and he had trouble getting the key into his car door. Once he was inside his car, bag on the passenger seat, he allowed all of his anger and fear to swell up. He shook for a while, adrenaline putting a sour taste in his mouth.

I did it. I really fucking did it.

Gabe genuinely had no idea how the next three weeks would play out. Leaving proved he was serious, while staying would have shown her otherwise. Without him around to pay for shit, she'd start to understand. She'd either go to rehab and get clean, or she'd face the consequences.

Debbie had exactly three weeks from today to choose her own future.

Because Gabe had already chosen his.

21

K araoke was all Tristan hoped for and more. Big Dick's had been packed with more than just hot gay men. Drag queens and quite a few women—gay or straight, he wasn't always sure—were among the throng. Gabe said it wasn't unusual, and quite a few really good singers got up on the platform.

A bunch of stinkers too. Tristan didn't care. He was spending time with Gabe, and nothing else mattered. A friend of Gabe's had come out too. A hot blond named Jon—the best friend Gabe told him about, and a fellow model.

Meeting him had made Tristan even more insistent on learning the secret of Gabe's porn experience, and on the ride back to Gabe's house, he decided he wasn't letting Gabe put it off any longer.

He waited until Gabe pulled alongside the curb in front of the house before saying, "I want to see one of your porn videos tonight."

Gabe's slow, deliberate head turn made Tristan squirm in the best possible way. Gabe's dark eyes glittered from the streetlights. "Oh yeah?"

"Oh yeah."

"You're really sure you want to see me fucking other guys?"

"Positive." Tristan clasped his hands tight. "It's just sex. It isn't like what we have. You love me, not them."

"You never stop amazing me, do you know that?"

He ducked his head, cheeks hot. Gabe touched his chin, urging him to look back up. Gabe smiled in the dim light. "Let's go inside," he said.

"Yes, please."

The house was dark, no one home. Because of the karaoke special, both Bear and Richard were closing up the club. Tristan could have jumped Gabe right in the entryway, but he wanted to see a scene more. He'd never—to his knowledge—given much thought to the idea of dating a porn star. Hell, he never imagined meeting a porn star, gay or straight, let alone falling in love with one. And he really wanted to see his boyfriend in action.

Does that make me kinky or downright insane?

Gabe closed his bedroom door. His hand hovered near the lock briefly—a moment that Tristan caught. He didn't lock it. Tristan imagined his dads were really good about personal boundaries.

He kicked off his shoes and socks, then bounced up onto Gabe's big bed while Gabe booted up his laptop. Tristan had half a mind to simply skim down to his briefs, but he didn't want to seem overeager. Not that he thought Gabe would mind, so he did strip off his shirt and belt.

Gabe quirked an eyebrow at him. "Getting comfortable?"

"Yep." He settled back against the pillows, ready and excited.

After he found what he was looking for, Gabe also skinned down to just his jeans. The bare-chest-and-denim look worked for him, especially combined with that delectable black scruff. He joined Tristan against the pillows then balanced the computer's lap tray on both of their thighs.

Tristan looked at the URL. MeanGreenBoys.com. He'd never heard of them. Then again, he wasn't exactly a porn connoisseur.

Dozens of studios had probably popped up since his college days surfing free sites, and even back then he didn't pay much attention to who made which clips. All he cared about was the sex.

Tonight he cared about the sex, but he also cared about Gabe. He wanted to see Gabe perform, see how he interacted with the other models, and to understand what he liked about porn.

"This is one of my first scenes," Gabe said. "I shot it with a guy named Ricky. He left for a different house about a year ago."

A little thrill shot through Tristan. He did the honors and pressed play. After a moment's pause, the scene opened with Gabe and Ricky sitting on a couch somewhere, bare-chested and grinning. The edited bits of the interview were kind of cute, as they talked about each other and what they liked to do in bed.

Tristan concentrated on Gabe. He looked almost exactly the same. His hair was a little longer and it curled around his ears. He wasn't bashful like Ricky. He answered the questions with a genuine smile, but something seemed...fake. Maybe because he knew Gabe so well he could see that he was very definitely acting. Saying the words the audience wanted to hear him say.

They segued right into making out and rubbing cocks over denim. Tristan's own dick took notice, slowly thickening as the scene progressed. Gabe devoured Ricky like a predator—testing him to see what made him squirm and squeal the most, attacking those erogenous zones with vigor, making Ricky putty in his hands, until he was begging to be fucked.

Gabe made him suck his cock instead.

Tristan rubbed his own cock through his jeans, kind of wishing he'd taken the fucking things off before sitting down. A quick glance showed Gabe's tented too, and he was glad that Gabe was getting turned on by this.

Watching another guy suck on Gabe's balls made Tristan gasp out loud. It didn't go unnoticed by Gabe, who slid closer until they were hip to hip, thigh to thigh. Shoulder to shoulder.

In the video, Gabe ordered Ricky to put his knees on the couch cushions and bend over.

Heat coursed through Tristan, warming his chest and gut. He placed a flat palm on Gabe's stomach, needing to touch him somewhere. Real Gabe pushed the laptop tray over onto Tristan's stomach, while Video Gabe pushed into Ricky.

Ricky moaned.

Real Gabe undid Tristan's fly and pulled out his hard cock. He spit on his palm, and then began a long, steady stroke. Tristan wanted to close his eyes and revel in the hand job, but he couldn't take his eyes off the screen.

His body knew what it felt like to be fucked by Gabe. Gabe was intense but always loving and tender—a perfect combination of things that made Tristan feel treasured. Video Gabe fucked like all he cared about was getting off. Sure, he was touching Ricky, kissing his neck, jacking his dick. All the usual things to keep a partner in the moment. It was different, though. Distant.

And sexy as all fuck.

Tristan trailed his fingertips down Gabe's abs, then right under the waistband of his jeans. Into his underwear to clasp hard flesh. Gabe grunted and pushed into his hand. The restriction of his clothes made it even more fun to tease. To pinch the tip and tickle around the crown. To trace lines along his length. To drive Gabe fucking nuts with the pressure.

The performers switched positions several more times, ending up with Gabe fucking Ricky over the arm of the sofa. Ricky came all over the place, and then dropped to his knees to suck Gabe off.

Real Gabe stopped stroking him the moment Video Gabe came all over Ricky's face, and goddamn, Tristan was so close to coming himself. His balls buzzed with the need. His chest was tight. A few more solid strokes.

Except Gabe didn't let him. He closed the laptop and put it on the floor, then tackled Tristan with a growl. He rolled him so

Tristan ended up on his stomach, cock trapped between the bedspread and his belly. Gabe stretched out on top of him, hard cock riding the crease of Tristan's ass.

Tristan turned his head for a sloppy sideways kiss, nipping at Gabe's lips and chin. Gabe bit his shoulder then began a slow journey down Tristan's back. Gabe's tongue left a cool, damp trail along his spine. He paused to play around the small of his back, laving the skin and waking all of Tristan's nerves. He wanted their pants gone so they were skin to skin, but Gabe seemed to have ideas of his own.

Gabe slid down until his chest was resting on Tristan's legs. He tugged Tristan's jeans farther down, baring his butt. Anticipation tightened Tristan's belly, and the first swipe of Gabe's tongue across his ass cheek made Tristan jump. He tried to see what Gabe was doing, but it hurt his neck, and then Gabe licked his other cheek. Tristan dropped his head to the mattress and gave in to Gabe's explorations.

Long, slow licks across his ass. Light nips and bites that barely stung and made his nerves sing. A single swipe from behind his balls, all the way to the top of his ass. With Tristan's legs pressed closed, Gabe didn't have a lot of room, but he wasn't making an effort to free up space.

Tristan figured out why when Gabe pulled his cheeks apart and licked at his hole. Gabe's unshaved skin created a delicious abrasion that slowly drove Tristan nuts, while Gabe's very talented tongue worked his entrance. The combined sensations echoed in Tristan's cock, which desperately needed friction of its own.

The onslaught continued, creating a burn that turned into bliss as Gabe worked his tongue inside. Just the tip, but it was enough to make Tristan whimper with need.

"Please," Tristan said.

Gabe stopped, and Tristan immediately wanted that burn

again. "Please what?" Some of the forceful top from the video was in Gabe's voice.

Goose bumps prickled down his spine. "Fuck me."

"I am so down with that, sunshine."

Gabe climbed off. Tristan scrambled up long enough to shuck the rest of his clothes. Instead of going to his hands and knees, he waited for Gabe to strip and glove up. Taking his cue, Gabe stretched out on his back. Tristan sat on his thighs, knees braced on either side of his hips. Gabe grinned up at him, dark eyes gleaming with desire and love. Two things Video Gabe hadn't shown.

This was all for Tristan.

This was all them.

"Here," Gabe said. He pumped some lube onto Tristan's fingers. "Prep yourself."

The naughtiness of fingering himself while Gabe watched made Tristan gasp. He rubbed the lube around a bit on his fingers, getting it warmer, adoring the way Gabe watched him so intently. Tristan planted his left hand next to Gabe's shoulder and bent forward, opening his cheeks so he could press a slick finger against his already wet hole. The familiar touch sent his heart galloping. The first breach broke sweat on his neck and shoulders.

"Fuck yourself on your fingers," Gabe said. "Just like that, sunshine."

Tristan did, reveling in the sensation of being filled, pumping in and out until he could work a second finger in. He humped his own hand, stretching himself for Gabe's dick, aware that Gabe was watching and enjoying every single second. Each part of Gabe was amazing, and Tristan went nuclear when he finally bore down on Gabe's cock. That first, eye-watering stretch that became an addictive fullness. The heavy slide in and out of his body. The faint sting of sensitive skin against Gabe's coarse hair.

The way his balls rubbed against Gabe's belly had Tristan's release edging closer and closer.

He needed the moment to last forever, to imprint itself on his heart because it wouldn't stay in his memory.

And then Gabe started jacking his cock, and Tristan gave in to the pleasure coursing through his body. His stomach tightened, his balls drew up, and then he shouted out his climax. Gabe slammed into him, fucking him through it, while he splattered Gabe's chest and chin with come.

"Oh fuck," Tristan said, gasping for air. "Fuck."

"So gorgeous," Gabe whispered.

A tremor of emotion surprised Tristan into rising up, off of Gabe's cock. His ass gave a twinge at the abrupt withdraw, but it was the best kind. The twinge of a well-used, satisfied ass. Tristan swung a leg over Gabe so he could kneel next to him, tugged off the rubber, and sucked him into his mouth. He tasted Gabe over the harsher flavors of lube and latex. Hot skin rolled over his tongue and nudged into his throat.

"Fuck, Tristan. Coming!"

Tristan stayed put, milking Gabe's orgasm for all it was worth, swallowing down every bitter drop and loving it. He licked and kissed Gabe's cock as he quieted. Nosed the dark thatch of hair he loved so much. Then slid up to lick his own come off Gabe's chest, dipping his tongue into every plane and angle, leaving nothing behind.

So fucking good.

Gabe tugged him up so they were chest to chest, sticky and sweaty and so perfect. Gabe's cheeks were flushed, his mouth still open, his face a picture of surprise.

"We should watch porn together more often," Tristan said.

Gabe chuckled, then tapped Tristan's chin. "I didn't want you to do that."

"Do what?"

"Swallow."

"Why not? I love to swallow. You taste great."

"Porn, remember?" Gabe kissed the tip of his nose. "We're as safe as humanly possible on set, but—"

"Hey, stop." Tristan put a finger over Gabe's lips. "I didn't forget. I know there will always be a tiny risk, but I am of sound mind and body when I say it's an acceptable risk for being able to feel you coming in my mouth."

Gabe shivered. "God, when you say shit like that..."

"Yeah?"

"Yeah. I love you."

"Love you back." He dropped kisses all over Gabe's neck and upper chest. "Can we take a shower? As much as I like this, I feel all sweaty and gross from dancing earlier."

"Sure thing."

Gabe paused with his head out the bedroom for a beat, probably listening for his dads so they didn't flash the pair on their way across the hall to the bathroom. The brief moment of shyness from a porn star was all kinds of cute.

He watched Gabe's ass on the quick walk, admiring the taut globes and smooth skin. Eyes, mouths, abs and cocks were all sexy as hell, but Tristan's biggest downfall was a hot ass, and Gabe definitely had the best.

Despite the last few years and his struggles, Tristan couldn't help but think all the pain had been worth it because it led him to Gabe.

He's mine. Please, God, don't take him away from me.

He'd lost enough already.

Gabe waited until breakfast the next morning to bring up his Puppy Farm news. He hadn't told Tristan about the offer yet. He'd been waiting for the exact details from Chet, and he'd gotten them yesterday afternoon. Bear had wandered into the den, and

Dad was still asleep. He and Tristan were alone in the kitchen eating pancakes.

"So you know how you're into the fact that I do porn?" Gabe said. He'd barely eaten thanks to a knot of anxiety currently residing in his gut.

Tristan looked up with a piece of pancake stuck on his fork. "Yeah."

"A few weeks ago my producer got an offer from another studio for me to do a video for them."

"Really?" The look of surprised delight on Tristan's face made the knot of worry unfurl. "Which studio?"

"Puppy Farm. They're pretty new, and they do a lot of artsy stuff, but they're winning awards and getting noticed."

"Porn has awards?"

Gabe laughed. "Yes, the adult industry has awards like other industries. Ours just aren't televised live on ABC."

"Well that's kind of awesome that you specifically were requested."

"It is. And now I finally have the details. Their studio is in New York State, and they'll pay for me to take a train from Ardmore. It's the nearest station outside of Philadelphia. The only thing is I leave Thursday afternoon, and I won't be home until Sunday."

"It takes that long to film a scene?" Tristan finally ate the piece of pancake.

"Their director is known for being a bit of a perfectionist, so he always plans in time for reshoots and getting extra footage."

"Do you know who you'll be shooting with?"

"They want me with one of their hottest stars. A kid named Aaron Troy."

Tristan's eyebrows popped up. "Can we search him online? I want to see what he looks like."

"I had a feeling you'd ask that." Gabe found the promo shot he'd saved to his phone. Aaron was nineteen, slim and twinky, with a head full of curly blond hair and a long, uncut cock. Not that said cock was getting anywhere near his ass, but he'd have to work a bit to suck it.

"He's cute," Tristan said.

"Notice anything else?"

He plucked the phone from Gabe's hand to study up close. "Eyebrow stud?"

"Nope."

"Is there a scar somewhere I don't see?"

"He looks like you."

Tristan squinted at the photo. "Oh. Oh! Damn, that's going to be hot to watch."

"I guess I have a type."

"That's not a bad thing." He gave the phone back. "So will you still be able to Skype while you're away?"

"I don't see why not. I'll miss not seeing you in person, though."

"It's only for a few days. We don't see each other every day as it is."

Gabe very badly wanted that to change in the future. The biggest question was when. He couldn't invite Tristan to live with him here. He definitely had to wait until the Debbie issue was sorted out, so Gabe had his own place again. Be it the house or an apartment, he wanted a home for himself and Tristan.

"What?" Tristan asked.

"What what?"

"You got all distant and dreamy for a second. Thinking about the hot ass waiting for you in New York?"

"Thinking about the hot ass sitting next to me."

"Anything in particular about it?"

Gabe decided to go for broke. "I'm thinking one day I'd like to do this all the time. Sleep with you. Wake up with you. For us to have a real life together."

"You mean that?" Tristan's blue eyes went watery. "For real? You want your life to be with me?"

"Of course I do."

"Even with all of the other hot guys you work with that don't come with built-in health issues and frustrating memory blips?"

"Hey." Gabe squeezed Tristan's hand. "Stop. I don't want any of the guys I work with. Never have, never will. And I went into this knowing full well about your baggage. I'm in, Tristan. Please stop doubting that."

"I'm sorry. Am I ruining this? Was this a moment?"

"It is a moment, and you're not ruining anything. Yes. I think about our future together a lot. I think about you being able to leave Benfield behind for good."

"I think about that too. Sometimes living anyplace else feels like a dream I'll never get to experience. Moments like this are vapor. Too thin to last for long, because what's real is that room covered in paper and my bad memory."

"Your memory is getting better. I remind you of things so rarely now, because you're able to figure it out yourself." Gabe didn't want to think about last week's seizure. He wanted to believe it had been an isolated incident, never to be repeated.

"It's a scary move. I mean, my parents pay for my care. What happens if I leave, and then I suddenly get worse? I can't afford a place like Benfield on my own, considering I've never had a job in my life."

"Really?" A tidbit about Tristan that Gabe hadn't known. "Not even in high school? Summers at college?"

Tristan blushed. "No. My parents are loaded, remember? They wanted me to focus on studying and shit, so they didn't make me get a job. They did, however, make me take summer classes, which kind of sucked."

"Summer school? Gross."

"Helped me learn how to speak fluent French and Spanish."

"You're kidding." The depth of things he still didn't know about Tristan kind of shocked him.

"I was supposed to start learning German the summer of the accident. I didn't retain much from the few classes I managed."

Accident.

"Tristan, why do you do that?"

"Do what?"

"Call it an accident." It bothered Gabe every single time he heard it, and he was done keeping quiet. "It wasn't an accident."

Tristan shrugged and leaned back in his stool. "Because I don't remember anything about it. It's like I wasn't even there. I could have been in a bad car wreck for all I really know."

"Noel would never lie to you about what happened."

"No, I know that. He knows it was a deliberate attack, and in my heart I believe him, but I don't know it. I guess thinking about it as an accident is easier than admitting someone intentionally tried to kill us both." Tristan's voice broke, and those big eyes were shining again.

Gabe stood up and tugged Tristan into his arms. He hated upsetting Tristan with the subject but he wasn't sorry he'd brought it up. "It wasn't an accident. You were bashed."

Tristan nodded, his face pressed against Gabe's neck. Warm breath came out in short pants, heating his skin.

"I need you to say it."

"I can't."

"Yes, you can."

Tristan made a soft, strangled sound, followed by a sob.

Shit.

"I've got you, sunshine," Gabe said. "You're safe. It's okay to say it."

"It wasn't an accident," Tristan whispered. Tears dampened Gabe's neck. "I was bashed. Goddammit."

"It's okay."

Gabe held on while Tristan got it all out, hating himself for bringing his boyfriend to tears, and hoping they were cathartic tears. Some terrible truths needed to be acknowledged and spoken out loud in order for a person to really heal. Tristan had more healing to do than most, and Gabe wanted him to have every possible tool to do so. Even if those tools hurt once in a while.

He whispered support and rubbed Tristan's back until he settled.

"You guys must be so sick of me sobbing like a girl all the time," Tristan said as he pulled back. His face was blotchy and his eyes were swollen, but he looked...different. A little more assured.

"Never. Tears don't make you weak. They make you human."

"Yeah, well, when was the last time you were seriously human through tears?"

Gabe didn't even have to think. "The second time Andrew broke my heart."

Tristan frowned. "Andrew?"

Thinking about Andrew didn't hurt like it used to, and Tristan deserved this story. "I met him when I was eighteen. He was thirty-three. I thought we were in love, but I was just sex to him. We'd been seeing each other for a year when I had a particularly nasty confrontation with my mother. I went to Andrew and told him about her. A few days later he dumped me over email."

"Fuck." Tristan grabbed his hands and squeezed. "What an asshole."

"Yes and no. I wasn't out yet, and I wanted so badly for someone to love and accept me that I saw more into our sex than was there. He wasn't out, either, and I was only ever a booty call to him. Anyway, a few years ago I ran into him at Big Dick's. We ended up fucking at my place. It was great, just like I remembered. Considering where I'd found him, I thought he'd finally come out. Afterward he took a phone call from his wife."

"Shit."

Gabe shrugged. "My own fault. But after that I was so upset I did some risky things, and ended up with a case of oral gonor-rhea. That woke me up to what I was doing. I met Jon and started porn not long after. Sex without the same risk."

"But that's not why you do porn now."

"No, now I do it so I can keep our bills paid. Helps with what waiting tables doesn't cover."

"Does your mother know? That you do porn?"

"Hell no. If anything is guaranteed to make her flip the fuck out, it's that. Besides, she'd find a way to make it about poor her, somehow. She's always the victim."

"I hate that you've had to deal with her for so long." Tristan ran a palm up his arm to his bicep. "But you did something, right? That seems familiar. You moved here?"

"Right. I moved here and I gave her three weeks to go to rehab or she's out."

"Good. You need to live for you."

"I am now." Living for himself and for Tristan.

Gabe was finally ready to believe in a happy future—the kind they both deserved so fucking much.

22

By Saturday evening Gabe was a special kind of exhausted and, for the first time in his life, bored with sex. Rumors that Stuart Rhodes was a perfectionist kind of director had not been exaggerated.

Gabe's arrival Thursday night had been a quiet affair of a late dinner and meeting both Stuart and his director of photography Lucy James. Stuart's home was a historical farmhouse in the middle of nowhere, with an ancient barn that had been the site for more than one Puppy Farm scene. The next morning, he met Aaron, who surprised him by only being five five. But he was an excitable ball of energy and very eager to work with Gabe.

Their first day had been spent videotaping their meeting, a lot of chatter, and then shooting promotional stills all over the property, including in the barn. Gabe was no model, and he'd never endured six hours of photography. He was beyond bored by the whole thing but Aaron kept him entertained with stories about other shoots and the models at Puppy Farm.

Filming the actual scene on Saturday was an experience in patience, muscle tone and endurance. From ten in the morning until seven at night, with two breaks for meals, before Stuart finally called it a wrap. They filmed more footage than could possibly be used in a thirty-minute video, changed locations multiple times and reshot several things from different angles.

More than his own exhaustion, Gabe felt for Aaron. The kid had taken it like a champ for the better part of six hours, and he never once complained. Gabe had mad respect for anyone who did this on the regular.

After he showered, Gabe collapsed onto his bed on the second floor of the farmhouse. The room was unusual in that it had a staircase in the corner that led to nowhere. It simply curved into the ceiling and stopped.

He hadn't managed to check his messages since their last break three hours ago. He'd sent a brief status update to Tristan, then deleted two missed calls from Debbie. She still called him, left no voice mails and hadn't responded to his ultimatum.

Two weeks left before she forced his hand.

A voice mail from an unknown number made his breath catch.

"Gabe, listen, it's Shane. Noel's being an asshole right now, so I had to get your number from Chet, who couldn't help but hit me up to work for him again. Anyway, that's not why I'm calling. Tristan had another seizure this afternoon."

A cold hand grabbed Gabe's heart and squeezed.

"He's fine. He was at Benfield when it happened so they're keeping an eye on him, and his doctor's on the way. Noel and I are here too, and Noel said something about Tristan telling him you were working out of state this weekend and not to bother you, but I had to tell you. I know Noel gets jealous over Tristan, but you're his boyfriend and you deserve to know. Text me when you get this."

Anxiety and rage warred inside of Gabe for a long, torturous moment. Another seizure was not good news in any way. Noel keeping it from him was something they'd address in person, and Gabe was hundreds of miles away with no car.

He texted Shane back with shaking fingers, somehow managing a clear message that he was figuring out how to get back.

Then he called the train station.

Tristan worked hard to orient himself. Sleep simply wouldn't let him go so he could wake up and find out why he felt so strange. Sluggish. Like he'd gone on a bender and woken up with all of his limbs asleep. The smell and bright lights told him he was in Benfield. Nearby musical sounds reminded him of a game Noel liked to play on his phone.

"Noel?" There. He got his mouth to work.

"Tris, hey."

Yeah, Noel was there. He tried to ask what was going on, but his tongue mashed up the words into nothing.

"You're okay. You had another seizure, that's why you feel weird."

"Shit. Gabe?"

"He's out of town working, remember?"

"He's on his way back." New voice. Familiar voice. Shane. Shane was there.

"What?" Noel asked. "You called him?"

"He deserved to know, whether he's working or not. He texted me a little while ago. He managed to get a train ticket back tonight."

Gabe. I want to see him so bad.

Gabe would make it all okay. He'd make the seizure less scary.

Tristan managed to peel his eyelids apart and keep them that way. Noel and Shane stood on the same side of his bed. Noel was in his uniform, which was weird. "Your clothes?"

Noel glanced down. "When I got the call, I changed into my

uniform so I could go straight to the station from here. I wanted to stay as long as I could."

"Which won't be for much longer," Shane said. "It's pushing ten."

Fucking weird overnight shift.

"Gabe's coming," Tristan said. It made Noel leaving okay. Plus he was in an assisted living center with nurses and a doctor on call. He was covered.

"Apparently," Noel said. "I talked to Dr. Fischer. He's prescribing the phenobarbital."

"Side effects bad." He couldn't remember them, only that he hadn't liked the idea. Something about sleeping.

"Seizures are dangerous, Tris."

"No shit. Don't remember having them."

"That's not unusual."

"Bet you said that last time."

Noel's lips twitched. "I did."

"Sorry I scared you."

"You didn't do it on purpose. None of this is your fault."

Tristan was beyond sick of hearing those words. He was certain he'd heard them more times that he'd forgotten over the years. No fault didn't remove the guilt of causing so much fear and concern for the people he loved.

"Do you need anything?" Shane asked. "I came in my own car, so I can stay or go to the store or whatever."

He managed a real smile for Shane. "You called Gabe. That's all I want right now."

"I'll chill until he gets here, then. It's gonna be a few hours."

"Okay." He and Shane weren't besties, but they were getting along better lately. Probably because Tristan didn't need so much of Noel's attention now that he had Gabe.

"I'll call in the morning to see how you feel," Noel said.

"How about I call you if I feel anything other than a hundred percent better?" Tristan countered. He didn't want Noel hovering. Not this time.

Noel's eyebrows went up, but he didn't argue. "Get a good night's sleep, okay?"

"I'll do my best."

Tristan ignored Noel and Shane's cutesy good-bye kisses and whispers. He didn't need Shane to stay. He also didn't want to be alone. Not until he felt less swimmy and more sure of himself. That would probably come with more rest, and all he wanted was to talk to Gabe. To hear Gabe reassure him that everything would be okay.

Once Noel was gone, Shane sat on the desk chair and said, "So now that your keeper has bounced, how do you really feel?"

Being honest with Shane was fine. Shane didn't hover over him like Noel. "Okay. Sluggish. I know I need sleep, but a tiny part of me is scared that if I close my eyes I won't wake up again."

"Understandable, given the circumstances. I can hang out if you want to take a nap until Gabe gets here."

Maybe it was an aftereffect of the seizure but Tristan couldn't seem to stop from saying what was on his mind. "Why are you being so nice to me?"

Shane blinked. "Because you're my friend? You're important to Noel, so you're important to me."

"Oh. Thanks. Ditto."

"It's pretty refreshing for me to walk into your room and you know who I am."

"It's cool knowing who you are too. Remembering names and details, and not just a vaguely familiar face." Like the very interesting detail that Shane had done porn with Gabe. Shane was drop-dead gorgeous with a dancer's body he knew how to use, but Tristan couldn't picture it. And he hadn't watched any of Shane's scenes yet—at least, he was pretty sure he hadn't. Nothing seemed familiar.

Shane's phone rang. "Hey, man." He listened. "Yeah, I'm still with him."

He held the phone out to Tristan.

Tristan took it. "Gabe?"

"Hey, sunshine," Gabe said. His deep voice rolled over Tristan and settled some of his anxiety. "How are you?"

"Exhausted. Hearing your voice helps."

"I'm glad."

"Noel went to work, but Shane is staying until you get here."

"Good. My train just left the station in New York. I'm about two and a half hours from the station in Ardmore, then maybe another hour to get back to Harrisburg."

"I can't wait up that long."

"You don't have to. Just know I'll be there when you wake up."

"Okay. Love you."

"Love you back."

After Gabe hung up, Tristan handed the phone over to Shane. "Thank you for telling Gabe."

"You're welcome," Shane said.

Tristan felt better after talking to Gabe, but he was also too scared to sleep, so he floundered for some kind of conversation. "Gabe and I watched one of his scenes together."

Shane dropped his phone. It hit the linoleum floor with a clatter. "Really? Together?"

"Sure. I wanted to see something he'd done. Or someone, I guess." Tristan grinned, amused by the confusion and surprise on Shane's face. "What? You and Noel never watched one of yours?"

"Not together. I mean, after I told Noel about it, he went through my gallery shots on his own. I don't know if he's ever actually watched a scene, though." His lips twisted. "Really? You guys did?"

"Oh yeah." Tristan had the vaguest recollection of that night. Mostly he remembered the emotions. "Best sex ever."

"Hey, if it works for you, go for it. I don't think Noel would be so eager, though. We don't really talk about it. It's my past. The old Shane."

"I get that. Noel is crazy private anyway. I'm amazed he's so decent to Gabe, considering you two have fucked each other."

Shane nearly dropped his rescued phone again. "Have you always been like this?"

"Been like what?"

"I don't know. Blunt?"

"Before the acc—" *No. That's wrong.* "Before the bashing, I was like this all the time. Drove Noel nuts."

"I bet. He loves seeing the old you coming back out."

"I love it more, believe me. I feel like I'm waking up after a long, uncomfortable nap. It's pretty great." He took in Shane's slouched shoulders and obvious fatigue. "I bet you're loving it too. I don't need as much of Noel's attention as I used to."

"Doesn't mean he isn't giving it to you anyway."

"I know. He's a creature of habit. It'll take a while for the mothering instinct to wear down to less obnoxious levels."

"Yeah, right, I'll hold my breath. I mean, I get he has power of attorney but he can step back a little bit."

Power of attorney. Power of attorney over what?

Tristan's gut sloshed with acid. "Shane, what does that mean? He has power of attorney over what?"

Shane's eyes popped wide, and his mouth fell open. "Shit, he didn't tell you, did he? I'm going to fucking kill him."

"Why?"

"I am not supposed to be the one telling you this." He looked so miserable that Tristan felt sorry for forcing the issue. But he had to know. "Your parents gave Noel power of attorney over your medical care. They didn't want to have to make those decisions anymore."

The magnitude of those words slammed down on Tristan like a crashing ocean wave, tossing him around and drowning him in grief and loss. His parents had cut ties with him in every way except financially. They probably had no clue he was on the drug trial, or that his memory was improving. They didn't know because they didn't fucking care.

His throat closed, and he swallowed hard against rising bile. "When?" was all he could force out.

"July."

"That was fucking months ago!" His chest tightened, and he rolled onto his side, his stomach already folding in on itself.

Shane shoved a trash can under his head in time to stop him from barfing on the floor. He coughed and heaved until he had nothing except tears and a sour taste in his mouth. The trash can went away, and then Shane came back with a wet washcloth and glass of water. The tender way he wiped Tristan's face and helped him swish out his mouth had more tears rolling down his cheeks.

"I'm so sorry, Tristan," Shane said. He seemed near tears himself. "I don't know why he didn't tell you sooner."

Tristan knew. Noel was doing what he always did—trying to protect Tristan from the realities of the big bad world—and he was fucking sick of it. Sick of Noel orchestrating his life and deciding who knew what. He couldn't know about the power of attorney. Gabe couldn't know he'd just had a seizure.

"Goddamn him," Tristan snapped. "He should have fucking told me when it happened."

"To be fair, your memory hadn't improved yet. He probably figured if he told you, you'd forget, and he'd have to keep doing it. Keep causing you this pain."

"No. I've been improving for weeks. He could have told me anytime and he chose not to. He couldn't be fucking bothered to tell me my parents wrote me completely out of their lives and no longer give a shit if I live or die. Fuck!"

"Tristan?" One of the night nurses stuck her head in from behind the half-closed door. Dark hair. Instant dislike. Debra. "What's going on?"

"Go away."

Shane got up and walked to the door. Tristan curled onto his side, away, not caring what he told her. Every single part of his body hurt, and he couldn't shake the pressing sense of betrayal. Noel had kept a huge secret from him.

How could he do this to me?

He wasn't really crying, but he couldn't seem to stop the tears that leaked from the corners of his eyes and rolled down his nose and cheek. Eventually Shane returned to that side of the bed.

"Can you go away?" Tristan asked. "And tell Noel not to visit me tomorrow."

Shane nodded. "Yeah. I'm really sorry."

"Me too."

He tried to stay awake for a while, but he was too exhausted and emotionally wrung out to keep his eyes open for long. Eventually they closed, and he sent a silent prayer that when he opened them again, Gabe would be the first thing he saw.

Debra didn't seem surprised at all to see Gabe strolling into Benfield at two thirty in the morning. Noel had probably warned her that Gabe was going to show up at some ungodly hour, and bless the staff for allowing visits whenever a resident needed the comfort of a friend or relative.

The hallway lights were dim and silent, and his sneakers squeaked on the linoleum floor. Tristan's door was almost completely shut. He pushed it open far enough to slip inside. The bathroom light was on, the door half-closed, casting enough light for him to find his way around. Tristan lay curled on his left side, away from him, a blanket tucked up around his shoulders.

Shane had called him while he was still on the train, and what he'd said had enraged Gabe. Finding out your parents had severed all ties to you was one thing, but finding out from your best friend's boyfriend? Unforgivable. If Gabe had ever needed a reason to be pissed at Noel, he finally had one.

If he tries to defend himself over this, I will punch him in the fucking face.

Even asleep, Tristan looked unhappy. His eyes were scrunched, his lips pinched. Gabe hated waking him. He needed his sleep after the seizure. So he quietly moved the desk chair next to the bed and sat.

As if sensing his arrival, Tristan grunted. His eyelids slowly worked themselves open, and Tristan blinked bloodshot eyes at him. Eyes that went briefly wide.

"Hey, sunshine," Gabe said.

Tristan's gaze went distant, his mind working to orient himself and what had recently happened. Gabe saw the moment it clicked. Tristan's entire face fell, overtaken by the weight of grief and betrayal.

"I know what happened," Gabe said. "Shane told me all of it."

When Tristan didn't speak, Gabe toed off his sneakers and climbed into bed with him. He curled up behind Tristan so he could wrap his arms around his boyfriend and hold him tight. Shield him from the world for just a little while. Tristan trembled, his hands wrapped around Gabe's.

Gabe didn't know what else to do, so he held on and let Tristan work through whatever was going on inside his head.

Even though he'd napped on the train, fatigue stole back in and Gabe let his eyes close. Tristan stilled.

The next time Gabe opened his eyes, sunlight was streaming in through the room's only window. His neck was sore from sleeping in one position for so long, but it was worth it. Tristan's hold on his hands had loosened. He freed his right hand and rubbed Tristan's shoulder.

Tristan inhaled a long breath, then exhaled deeply. "Time is it?"

"No idea." Gabe didn't care. If Tristan had missed breakfast, he'd take him out somewhere. His entire day was free, since he hadn't expected to leave New York until this afternoon.

"I feel like I've got a hangover, only I don't drink anymore."

"Not surprised. You had a shitty night all around."

"I know I did. I feel it, but the details are fuzzy."

Gabe explained the seizure, and then Shane's big reveal.

Tristan grunted. "Yeah, shitty doesn't quite cover it. I don't know who I hate more right now. Noel or my parents."

"You don't hate Noel. You're furious and you feel betrayed, but you don't hate him."

"I guess."

"And you're allowed to be pissed at him, Tristan. What he did was cruel, no matter what his intentions were."

"Yeah." He let out a bitter laugh. "I kind of feel sorry for Shane. It wasn't on him to tell me."

"Shane and Noel can work that out between themselves. I'm only worried about you."

"I was so upset I think I threw up. I'm not sure."

"It's okay." He kissed the side of Tristan's neck. "I want you to know one thing, okay?"

Tristan wiggled around so he was facing Gabe. His eyes were swollen and his face sleep rumpled, but he was attentive.

"Your parents aren't worth getting upset over," Gabe said. "They signed away the chance to ever know the beautiful, kind, vibrant, talented man that I have the great privilege to love and call my boyfriend. They lost something huge, and I don't want you to ever feel like you deserved it or you did something wrong. All you deserve is to be loved. I love you. And Noel made a huge mistake, but he loves too."

After a long moment of silence, Tristan smiled. "Thank you for that. You're right. God, why do parents have to be so complicated?"

I wish I knew.

"Come on," Gabe said. "Let's get you up and showered. I'm taking you home for the day."

Tristan's smile widened. "Really? You don't have to work?" His smile dimmed. "Shit, your shoot. You didn't have to cancel anything, did you?"

"No, we finished last night. The only thing I missed today was brunch."

"Oh good. Can you tell me about it?"

"How about I fill you in over breakfast?"

"Okay." Tristan pressed a gentle kiss to his lips. "Thank you. For being here."

"I'll always be here when you need me, Tristan. I promise."

After Tristan disappeared into his bathroom to shower, Gabe checked his messages. He had a text from Noel: *Please tell T I am so sorry & I really want to talk to him.*

Gabe thought a moment so he didn't respond out of anger. He replied: *No. He'll contact you when he's ready.*

Then he let his petty side out to play and added: *Asshole.*

For once, Tristan was going to control his own life and make his own decisions. He'd talk to Noel when he was damned good and ready, not because Noel wanted to assuage a guilty conscience. Tristan fucking deserved that and more.

23

Thanksgiving ended up being far more awkward than Gabe expected. Tristan didn't ask him to uninvite Shane and Noel, but he actively avoided them the entire two hours the pair spent in the house. Gabe had never seen Tristan's inner Angry Bitch until now, and he kind of felt sorry for Noel. Noel was visibly miserable over Tristan ignoring him for the last five days.

Gabe didn't interfere, though, and neither did Shane. This was for Tristan and Noel to work out.

After everyone ate and their guests left, Gabe and Tristan spent the rest of the day in the den, watching Christmas movies with Bear and Dad. All of the early, black and white classics, a lot of which Tristan had never seen. Exposing him to the cozy charm of *White Christmas* was a lot of fun and smoothed out the feathers that Noel had ruffled by showing up.

Gabe's biggest surprise came the next morning when Bear knocked on his door and said he had a visitor downstairs. He left Tristan sleeping in bed, threw on some clothes and padded down to the living room, incredibly curious who was bothering him at eight o'clock in the morning.

Debbie was sitting on the sofa, her hands folded in her lap.

She was dressed, her hair smooth, and he swore she was wearing makeup. She smiled brightly when she saw him.

"I know it's a day late, but happy Thanksgiving, Gabriel," she said.

"Uh, yeah, you too."

Bear hovered near the arch that led into the kitchen, and Gabe appreciated the backup.

"I came over to ask you something," she said.

"Okay."

"Will you drive me to Baybrook House?"

Gabe nearly fell over as the weight of the request smacked him in the gut. She wanted to go to rehab. She wanted him to drive her there so he knew she'd go through with it. He couldn't process anything in that moment, so he settled on staring. Waiting for the shock to wear off and let him react.

"I've hated these two weeks, you cutting me out," Debbie said. "I know I've screwed up beyond the point of forgiveness, but I love you so much. I want to do this. I want to give you a chance to love me again."

His heart twisted. "I do love you, Mom. That's why I did what I did and said what I said."

Her eyes glittered with tears. "So you'll do it? Take me to New Jersey?"

"Of course. Yes." His eyes stung and he blinked hard. "When?"

"As soon as you have time. I've been sober for the last eight days. It wasn't easy, believe me, but I stopped drinking. I took some stuff to a pawn shop like you said. I even vacuumed the entire house yesterday."

He laughed at that, because he couldn't remember the last time she'd used the vacuum. "I am so proud of you. You have no idea."

She stood, still grinning. "You don't know how much I needed to hear you say that. I'm doing this for me, but it's for you too. I'd rather be a part of your life than hold onto old grudges." She glanced at Bear. "I'm sorry, Bernard. So sorry for how I've treated you both."

Bear nodded.

"We'll go today," Gabe said. He wasn't giving her a chance to change her mind.

"Don't you work at noon?" Bear asked.

"I'll call in sick. I haven't called in a sick day since I started there."

"Don't put yourself out for me," Debbie said.

"He's been putting himself out for you for years," Bear snapped.

Debbie flinched. "I never asked him to."

"But you never thanked him for it, did you?"

Gabe hated hearing Bear turn his temper onto Debbie, but he also knew better than to get in the middle when his parents went to war.

"I know I was wrong," Debbie said. She seemed stuck between contrite and annoyed—two things that never ended well with her. "I'm a terrible mother, okay? Is that what you want me to say?"

"No, it's not. I want you to apologize to our boy for how you treated him. He's worked his ass off taking care of you. He might as well have set the money on fire for all the good it's done him."

"I'm sorry—"

"Stop apologizing to me, woman! Apologize to your son."

"Do not order me around. You lost that right when you screwed another man behind my back."

Gabe retreated slowly, intent on the stairs. He didn't want to witness this. Good news was slowly disintegrating into reruns of old drama, and he was tired of it.

"Right, let's make sure we turn this into another episode of Poor Debbie," Bear said. "This is supposed to be about Gabriel, not you."

"It is about him."

"Then act like it."

Gabe's back hit the banister. A warm hand came down on his shoulder. He looked up, expecting Dad. Tristan blinked down at him, worry all over his face. God, he didn't want Tristan to hear this. Tristan didn't need any more ugly in his life.

Debbie crossed her arms as she turned to face Gabe. She froze, her attention past him. On Tristan. Her demeanor changed instantly, from furiously rigid to openly welcoming.

"Who's this?" she asked.

Bear appeared in Gabe's line of sight while still keeping his distance from Debbie. He frowned, clearly unhappy that Tristan had witnessed their family dysfunction.

"My boyfriend Tristan," Gabe replied.

"Hello," Tristan said weakly. His hand squeezed Gabe's shoulder.

"Hi," she replied. "I'm Debbie Harper, Gabriel's mother."

No fucking shit.

No one said anything, and the awkwardness level of the entire situation rose several notches.

"Anyway, I stopped by to give Gabriel some good news," Debbie said. "So I guess I'll leave."

"Pack whatever clothes you want to take with you," Gabe said. "I'll be by before lunch to pick you up."

"Okay. I love you."

"Yeah."

Her departure settled the tension around Gabe, and he sagged against the banister.

Tristan came down and cupped his cheek with one hand. "Are you okay?"

"I'm not sure. I think so." He pressed into Tristan's touch. "She's agreed to go to rehab, and she asked me to drive her there."

"Really?" Tristan yanked him right into a tight hug. "That's great news! Oh my God." He pulled back. "Wait, are you okay with driving her?"

"Yeah, I am. Honestly, it's the only way I trust that she'll get there."

"I don't blame you."

"Be careful with her," Bear said. His tone was flat, his expression hard to decipher. "Don't let her manipulate you."

"I won't," Gabe replied. "But I need to see this through."

"I know you do. You're a good kid."

Bear wandered off.

"I guess I should take a shower and get ready to go," Tristan said.

Gabe hated it every single time Tristan had to leave. "I would have had to work today, anyway. Paulo will be pissed at me for calling out on Black Friday, but this is more important." The trip to the rehab facility would take about five hours round trip, and he'd come home mentally exhausted. The idea of coming home to Tristan held so much appeal the words were out before he could think. "You can stay here while I'm gone. Watch TV or read or something."

Tristan tilted his head, considering the offer. "Do you think your dads will mind?"

"No. They both really like you."

"Then I'll stay. I like your room. It's familiar. It's everything I remember so clearly before the acc—the bashing."

Gabe grinned. "Then stay. Eat. Hang out."

"Awesome. And now I know I can be here when you get home. I doubt this is going to be a fun road trip."

"No, it won't. But I hope it's worth it in the long run."

"So do I."

Gabe left on his errand after a quick breakfast of scrambled eggs and bacon. Tristan savored every morsel of the homemade food. The meals at Benfield were decent enough, but it was cooked in mass quantities. Something about watching three eggs being whisked at a time just made them taste better.

Tristan made himself comfortable in Gabe's room and started channel surfing. His habit of jumping from one thing to next had always driven his roommates nuts. Especially Chris. He was "pick a channel and watch it", while Tristan flipped to the next program once a commercial started.

He hated commercials.

They even had commercials for programs online, which didn't seem quite fair but whatever.

A home renovation show with hot twin brother hosts caught his attention until the first commercial break. He hopped over to a game show, and then a sitcom he didn't recognize. Rinse, repeat. Another change landed him on a program with a blond cop in uniform who made him instantly think of Noel.

His heart ached with how much he missed Noel. He also burned with anger over the secret Noel had kept from him. He couldn't avoid Noel forever. Their friendship meant too much to him to ruin it over this. But he was making a point, damn it.

I'm also being kind of childish.

Problem was he didn't have a cell phone. He needed to get one now that he was spending more time away from Benfield. Even a cheap pay-by-the-month phone, so he didn't feel so disconnected when he was alone.

He checked the front cover of his latest notebook—something he still carried and took notes in, although less frequently. He was able to recall so much without help, but some habits would be hard to break. The notebook was a touchstone of sorts. And Noel's cell number was written in it.

Tristan took the notebook downstairs. Bear was watching TV in the den, his feet up on a big ottoman.

"Bear?"

He immediately muted the sound. "What's up, kiddo?"

"I was wondering if I could use the phone. I need to call someone."

"Sure. Room to the left of Gabe's is our office. There's a land-line in there."

"Thank you."

"Sure thing. You gonna make amends with your friend?"

"Yes." Something about Debbie's visit had inspired Tristan to forgive. "It's time. I don't want to keep punishing him."

"Good boy."

The unexpected praise warmed something inside of Tristan. Knowing a parent was proud of him for something as simple as ending an argument meant the world to him. It was something his own parents would never give him, and he was okay with that. He'd been accepted into Gabe's family without hesitation.

The door next to Gabe's was shut, and he felt weird opening it, even with permission. The office wasn't quite what he expected. Two recliners with lap trays for computers. A bookcase full of all kinds of books. Mostly queer books, from nonfiction to fiction. And the walls. Painted a pale blue, they were covered in framed photographs of men in various stages of dress. All of them were artsy, none pornographic.

"I could work in an office like this," he said to the beauties all around him.

The phone was shaped like a pair of red lips, and it made Tristan laugh out loud. He shut the door, sat on one of the recliners and dialed Noel's number.

On the fifth ring, he'd resigned himself to voice mail. It was an unknown number, after all. Then, "Officer Noel Carlson."

The sound of his voice made Tristan's heart skip. "Hey."

"Tristan? Hey, how are you?" His relieved, eager tone rein-forced the decision to call.

"I'm good. I'm sorry I was such a jerk at Thanksgiving."

"Don't apologize. I know you're mad at me, and I do not

blame you. Not even a little bit. I'm so sorry I didn't tell you about the power of attorney."

"You don't have to explain why you didn't before the trial started working, but after?"

Noel was silent for a long while. "Same reason as always, I guess. I wanted to protect you. I knew finding out that your parents wanted out would hurt you."

"Yeah, well, finding out from Shane hurt even more. He assumed I knew."

"I know. It wasn't his fault, and he was justifiably pissed at me for a few days. I put both of you in that position, and I'm sorry."

"You don't have to protect me anymore, Noel. Not from anything, but especially important stuff. We've never kept secrets from each other, and I hate that you kept this from me."

"I know. All I can say is I'm sorry."

Tristan harrumphed. "That's not all you can say."

Another pause. "I'll never lie to you again?"

"Bingo. Now once more with feeling."

"I swear I'll never lie to you about your life, or keep life-altering secrets from you. Hand to God."

"That's better. Okay. I forgive you."

Noel let out an audible sigh. "Thank you. I've missed you."

"Me too."

"So why'd you finally decide to forgive me?"

"Gabe's mother."

"Huh?"

Tristan briefly explained the situation without giving away too many details. It wasn't really his family drama to share, after all. "Gabe's wanted this for so long, and his mother was brave enough to try. I realized some things are more important than grudges."

"I'm glad. For us and for Gabe. I mean it."

"Thanks."

"So if he's driving to New Jersey, where are you? I don't know the number you're calling from."

"I'm at his dads' house. He offered to let me stay for the day, instead of dumping me back at Benfield. How could I turn that down? They have way better cable here."

Noel's laughter rumbled over the line. "Sounds like you're settling in."

"I kind of am. His dads are awesome, especially Bear. I'd ask Bear to adopt me if I wasn't fucking his son."

This time Noel sputtered. "Jesus, don't do that when I'm drinking."

"Ha! And I wasn't even trying for a spit take. What are you drinking?"

"Iced tea. Coffee hasn't finished brewing yet."

Friday midmorning. Noel was off on Thursday nights, but he usually slept in when preparing for going back to work Friday night. "I woke you up."

"It's fine. I'll take a nap later before I go in. I'd rather do this than sleep."

"Good answer."

"So do I have your permission to visit on Sunday like usual?"

"Of course you do, dummy. And can you do me a favor? Tell Shane thanks for taking care of me Saturday when I freaked out."

"He told me about that." Tristan could hear the cringe in Noel's words. "I'll pass along the message."

"Cool." Shane and Saturday brought back a sliver of their conversation. "So how come you and Shane haven't watched one of his scenes together?"

"I—what? Really, Tristan?"

"It's a legit question. Me and Gabe watched one of his together, and it was totally hot."

"Okay, two things to end this particular conversation. One, I'm not you. Two, Shane is not Gabe."

Noel code for "drop the subject, I don't want to talk about it".

"Duh and duh," Tristan replied, "but I get the point."

"If you're watching his scenes together, it must really not bother you that he still does porn."

"It really doesn't. I mean, I know he doesn't want to do it forever. And if his mom can get clean and start supporting herself again, maybe he can quit if he wants. Plus, it's not like he won't still get residuals from his old stuff."

"This is true."

"Doesn't Shane get those?"

"No. He was always paid upfront."

"He needed the money because his brother was sick." A month ago, Tristan wouldn't have remembered that. He wasn't sure when was the last time he'd been told. Knowing it and recalling it was enough.

"Right."

"Then I guess it makes sense you and Shane kind of ignore it. So do you guys watch other porn?"

"Your obsession with our sex life is disturbing," Noel said with laughter in his tone. "I've missed it."

"I know, right?"

"So you want to hear about a call we responded to the other night that involved a turkey on someone's roof?"

"Definitely." Tristan relaxed into the recliner, more than ready for one of Noel's fun work stories, delighted to have his best friend back.

The drive to New Jersey wasn't as painful as Gabe expected it to be. He and Debbie spoke very little. They listened to the radio, occasionally commenting on the countryside. She fidgeted a lot, which didn't surprise him. This was a huge step for her. If she left rehab before the four weeks were over, she was done. She wasn't coming back into the house.

Shit's finally real and she knows it.

His phone's GPS got them there with no fuss. A white gate protected a long, winding driveway that led to a huge white building in the middle of a well-tended field. Splotches of trees and frozen flowerbeds were coated with a thin dusting of snow. He followed signs to Inpatient Drop-Off under a carport. Big glass doors hid whatever was inside.

Debbie stared out the windshield with wide eyes. "How can you afford a place like this?"

No way was he telling her about Chet's generosity. She'd probably blame herself for Gabe accepting charity, or something. "It's taken care of. Don't worry about it."

"Gabriel—"

"I mean it. All you need to think about is getting better."

Gabe double-parked and shut off the engine.

"You're coming in?" Debbie asked.

"Yes. We're both seeing this through."

He got her suitcase from the trunk. She hesitated before taking that first step toward the front doors. He followed, knowing how hard this was, and so grateful to see her going on her own steam. She straightened her shoulders right before the doors slid open on a track.

The foyer had white stone floors, blue walls and a simple wooden admittance desk in the center. No chairs, no magazines. Nothing to suggest people were kept waiting. A petite brunette behind the desk smiled brightly at them.

"Welcome," she said. "My name is Alice. Have you come to begin your journey with us today?"

"Um, yes," Debbie replied. "My name's Deborah Harper. You're expecting me."

Alice typed something into a computer. "Yes, we are. Your room is ready for you, Ms. Harper. I need to fill out some paperwork, and then we'll get you settled."

"Okay."

Gabe waited through the paperwork, which Debbie completed with amazing calm.

To him, Alice said, "I'm sorry, but after this point, Ms. Harper won't be allowed visitors for the first fourteen days of our program."

"I know," Gabe said. He'd practically memorized the pamphlet before giving it to his mother. He turned to Debbie, whose eyes were wet. "You can do this, Mom. I know you can."

"You believing in me is everything, Gabriel," Debbie said.

She didn't try to hug him, and he was glad. He couldn't remember the last time they'd shared a genuine hug, and he didn't want their first to be here. He waited until a pair of double doors swung shut behind Debbie and Alice, and then he left.

The drive home was a blur of conflicting emotions, and finding Tristan napping on his bed was the very best thing to come home to. Gabe kicked off his shoes and curled up behind Tristan, pulling him close. Tristan snuffled, then settled.

For the first time in a long time, Gabe truly believed everything was going to be all right.

24

Tristan was a giant bundle of nerves by the time they pulled up in front of Bear and Richard's house on Monday night. Gabe had decided to keep living there while his mother was in rehab, and Tristan was all for it. He'd been to the other house once, and the place was depressing. Plus he loved seeing Gabe's dads.

Shane had picked him up from Benfield for Gabe's birthday outing at Big Dick's. Shane was on the schedule to dance tonight, so he was dropping him off and heading over. Tristan would ride to the club with Gabe. The only person he wished was with them was Noel, but he had to work. He'd yet to manage seeing Shane dance at the club.

Tristan clutched his carefully wrapped package to his chest as he walked toward the house. He wasn't nervous about going to the club. That excited him to no end. He couldn't wait to dance with Gabe.

He was scared about the gift he was giving to Gabe. He needed Gabe to love it, and he really hoped he hadn't fucked up by enlisting Bear's help. No matter how many times Bear had said Gabe would love it, Tristan wouldn't believe it until it happened.

Gabe met him at the door, and Tristan resisted the very real urge to drool. His facial scruff had grown out a little bit, and he wore a black sleeveless tee over black jeans. The entire package made Tristan feel a little basic in his blue jeans and shimmery purple tee.

"Hey, sunshine," Gabe said, all smiles. He planted a hearty kiss on Tristan that made him want to drag Gabe upstairs.

"Happy birthday," Tristan said.

"Thanks." He let him inside the warmth of the house so he could shut the door.

Tristan clutched the gift tighter, his nerves jumping all over the place. "Are your dads here?"

"They both left for the club already. I'm sure they're scheming the best way to embarrass me tonight."

He hooked his thumb in one of Gabe's belt loops. "So we're alone?"

"Don't tempt me if you want to go out to dinner. We have to be at the club by ten, Bear's orders."

"Damn."

Gabe traced a finger down the front of Tristan's shirt. "Think of the anticipation for when we get home tonight."

"I don't know if I'll be able to wait with that outfit you're wearing. I may have to drag you into the bathroom with favors."

Gabe licked his lower lip. "I've never been with anyone in there."

"Never found anyone to take?"

"Not exactly." For a moment, he seemed uncomfortable and Tristan regretted bringing it up. "I'm the owners' son, so I didn't... I don't know, I didn't want to look like a cliché."

"Oh." Tristan didn't remember it, but he'd read his notebooks enough recently to know that he'd gone into that bathroom once, very intent on a hookup, only for it all to end badly. On the plus side, that night was how he met Gabe.

Does that make me a cliché?

"Hey, I'm not judging you or anyone else who goes in there," Gabe said. "It's just how I think of me, as an owner's son. Everyone else is free to do what makes them happy."

The explanation didn't stop Tristan from feeling like an idiot for suggesting the bathroom hookup in the first place. "Okay."

"You sure?"

"Yes." *No. Whatever. It's my insecurity.* "I brought you a birthday present."

Gabe's sly smile went along well with his quick grab of Tristan's ass. "I know."

"A different present." He held out the oblong package. "Happy birthday."

"I'm intrigued." Gabe accepted the brown paper-wrapped object with care, because it was a little heavy. The size and shape were reminiscent of a large board game, but that definitely wasn't what was inside.

He carried the package into the living room and sat on the sofa with it in his lap. Tristan hung off to the side, ready for his boyfriend to either love it or break it in horror. Gabe slowly peeled back the taped corners, as detail-oriented in unwrapping as he was with eating, and the pace was killing Tristan. He rocked on his heels, hands locked behind his back.

Gabe finally had all of the tape undone, and he whipped off the sheet of paper in one smooth motion. The wood frame was upside down, so he had to flip it over to see the final product. He froze, and Tristan couldn't breathe. Gabe stared.

And stared.

Fuck, he hates it.

Weeks ago, as soon as he learned when Gabe's birthday was, he'd enlisted Bear to find a dozen different photos of Gabe, ranging in age from infant to present day, plus a few others. Tristan had sketched each of the images into a kind of infinity loop, with the center Gabe as he was today. In the middle of one loop he'd sketched Debbie, and in the other Bear and

Richard. His parents. The people who'd made him the man he was.

Tristan had used colored pencils to fill the piece with as much detail as possible, and then used his allowance to have it professionally framed.

Gabe stared at it for so long that Tristan's cheeks flushed, and his heart slammed into his ribs.

I fucked this up.

And then Gabe finally raised his head. Twin streams of tears ran down both cheeks. His expression was so innocent, so young and enamored, that Tristan didn't know what to do or say.

"This is..." Gabe's voice broke. He never floundered for words. Never. "It's priceless, Tristan, thank you."

All of Tristan's panic evaporated, leaving pure joy behind. "Really?"

"Yes. It's so beautiful I can't even..." He held it gently by the sides of the frame, as if he expected it to shatter under the slightest pressure. "I love it."

"Oh good." Tristan sat next to him. "I was terrified you'd hate it."

"Never. You are so talented. Shit, you could make this into an actual business. Take commissions to do art like this for other people."

The idea had never really occurred to Tristan. He loved drawing. He wasn't very good at much else, and finding a regular job would be difficult with his limitations. Working for himself was a good way to stop relying on his parents for money. To finally be independent.

"I wouldn't know how to start," Tristan said.

"A website, definitely, and maybe become a member of some artsy sites online. We can figure it all out together. And my friend Jon is pretty savvy with computers. He might be able to help."

Tristan's mind was spinning with the possibilities. "I wouldn't know what to charge."

"We'll figure it all out. You have to factor in your expenses, the cost of framing, the time spent, all of that stuff goes into pricing." Gabe carefully placed the art on the coffee table, then yanked Tristan into a tight hug. "Thank you so much for this."

"You're welcome." Tristan inhaled the spice of his aftershave and the deeper musk of Gabe himself.

They stood like that for a while, enjoying the simplicity of a hug. He'd done good. Gabe loved his present. And he had an idea for making his own money. Tristan couldn't remember being so deliriously happy in his life.

Gabe's stomach rumbled, and they both laughed. "Guess that's our cue to head out to dinner," he said.

"I could definitely eat. I'll need the energy to burn off later on the dance floor."

"And even later when we get home."

"Yes, please."

Gabe chose Fire House Restaurant on Second Street because he'd heard only great things about it from acquaintances. Multiple floors of dining in a renovated firehouse was something he wanted to experience, and the food he and Tristan ordered was amazing. After sharing a bowl of their crab, spinach, artichoke dip, Gabe had feasted on an eight-ounce filet with a crab cake. Tristan had teased him about his serious case of crabs, and Gabe nearly inhaled his Coke. Tristan ordered the Tuscan lasagna. They tasted off each other's plates, and it was all fantastic.

He could have eaten those crab cakes all day long, but the club was waiting, and they were pushing it in terms of getting there on time. Gabe could have skipped and been happy, but this was for Tristan and his dads.

They made it to Big Dick's at five after ten, which wasn't

terribly late. Bear still made a show about tapping his watch when he waved them both inside. Bear wasn't decked out in a hula shirt or anything, and that gave Gabe a sliver of hope that the night would progress as usual for a Monday.

His hopes were dashed the instant he stepped inside the club. Walsh, one of the other bouncers, immediately shoved him into a blue Hawaiian shirt. Tristan willingly put on a matching yellow one, and they both got red leis. Everyone in the place had leis of some color or other. Gabe laughed out loud at the adorable dorkishness of the entire thing.

"Holy shit, look at the dancers," Tristan said.

In the back of the room on raised platforms, six dancers gyrated to the music wearing extremely short grass skirts and coconut bras. Shane was easy to pick out, his movements as precise as they were spontaneous. The guy had serious dance moves, that was for damned sure.

"Birthday boy! Birthday boy!" The chorus rose from behind the bar. Dad, Pax and Nicky were all back there, making drinks as quickly as they could be ordered.

Gabe flipped them all off, then steered Tristan toward the thick of the dancers. Frequent calls of "Happy birthday, man!" and "Yo, birthday guy!" made him suspect that Bear had told everyone to keep an eye out for the tall guy in the ugly blue shirt, because Gabe didn't know any of them.

A few of the regulars he greeted with hugs and kisses. He introduced Tristan to them, all the while holding Tristan's hand in an iron grip. Tristan was his, and he didn't want anyone thinking otherwise and trying to poach.

Tristan decided they'd gone far enough. He tugged hard on Gabe's hand, spinning him around to come hip to hip with his boyfriend. Gabe draped both arms over Tristan's shoulders. Tristan grabbed his waist, and together they danced. They swayed, groped, frotted and kissed for the world to see, because they loved each other and this was perfect. It was everything

Gabe had ever wanted, Tristan moving in his arms, enjoying the life he'd been blessed with.

Gabe acknowledged more birthday shouts as they moved deeper into the night, pausing once in a while for water breaks at the bar. Gabe didn't feel like drinking tonight. He was already high on Tristan, and that was all he needed.

At midnight—Gabe knew because he'd just glanced at the clock behind the bar during their latest water break—the music faded away. A small uproar came from the crowd. Dad stood on the platform next to Shane and Cory, and he had a microphone.

"Oh shit, can I hide now?" Gabe said.

Tristan followed his gaze, then busted out in delighted laughter. "Oh no, you're staying right here, birthday boy."

"Will my son please find his way to the center of the dance floor?" Dad said, his voice booming over the loudspeakers.

A few people hooted.

Gabe wanted to die. He decided to drag Tristan along with him for moral support. A small hole appeared for them to stand in, and all eyes were on them. Despite knowing thousands of people saw him fucking on their computers, being the center of attention like that made Gabe's stomach churn with nerves.

"I know you hate being fussed over," Dad said, "but this is a milestone birthday. You've hit the quarter century mark, my boy, so I'm going to fuss. I'm also going to embarrass the hell out of you, so enjoy the ride."

"I'll get you for this," Gabe shouted.

Dad gave him a thumbs-up, then signaled to someone.

Music streamed over the speakers, a slow and sensual beat. The crowd to his left parted, and a drag queen decked out like Marilyn Monroe sashayed slowly toward them. She held a microphone up to her red, red lips and sang a slow, breathy rendition of "Happy Birthday" that reminded him of the one the real Marilyn did for JFK. She trailed satin glove-covered hands across Gabe's shoulders while she sang, and she even spared a wink for Tristan.

The song was short, but Gabe's hopes for brief torture were dashed when "Marilyn" segued right into "I Wanna Be Loved By You".

The crowd ate it up. Even Tristan seemed enamored by the performance, and Gabe had to admit, she had a great voice. He didn't know who she was behind the makeup, but damn.

As the song ended, her audience roared. Cheers and applause exploded. She leaned in without the mike and said, "I'd offer to take you into the bathroom for a quickie, honey, but it looks like you've got a sweet something. Congrats and happy birthday."

Gabe laughed. "Thanks. You're really good."

"Don't I know it?"

"Marilyn" bowed for her audience, and then melted into the crowd. The regular dance music came back up, and everything returned to normal. He and Tristan swung back into the beat.

"That was fucking hot," Tristan said. The half chub he was rubbing against Gabe's thigh punctuated that statement.

"Yeah it was."

A little more dancing and Gabe's cock was fully erect and pressing tightly against his jeans. Tristan was beauty in motion, his eyes so clear and shining, his mouth open and smiling. So fucking amazing that Gabe was seriously considering breaking his no bathroom sex rule.

Except the bathroom wasn't the only place they could go to be alone for a little while.

"Come with me," he said to Tristan. Gabe took his hand and led him off the dance floor.

Dad was back behind the bar when they passed, and he winked at them both. Gabe flipped him off as he led Tristan through the doors marked Employees Only.

"Where are we going?" Tristan asked.

"There are a few perks to being the son of the owners."

"Such as back room access?"

"Yup."

They passed the break room and the kitchen, which was closing down for the night. Usually no one paid him any mind. The staff was used to seeing him. But they weren't used to seeing him with someone else, so he got a few curious looks.

Beyond the kitchen was a narrow winding staircase that led up to Dad's office. He and Mario did all of the club's major business up there, and while Gabe had no managerial duties, he'd still been given the code to the lock pad on the door. And he knew that his parents kept a supply of condoms and lube stashed in one of the filing cabinets.

"I feel like I'm walking up the stairs of some kind of castle tower," Tristan said, his voice a harsh whisper in the echoing stairwell.

"About to be ravished by a handsome prince?"

"Yes, please."

The stairs ended on a small landing with two doors. One was to a private bathroom—his entire life, Richard Brightman had a phobia of public restrooms, so he'd built one for himself and select others on the second floor. The other was the office door. Gabe punched in the code then turned the handle.

"You're going to ravish me in your dads' office?" Tristan asked. "That's so fucking hot."

"Best I could do, since the kitchen crew is still here." He turned on the light, tugged Tristan inside then shut the door. It auto-locked so he didn't have to do anything else except pull Tristan into his arms. "I'm going to bend you over the desk, put my fingers in your ass and then give you the hottest quickie of your life."

Tristan licked his lips. "Oh hell yes."

Gabe silenced him with a hard kiss that Tristan returned with equal force. This wasn't going to be soft and sensual. This was going to be a full-on fast fuck, and he loved that Tristan was very much on board with it. He kissed Tristan across the spacious room to the walnut desk, tongue delving deeply into Tristan's mouth, licking and stroking. Filling his senses with Tristan's taste and smell.

Their cocks rubbed together, heightening Gabe's awareness of his boyfriend and his very real need to fuck him. To plunge hard and deep into his body. To feel Tristan tight around his cock, shaking with pleasure and pleading to come. Gabe loved coming inside of Tristan. Didn't matter if Tristan had already shot. He let Gabe go until Gabe found his own release.

One day, when porn is behind me, I'll shoot inside him for real.

The thought forced a growl from deep inside of Gabe. A possessive, alpha growl that showed he knew what he wanted and what was his.

Tristan moaned, and Gabe swallowed the sound. Gabe spun Tristan around so fast that Tristan planted both palms to keep from falling sideways. Gabe undid his belt and jeans, then shoved everything to his ankles, baring Tristan's ass and legs. Christ, he loved spreading those pale cheeks and driving Tristan mad with his tongue. Rimming him to the edge and then stopping before he fell over.

Not tonight.

Gabe found the stash of condoms and lube sachets in the storage cabinet on the far wall. Certain supplies were kept under lock and key so the staff didn't help themselves too much. Tristan held position, already panting with anticipation.

"You are so fucking hot, standing like that," Gabe said. "Waiting to be fucked."

Tristan cocked his hip a bit, showing off his straining cock. "Less talking, more fucking."

"You got it, sunshine."

Gabe shoved his own jeans and briefs down to midthigh, just far enough to make things easy. It was sexy as hell that they were both still wearing their silly Hawaiian shirts and leis. Tristan wiggled his ass, which was rounding nicely as he continued to put on weight. Gabe gloved and slicked quickly, then spread the last of the lube onto his fingers. He pressed two against Tristan's hole, earning him a delighted squeak.

"Tell me," Gabe said.

"I need you in me. Fuck me, baby."

Tristan rarely used endearments, and that one shot right to Gabe's heart. He pushed first one, then two fingers inside Tristan's tight heat. Tristan breathed out hard on a long groan, arching his back to ease what probably stung a little. He went down on his elbows, putting more weight onto his forearms and giving Gabe more room to play. He fucked Tristan with his fingers just long enough to get him good and wet.

He lined up his cock and pushed halfway inside.

Tristan moaned. "All of you."

Gabe leaned down to press a kiss to Tristan's trembling shoulder. "You sure?"

"Yes."

He kissed Tristan again then slid his in cock deeper, finally stopping when his hips were flush with Tristan's ass. Tristan clawed at the desktop, panting and making soft noises that seemed to be a mix of discomfort and absolute joy. Trusting Tristan to say something if it got bad, Gabe began to fuck him. Long and steady at first, until Tristan threw back his head and cried out with absolute pleasure.

Then Gabe let go. He fucked his boyfriend hard and fast, skin smacking, balls slapping. He kept one hand on Tristan's hip and planted the other on his right shoulder, giving him all of the control. Allowing him to plunge in deep each time, and each thrust had Tristan keening. Then swearing.

Gabe wasn't going to last long. It felt too damned amazing, and every noise Tristan made echoed in Gabe's balls.

"So close," Tristan said. "Fuck."

Gabe went harder, and Tristan cried out. He slid his damp palm from Tristan's hip to his cock, and he'd barely brushed the taut skin before Tristan was coming. He went so tight around

Gabe's cock that he had to stop fucking him, and then Gabe's senses short-circuited with pleasure. He pumped into the condom, his skin buzzing, everything a little bit gray for the briefest of moments.

"Holy shit," Gabe said on a wheeze.

Tristan trembled beneath him. Gabe gently eased out. He took care of the trash, then tucked himself back in. Tristan had flattened out against the desk, arms under his head. Gabe's heart lurched.

"You okay?" he asked as he returned to Tristan's side. "Did I hurt you? Tristan?"

"Didn't hurt me," Tristan said to the desk. "All jelly now. Gonna stay here a while."

Gabe's chest puffed a bit with pride. "This was supposed to be a quickie. I don't really want my dad coming up here and seeing you with your ass hanging out."

Tristan snorted. "Yeah, not a good idea."

"Come on. You can clean up in the bathroom next door."

He helped Tristan peel himself off the desk, then checked that the coast was clear before Tristan limped out to the bathroom. Gabe stayed behind to clean the desk with a few sanitizing wipes and scent the air with lavender spray. He waited for Tristan on the landing, his blood humming with joy and the very real need to roll over and take a nap. His thighs were sore, and he'd probably have bruises on his lower stomach tomorrow.

All worth it to see Tristan so completely blissed out.

"Enjoying your birthday so far?" Tristan asked when he rejoined him. His cheeks were still rosy, his eyes shining, and he looked very, very satisfied.

"Every single second of it," Gabe replied. "Even the public serenade was kind of fun."

"What's been your favorite so far?"

He slipped his arm around Tristan's waist simply to feel his boyfriend's warmth. "I want to say fucking you just now, but honestly? That picture you drew. I can't tell you how much I love it."

"I'm glad." Tristan brushed his nose against Gabe's. "I love you."

"I love you too. For as long as you'll let me."

"Oh, I'm pretty positive I'll let you for a long, long time."

Gabe gifted him with a tender kiss. "Good answer."

EPILOGUE

S *ix Months Later*

Tristan laughed as Buzz tackled Woody from behind, sending the two cats tearing out of the living room to battle it out in the master bedroom. The pair of rescue cats had been Gabe's idea. He'd come home with them last week, and Tristan's heart had melted. Buzz was snow white with a little patch of black near his left eye. Woody was a calico stripe with a very fluffy tail, and they'd been the perfect addition to the new apartment.

A new apartment currently filled with guests laughing over the antics of the two cats, while Shane and Noel's gray mutt Misty slept in the corner of the room. The gathering was a house-warming of sorts. He and Gabe had moved into the apartment three weeks ago, and they'd finally settled in well enough to invite their loved ones over for a potluck dinner, which was winding down as a few people went back for seconds or thirds. Bear had made a pan of his special lasagna, and Tristan had tried his hand at homemade lemon bars.

He thought they'd turned out pretty damn good.

"At least you never lack for entertainment," Shane said. He and Noel were curled up together in an armchair, because they didn't really have enough seating for everyone.

The apartment was open-concept, so the living room, kitchen and dining area were one big room, with the master bedroom and bathroom in back and a half bath near the front door. Tristan loved it because they could all be in the same room at the same time. For the first time, he was pretty sure.

Debbie, Bear and Richard were occupying the same space, which—Gabe had confessed to him that morning—had terrified Gabe. Debbie was five months out of rehab, living in a house with three other single women, and she'd maintained steady employment to pay her share of expenses. She'd been nothing but polite and well-mannered since she arrived.

Gabe seemed deliriously happy about the whole thing. He'd sold the old house and given Debbie half of the money to sock away for a rainy day. After he gave Chet back what he owed him, the rest of his half went toward their apartment and furnishing the whole thing. Tristan might have gone a little overboard in the decorating department, but he'd never had his own place before, and Gabe had let him control it all. Gunmetal grays, geometric patterns and hints of teal and purple were scattered throughout the place, and Tristan adored how it had turned out.

The drawing Tristan had made for Gabe's birthday hung in a special place over the electric fireplace's mantel.

Gabe's friend Jon, who'd come over with his friend Henry, had told Tristan, "I'm hiring you to decorate when I get my own place."

Tristan had taken the compliment and kept it close.

"So how's business been for you?" Bear asked. He ambled over to where Tristan was standing by the kitchen island picking at a plate of lasagna, watching his guests interact as they ate off TV trays.

"Slow but so far so good," Tristan replied. "We're working on some social media ideas so I can get my name out there."

"Word of mouth works wonders for a small business. Believe me."

Tristan had followed through with the idea of creating a business out of his drawings. He'd hired someone to build a website showcasing the work he'd already done, comparing the finished products to the photographs he'd used as inspiration. He even did a new one of Gabe from one of his Mean Green stills, to show variety. In the four months since going live, he'd gotten five commissions. Each customer had left glowing feedback on his site about the finished product.

The money he was earning helped reinforce his decision to leave Benfield and cut ties to his parents' financial support. Not that he was likely to have stayed at Benfield after the allegations against the night nurse Debra.

Tristan swallowed hard as old anger resurfaced. Feelings of intense dislike for the woman without knowing why. Back in March, the parents of nineteen-year-old resident Charlie had filed misconduct and abuse charges against Debra after one too many unexplainable bruises on their son. She was fired from Benfield and the matter was settled out of court. In her confession, she admitted that during Tristan's infrequent bouts of insomnia, he had twice witnessed her hitting Charlie when he wouldn't calm down.

Learning that had disturbed the hell out of Tristan. He'd witnessed something horrible, but because of his faulty memory, he hadn't been able to report it. Debra said that she quietly walked Tristan back to his room and watched him until she was sure the memory was gone, leaving him unable to record it in any of his notebooks. She also swore over and over that she'd never been physical with any other patient, including Tristan.

He still wasn't sure what to believe. Mostly he wanted to keep the incident in the past where it belonged. Benfield was no longer part of his life. His life was with Gabe. He wanted to live every single day in the present.

"Hey, you okay, son?" Bear asked. A warm, meaty hand landed on his shoulder. "You got all morose for a minute."

"Sorry, my mind wandered," Tristan replied. He clutched the silver and jade phoenix medallion Gabe had given him for Christmas—the same necklace he'd admired during their first date at the market. He didn't want to dwell on the bad things. He wanted to focus on what mattered. Everything and everyone who mattered was in his apartment. Shane and Noel, Bear and Richard, and of course, Gabe.

Gabe was still fiddling with the coffeemaker over on the back counter. Okay, so maybe the one Tristan had picked out was a little tricky compared to what Gabe was used to having. Tristan liked gadgets, and that machine could do espresso and everything.

"Need some help?" Tristan asked.

"I've got it," Gabe replied. "I can master a coffeemaker, thank you very much."

"Shout if you get stuck."

"Very funny. If I'm going to be any good at hospitality, I need to know these things."

"Once you're managing your own hotel, someone else can make the coffee."

"Yeah, but everyone starts somewhere, and I'll start here."

Tristan grinned. Gabe's unique combination of stubbornness and patience was one of his finest features. It helped him put up with Tristan's occasional memory hiccup, and it would go a long way toward Gabe's new future. He'd started taking hospitality classes at the community college, with the hope of one day working in a hotel or managing a restaurant. Gabe hadn't decided yet, but he'd made the first few steps toward a real career.

And he'd given Chet Green three months' notice. A few more

scenes and Gabe was retiring from porn. Tristan planned on being very, very creative in his methods of celebrating Gabe's last shoot at Mean Green.

Buzz pranced back into the living room alone. He looked around, then leapt up onto Debbie's lap and settled there.

"She's a different person," Bear said quietly. "Makes me glad for Gabe."

"Me too."

"I hope it lasts."

"Me too, times infinity."

Gabe would lose it if Debbie started drinking again. But it was the quiet, familial moments like this that, he hoped, made sobriety worth it—not to mention having a real relationship with her son and his partner.

Even if said partner still couldn't identify her on sight. They hadn't spent enough time together yet.

The phase two trial had ended ten days ago, and so far so good. According to Dr. Fischer, Tristan was one of their biggest success stories, despite remaining on the phenobarbital to combat his still infrequent seizures. He no longer received the trial drug, but his twice-weekly appointments with Dr. Fischer would continue for another six months. Follow-up was necessary in judging the overall effectiveness of the trial and the drug's ability to permanently improve memory.

Tristan had spent the first few days post-trial terrified he'd begin to regress. Sometimes details were fuzzy. Sometimes he choked on a name or specific information. He had zero memory of picking out their table lamp shaped like an old-fashioned film reel, but Gabe insisted that was all him.

It didn't matter to Tristan if he slipped once in a while. He was living with a man he loved more than anything else in the world, they shared a great place and they'd adopted two hilarious cats. A year ago, he'd never have believed such a thing was possible.

A year ago, he'd seen the world as a scary place full of strangers and unexpected danger. He couldn't see past the scope of his room at Benfield and the once-a-week visits from Noel. Today he saw a world full of promise and a future that could be anything he wanted it to be. He saw himself living in it, instead of hiding from it.

"I win!" Gabe said. "There will be coffee."

Tristan laughed at Gabe's delight. He went to his boyfriend and tugged him into his arms. Gabe squeezed his hips, beaming from defeating the dreaded coffeemaker. "There was never a doubt in my mind," Tristan said.

"Sure there was."

"Nope. Not one. You don't fail at anything you set your mind to."

"That's true. I knew the first time we met that I wanted you to be a part of my life."

"And you made sure I was."

"Well, I do have to give some credit to Noel for bringing you back to Big Dick's the second time."

"If you say so."

Tristan still didn't remember those moments, but he'd reread his journal entries and the emails enough that the details were imprinted on his mind. He wanted to know every moment of his life with Gabe, whether through the written word or his own memory. The means didn't matter. All that really mattered was the experience—and Tristan planned to experience every single thing possible and to love Gabe for as long and hard as life allowed.

He'd been giving an amazing second chance. No way was Tristan going to waste a moment of it.

Woody gave her signature yowl, followed by a thump from the bedroom.

Tristan laughed and went to see what his crazy cats were up to this time.

Don't miss Jon Buchanan finding love and acceptance in an unexpected place, and with the help of a fuzzy gray kitten, in **The Heart As He Hears It** (Perspectives #3), available now.

ALSO BY A.M. ARTHUR

Cost of Repairs

Cost of Repairs

Color of Grace

Weight of Silence

Acts of Faith

Foundation of Trust

Perspectives

The Truth As He Knows It

The World As He Sees It

The Heart As He Hears It

Belonging

No Such Thing

Maybe This Time

Stand By You

Restoration

Getting It Right

Finding Their Way

Taking A Chance

All Saints

Come What May

Say It Right

As I Am

Off Beat

Body Rocks

Steady Stroke

Hot Licks

Discovering Me

Unearthing Cole

Understanding Jeremy

What You Own

Fractured Hymns

ABOUT THE AUTHOR

A.M. Arthur was born and raised in the same kind of small town that she likes to write about, a stone's throw from both beach resorts and generational farmland. She's been creating stories in her head since she was a child and scribbling them down nearly as long, in a losing battle to make the fictional voices stop. She credits an early fascination with male friendships (bromance hadn't been coined yet back then) with her later discovery of and subsequent love affair with m/m romance stories. A.M. Arthur's work is available from Carina Press, Dreamspinner Press, SMP Swerve, and Briggs-King Books.

When not exorcising the voices in her head, she can also be found in her kitchen, pretending she's an amateur chef and trying to not poison herself or others with her cuisine experiments.

Contact her at am_arthur@yahoo.com with your cooking tips (or book comments). You can also find her online (http://amarthur.blogspot.com/), as well as on Twitter (http://twitter.com/am_arthur), Tumblr (http://www.tumblr.com/blog/am-arthur) and Facebook (https://www.facebook.com/pages/AM-Arthur/).

Get sneak peeks, character Q&A's and more at her Facebook reader group, Pot O Gold: https://www.facebook.com/groups/300209733646247/

Made in the USA
Middletown, DE
14 August 2023

36733179R00176